## By the Author

My Date with a Wendigo

Olivia

Thor: Daughter of Asgard

A Fae Tale

Cold Blood

A Second Chance at Life

Snake Charming

Visit us at www.boldstrokesbooks.com

# Praise for Genevieve McCluer

## *Cold Blood*

"The story is a good one, and I enjoyed it a lot. It doesn't hide what the plot is doing, though it still manages to throw in the odd surprise, and it moves at a pace fast enough to keep me wanting to read just the next bit. If you like vampires that hunt other vampires, moral quandaries, limbs going flying (and getting stuck back on again), and cute women falling for each other—grab this one."—*Lee Hulme's Book Reviews*

"I like Genevieve McCluer's writing style. It is fast and immediate and draws me in. I loved the nod to a previous novel, *Olivia*, and to some recognizable areas of the city. She makes monsters sympathetic characters and gives them entirely plausible lives alongside the other residents of Toronto. I like this world she has invented."—*Kitty Kat's Book Blog*

## *A Fae Tale*

"This is an unusual tale, but a very enjoyable one. It's funny and a bit kooky, but very sweet and romantic too. Genevieve McCluer writes great humorous prose and I found myself giggling out loud a few times in the course of reading this book. Her characters are well defined and fun, and she makes her secondary characters come to life as much as the main protagonists. An enjoyable read."—*Kitty Kat's Book Blog*

## *Thor: Daughter of Asgard*

"Norse mythology intrudes on a bubbly romance in this light adventure from McCluer...Readers will come for the gender bending mythology and stay for the light romance."
—*Publishers Weekly*

### Olivia

"There's a playfulness at times, but then the seriousness of the situation hits the reader square in the face. At the halfway mark it suddenly took off for me. There was one heck of a surprise, that I did not see coming at all. I enjoyed the story and would like to read more in this world."—*Kitty Kat's Book Blog*

### My Date With a Wendigo

"*My Date with a Wendigo* is a sweet, second chance romance at its furry little heart."—*Wicked Cool Flight*

# SNAKE CHARMING

*by*

Genevieve McCluer

2024

**SNAKE CHARMING**
© 2024 By Genevieve McCluer. All Rights Reserved.

ISBN 13: 978-1-63679-628-4

This Trade Paperback Original Is Published By
Bold Strokes Books, Inc.
P.O. Box 249
Valley Falls, NY 12185

First Edition: May 2024

**Credits**
Editor: Barbara Ann Wright
Production Design: Stacia Seaman
Cover Design by Jeanine Henning

# Acknowledgments

Thank you to Jessica, Daniel, and Alexandra for all of your support and help, and to my editor, Barbara, this book quite literally couldn't exist without your help.

# CHAPTER ONE

## *Elfriede*

I splash water on my face from the sink in the airport bathroom. My eyes are beyond bloodshot. Normally, the ten minutes it takes to stumble out of the plane and into the restroom is enough time to clear up a hangover, but that's after a short flight in Europe, not an entire trip across the Atlantic Ocean. Twelve hours of drinking to barely even dull the pain is apparently enough to leave me completely wrecked once we've landed. I doubt it'll last much longer, but it's certainly a novel agony.

I will never understand why indoor plumbing does nothing to me, but even being eight thousand meters above oceans or rivers makes it feel like my skin is trying to get up and run away and take a few extra pieces of me with it. Most of the pain is likely from that and not the drink, but it seems reasonable to assume that when I have no fresh blood in my veins and instead have a few gallons of alcohol, that likely explains some of the symptoms.

My reflection looks a complete mess. My chic, asymmetrical red hair that had taken stylists hours to get right looks more like a frayed mop, and my tailored silk button-up is half-undone and so twisted and wrinkled as to look like it tried to join my skin in its escape.

The hangover is finally clearing up a little, but it still feels like my head is ringing as I fix my shirt and tuck it back into my slacks. I put the rose-tinted glasses that drug dealer gave me back on, turning my blue eyes a vague purple. It covers up the red in my sclera, and vampiric eyes don't exactly handle the afternoon sun reflecting off snow well. Now for the big question. Do I head to the airport bar or try to find someplace to sleep? It would be lovely to take the edge off this headache, but I didn't have time or money to plan ahead and book a room, so I may want to get on that.

Toronto is supposed to be the city of miracles, isn't it? It's where half my nonhuman friends and a good deal of my gambling buddies ran off to. The former could be explained by them trying to get away from me, but I owed the latter money, so you'd think they'd want to stay close without a pretty compelling reason, so Toronto has to be something rather special. Or a very good con. There's no use lingering on the past. I can't change it any more than I can change a bet once the roulette wheel has started spinning.

I run my fingers through my hair, trying to fix it into something resembling presentable. I hadn't had time to grab a brush. Or a change of clothes. I can take care of the hangover and the bed at the same time. The airport bar is a bad choice, as most of the women there are going to be waiting for a flight, or even worse, straight, but there must be a decent joint nearby.

Taking a taxi from an airport is too long a wait with this hangover, and I've never minded walking. Cars are just a fad anyway. Give them another century, and they'll have gone the way of bell-bottoms and hat buckles.

Phones, on the other hand, may stick around. Mine will not, as it is well and truly dead, and is not giving me any helpful directions. So I do it the old-fashioned way and ask the first person I see walking in the half a foot of snow.

He stares at my shirt and slacks. He'd probably be concerned by my loafers as well, but they're hidden under the snow. "You don't think you've had enough?"

My breath probably still stinks of alcohol, and it would explain my ill-preparedness for the weather. I didn't think getting a drink would be this difficult. I lean in, smirking, putting my will into the words. "Give me any cash you have and point me toward the nearest bar."

His eyes gloss over, and he reaches into his pocket, handing me a twenty before pointing across the street. I don't see the bar, but it's not as if he could lie to me. Probably should've said "give me directions" instead of "point," but it's too late now. "Twenty dollars, really? God, I miss when people had cash. Well, thanks for the single drink."

Shaking my head, I cross the road and leave him blinking in confusion. I keep going and find the place a few blocks up. It's a sports bar, and I can hear people cheering from inside. Not exactly a dyke bar, but I'll take it.

I open the door and look around. There's a hostess up front, a few people at tables throughout, and a rowdy crowd gathered at the bar cheering on a hockey game. I take a seat at the bar next to a large, bewitching woman in a hockey jersey and order an appletini. So much alcohol used to be apple-flavored. It's weird that we're only now starting to get back to that. It's still nearly impossible to get decent applejack anywhere. "Hey there," I say to the hockey fan as flirtatiously as I can manage with my head still throbbing. A sip of the drink at least helps with that, though I'll need some blood to properly fix me.

She looks me up and down. I got lucky. Her face is gorgeous, with glistening green eyes and a strong jaw, and she has large, rugged hands and actual biceps. I can't build muscle anymore. I'm almost jealous. "I'm trying to watch the game."

I should've realized that. And I'm too spent to even consider staying here until it's over. "I'm sure you can record it. Or find it online." I smirk, letting my fangs show. I should really thank Stephenie Meyer or Anne Rice or Joss Whedon. It comes in waves, but every last one of them turned a generation of women into vampire fetishists. "I'm sure we can find something better to occupy your time."

She chuckles. "No offense, but I doubt you're as engrossing as a hockey match."

I've had worse insults but so rarely about my sexual ability. I've had experts study me. I am perfection in bed. "Oh, I can give you the reviews if you want. Most of the recent ones are on my FetLife profile. And I'm sure a night with an actual vampire can be quite engrossing."

She laughs again, and I expect her to doubt me. It's generally where I seal the deal. A show of strength, or if they seem flirty, a nip of their wrists and running my tongue along the trickling blood is always enough to take us back to a bedroom somewhere. Or a bathroom. Sometimes a closet. "Oh, it certainly can be. It's why I'm dating one."

What? I stare, trying not to let my jaw drop. "You..."

She nods, an awkward smile blooming. "Yeah. And she's a little possessive."

Who's already dating a vampire? We're nearly extinct. No one knows that many. I've only met a handful myself. "Really? And you're sure she's the real deal? We could always have a threesome. It's been centuries since I fucked another vampire. How did you even find one? There are so few of us."

She chuckles. "Maybe you *can* be almost as entertaining as a hockey game. You think vampires are rare?"

Did that flight take even more out of me than I thought? The world isn't making any sense. "We were hunted to near extinction just over a century ago. I should know. I ended up in bed with the people who were trying to kill me. There's no way we've bounced back from that."

"Honey, this is Toronto. You can barely throw a rock without hitting one."

"But we're endangered."

She snorts. "Maybe elsewhere. You must be new in town."

How on earth is that possible? Is someone just running around turning every other person they see? It doesn't seem sustainable, as much as we drink. "I just came here from Berlin. I'd heard a lot about this place. I was hoping to sample that famous Canadian hospitality."

The woman sips her beer and shakes her head. "You can sample it elsewhere. Maybe check the Community Center?"

I blink and shake my head. It's already starting to hurt again, and I don't think this one's a hangover. "The what?"

"God, you really are from out of town. You don't know anything about Toronto?"

Is this something I should know? Is it, like, a famous landmark? I've already come across as quite a few descriptors I'm not used to, and I'd rather not also seem like an idiot, so with nothing to say, I stay silent.

"Look up the Honeydale Mall. I know it says it's closed, but well, you'll be safe so long as you *are* a real vampire."

That would be a good lead-in to my normal tricks, but I feel the moment is gone. "My phone's dead."

"Jesus, you are just pitiful. Shit, sorry—"

"It's fine. Religious stuff doesn't hurt me."

Her expression grows more playful, and she looks me up and down, but there doesn't seem to be the usual lust I'd expect. "Maybe you do know your stuff." Was that a test? It does hurt some vampires, doesn't it? I swear that's not just in movies. I think I remember meeting one who was hurt by a cross, but it was centuries ago, and I suppose time could be playing tricks on me, as my memory is far from perfect, especially as much as I drink. "Fine, shut up, sip your weird appletini, and let me watch the game, and you can use my phone charger." She pulls a black brick from her pocket and slides it over. "And don't go running off with it. Not that I can do shit to stop you."

I sigh. This is so weird. Why does a human seem to know more about vampires than I do? There's already a cord sticking out of it, but it's for an Android, and I have an iPhone. "Do you have a different cord?" I ask, holding up my dead phone.

"You don't have your charger? Were you just dropped from a plane or something? It would explain the hair."

I shrug. I give up. I take a sip. It's good. And it's gonna have to last me.

She sighs. "You're lucky that apparently, all vampires have the same taste in phones." She grabs a tiny cord from her pocket. "I always keep it on me because she is incapable of remembering anything important in her massive purse."

"Thank you." I plug in my phone and watch it light up and proclaim that it's charging. "I'm Freddie, by the way." I can never take non-German accents saying Friede. It just sounds weird. I'd rather make it easier for them.

"Are you not gonna let me watch the game? I can take my charger back. The Maple Leafs are up by three, and I need them to stay that way."

Is she a gambler? I want to ask about the bet, maybe get in on the action, but I also don't want to have her take the charger back before my phone can even turn on, so I shut up, sit back on the stool, and try to take my time with my drink. I have maybe enough in my wallet to afford three more, if I'm lucky, and this isn't fast charging.

# CHAPTER TWO

## *Phoebe*

"That fucking bitch," I shout for what has to be the fourth time. Dozenth time. Fortieth time. "We were together for three fucking months."

"I know," Dinah says, rubbing my back from her seat next to me on my massive circular bed.

I grab a pillow and either scream or cry into it. I'd meant to do the former, but it comes away covered in tears. "I want to fucking kill her. I want to crush her fucking bones and swallow her whole."

The rubbing turns to a gentle pat. "Phoebe, I know. If you want to, I won't stop you. I'm not sure I'd have any room to judge."

I sit up, balancing on my tail, and glare at the self-flagellating little vampire. She's a quarter my size, with brown hair and a far too-young face. "He was trying to kill you. You're not even slightly a murderer. Can we deal with your self-hate issues later?"

"I don't hate myself," she mutters. "But, yes. Of course. I'm sorry, I wasn't trying to turn it on me. I was just saying that even as much as I hate killing, I'd understand you doing it. I had a roommate in prison who went away for stalking a guy. Everything she said was horrifying. I still can't believe none of us saw it in Paula."

I don't need any further cues to get back to my ranting. "I

was just fucking stupid. The bitch pretended to care about me for months, only for me to fucking find that she'd been lying the whole time. And she was posting pictures of me online! She's lucky I let her leave here in one piece."

"Can you actually swallow her whole?" Dinah asks.

I grumble and try to think of her dimensions as non-sexually as I can manage. "Probably. I can unhinge my jaw, but the human parts can make it kind of complicated."

She looks me up and down, from human head to snake tail. "Huh. I've never seen you do that."

"It's not exactly pleasant."

"Yeah, I guess it wouldn't be. Maybe just stop at the bone crushing?"

I grumble. "She deserves worse."

"Yes. She does." Dinah shakes her head. "That was reprehensible. Even if you were human, that would be beyond disgusting, but she's putting our lives at risk by posting pictures of a fiend online like that."

"Not like she gives a damn." I cross my arms. Crushing her bones is too good for her. I want her to suffer. "I didn't think she was the one or anything…" I trail off like I'm about to cry. Damn you, Aphrodite. I'm better than this. She's a miserable, psychopathic, evil bitch who was using me. How dare I be heartbroken! "It fucking hurts. I trusted her. I let her into my home. Into my life."

"I know." Dinah wraps an arm around me and leans against my shoulder. "I'm so sorry."

I grumble. "I know where she lives. We could burn it down."

"My parole officer would kill me."

"Just offer him some extra karma in your Shadowrun game."

She sits up, rubbing her chin as she considers that. "That might work. He's really been wanting to get some new cybernetics for his rigger. He's covered up a murder for less."

I giggle. I try not to, but I can't help it. I can*not* imagine Dinah helping me murder my ex-girlfriend. It's enough to actually make me smile for the first time all day. She's the least murderous person I know, and I know several people who have never killed anyone. "He can earn his damn karma with the rest of us. I know you'd never be willing to kill someone."

She studies the bed. It's big enough for a dozen of her. "She's really awful."

"And you're really good. Don't pretend otherwise. If I'm going to kill her, and I probably won't, then it won't be with your help. I just needed you to cry to."

She nods. She better not start pouting again.

"Fuck, I just, I need to get her out of my system. I…" Well, I certainly can't drink away my sorrows with my sober friend right next to me. She's never given me a hard time for it, but it always feels weird. "I need some meaningless sex. Someone I could never get attached to. Just some stupid, sexy asshole. And a fiend, so they won't fucking fetishize…all this." I gesture at my tail. "Drive me to the Community Center?" I smile as adorably as I can manage with a face covered in snot and tears.

Dinah hates driving. "Fine." She doesn't even complain. Wow, I didn't think looking all cute would work that well. "I'll have to run home and get my car, though. You gonna be okay on your own for a few minutes?"

"I'm not that pathetic."

"I could just have Rachel pick us up."

There we go. I knew she'd try to find a way out of it. "Fine. Call your wife. But I'm finding someone."

"How do you even pick up girls?"

Did she seriously just ask me that? "Dinah, you were in prison. You never…seems like there would have been some pretty prime pickings, and more than a few women willing to experiment."

"I would never!" Her face turns bright red. It's always adorable when vampires blush, until I start wondering whose blood that is running through them. "I was only interested in Rachel."

"You poor, sheltered thing. One woman for all eternity? I think thirty years is the longest I've ever lasted, and she was amazing in bed, and without that, I doubt we would've made it twenty."

She only reddens further. "Well I can assure you, Rachel has no issues there." She turns away as she pulls out her phone, calling the woman of the hour.

At least flustering Dinah takes my mind off my woes. *I can't believe I fell for those stupid lies. I'm smarter than this. I'm better than this. And now Paula is all I can fucking think about. If that's even her real name. She was lying to me the whole time. Why should I trust anything she said?*

"Okay, she says she'll be here in, like, ten minutes," Dinah says, interrupting my inner rant.

"Thank you." *Drinking is still sounding like a very tempting option. I have some absinthe that I was super excited to bring to Friday game night before Dinah joined, and now I haven't had a good use for it. I even bought sugar cubes to go with it, though that sounds like a lot of extra work if I just want to get drunk. Maybe I'll go with the chocolate vodka.*

"You'll get her out of your system," Dinah says. "Just be you, find some cute girl, and wow her."

"You're still trying to figure out how it works, aren't you?"

"I've never picked anyone up. I knew Rachel since I was five, and we were each other's first girlfriends."

*They're adorable. Such children.* "I know. Well, maybe you can watch me try and fail a few times." *I've never had much trouble getting laid, but that's normally been with friends or acquaintances. Just going out and getting it on demand isn't the easiest thing in the world. It's certainly worked at a few parties and the like, and the internet has made hooking up far easier, but it's never a sure thing.* "With the emotional wreck I am today, I'm not expecting much, but I need to at least try. I feel like absolute shit, and I just…I know probably the last thing I need is to go and be even more objectified, but at least it would be on my terms. She fucking put those pictures all over the goddamn internet, and it sounds like we got them removed—thank you for talking to your lawyer about that—but I need to feel wanted on my own terms, to be the one using someone. And I need the last person I fucked to not have been that lying bitch."

"So pick out a cute top?"

That's probably a good plan. The one I'm wearing now is as tearstained as this pillow. I slither to my closet and try to pick out something to wear. Damn it, and I missed a really easy joke in response to her. I don't know how I'd have phrased it, and it's too late now, but if I wasn't so mopey-brained, I'd have come up with something brilliant. I could've at least said I *am* a cute top. But the moment's passed.

I grab a sleeveless blue blouse and throw it on, trying to psych myself up for this. I never try to pick up girls, and the only place I can really go is the Community Center, which isn't exactly a prime dating location, but I need this so badly. I need a way to take her off my mind.

"How do I look?"

Dinah grins at me. "Clean up your face a bit, but that shirt looks amazing on you."

I smile back and don't entirely have to force it. Damn right, I look amazing. This is going to go perfectly. I'll find some super sexy girl, have hot meaningless sex with her, feel so much better, and never think about her or that gods-damned bitch ever again.

Dinah was right about my face, though. By Apollo, I'm all slobbery and swollen. How on earth is anyone going to want to fuck me?

Once I'm all cleaned up and have tried to talk myself into and out of this three separate times, I finally leave the bathroom, but someone knocks at the door. I feel my heart jump in my chest. I know it's Rachel, but I can't help but fear that it could be Paula coming back, trying to pull some excuse out of her ass or maybe some other obsessed fan to come and lie to me.

"That's Rachel." Dinah gets the door, and I grab my purse so we can head outside. I live on the ground floor of what was once a warehouse and has now been adapted into some potentially up-to-code apartments for fiends. My upstairs neighbor is a bunyip, and the noise can get a bit overwhelming, but the rent is affordable, and the place is spacious enough that I never feel too cramped.

Unlike in Rachel's sedan.

I coil my tail all around the back seat, and I still have to hold it to my chest to keep it from blocking the rearview mirror as she pulls out of her parking spot.

"So we're just going to the Community Center?" Rachel asks. "Dinah didn't tell me much."

"Yeah, sorry," I mutter. I hate troubling people like this. By now, Rachel probably counts as my friend too, but she still just seems like my friend's wife, so I extra feel like I'm inconveniencing her. "Just really needed to get out of there."

"And into someone else?" Dinah asks.

I roll my eyes but don't bother to deny the point.

"Dinah told me what she did. I'm so sorry. I heard Mrs. Gudaitiene was able to take care of it, at least."

"Not before plenty of people saw it." It was violating, but more than that, it put everyone in danger. If people know that fiends are real, there's very little telling where they may stop. I'm trying to not let myself think about it and just focus on getting over her, but it makes the betrayal so much worse than the already disgusting crime that it was. And I'm going out with two addicts, so I can't even drink. "Is there, like, a singles night or something there?"

"I don't think so," Rachel says. "Though honestly, I'm surprised there isn't with as many events as they have these days."

It's so rare that being a lamia bothers me. It's not as if I ever knew anything else, and dating has grown increasingly easy, but picking people up in person certainly hasn't. Especially if I don't want a bunch of people taking pictures of the weird snake girl. I will forever curse the invention of camera phones.

We park in front of the Community Center and hurry inside. Maybe I can just go to the bar and get lucky. I can buy Rachel and Dinah some food or something to keep them busy. I just have to find someone who isn't a complete creep. That shouldn't be too hard, so long as my definition of creep doesn't include criminals and murderers. That would leave my pickings awfully slim. But at least none of them would ever want to be tied to any pictures going online. I should never have dated a human. I know better than that. So that only leaves finding a cute, dumb, shallow fiend to take home.

# Chapter Three

## *Elfriede*

So this is the place? It's just an old, abandoned mall. This is the place where every monster—fiend should be going? Why fiend? Isn't that more of a demon thing? I don't get any of this.

There are five cars in the parking lot, and most of them look pretty run-down, like they could've just been abandoned here. I don't understand this at all. I breathe in, tasting other creatures on the air, hear faint sounds drifting out from inside, and smell blood. How long has it been since I had a drink? A real drink, not alcohol. I was so tempted to try to find someone at the airport or that bar, but that would mean potential witnesses, and I'm in enough trouble without attracting attention in a city that's already so deeply confusing.

All I can do is go in. I tell the cabbie that I already paid, and he gives me my change and drives off, leaving me to stare at the decrepit old building some more.

I've been to some divey bars in my time, shady back-alley places where the drinks all had to come from bottles or cans, and there were more drugs and illicit activities on the menu than food, but none of them worried me the way this place does.

I don't know how to act around monsters. Fiends, the weird hockey lady with the vampire girlfriend said, they're called fiends. I've known quite a few over the years but certainly none who would act like the term monster was offensive, and I've intimately known so many of them. Maybe it's a Canadian thing?

The building looks increasingly intimidating. What am I thinking? Why would I be scared of monsters? I've bedded so many of them. For that matter, I am one.

And they all came here. I'm not scared that I'll be eaten; I'm scared they came here for a reason, and they won't want me here.

I could run. I don't have to go inside. I can find someone and make them withdraw money from an ATM for me. It would be easy. If my card works here, I can deposit my money in my account, get a night at a normal hotel, order room service and drink them, and figure out what I'm doing from there.

But this is why I came to town. All the other people I've known came here. There's something about it that seems to call to us. I haven't the foggiest idea what reason there may be, but so many of us end up here that there must be an explanation.

And I may find it beyond those doors.

And I'll know why so many of my friends who wanted to come here vanished without even a farewell. The place is supposed to be a paradise. And it's not like I gave them reasons to stay around.

Great, this place is making me introspective. I've avoided that for far too long to let a mildly intimidating building be my undoing. I can handle this.

Though I would much rather handle it with my hair fixed and some clean clothes. I can come back later.

I turn around, trying to think of where I should go for that money. My phone has a charge now, so I may be able to look it up, but I didn't think to get a Canadian SIM card, so I'll have to use someone's internet.

I glance over my shoulder, back toward the Community Center, to see a couple women entering, laughing, happy, and smelling of drugs. Right, beautiful women and drugs! What was I thinking? Obviously, I should check out this Community Center before I do anything else. It'd be rude to be a new fiend in town and not at least pay it a visit before I figure out the rest of my stay.

The entrance isn't all that imposing. It's a graffitied old door that was once largely glass but has since been replaced with plywood, and it opens easily when I give it a slight tug. Inside,

I don't see the cute girls with their drugs, but I find a good deal more than I'd ever have expected to see, even if I were to live another thousand years.

Tables line the inside of the hollowed-out mall, and while they're all covered in sundry goods, many of them illicit and many of them dangerous, they are certainly not where my attention lingers. The people behind and around the stands, if one can even call them people, are in more assortments than I thought possible. Some look almost human, even more than I do, while others have far too many limbs in the wrong spots, horns, tails, fur, massive maws full of jagged fangs, or long talons looking ready to impale.

I've seen monsters before. None of these are the worst of those, but there's certainly the most variety. Part of me wants to run, but part of me is more curious as to why nothing is trying to eat me. The place is so full of so many wretched creatures that I assume I look like fresh meat. Am I too long dead? It would explain why no one has ever tried to eat me before. At least without asking first.

Which reminds me of why I'm here. I have forty dollars left, no idea if I can control any of these fiends, and a desperate need for blood, a change of clothes, and a bed to sleep in.

I had expected clothes to be the last thing I could get here, but some of the garments on display make me question that. Completely forgetting the horror of the situation, I wander toward a booth with some exquisite handmade clothes. It's not exactly my tailor, but they're very chic.

There's a black blazer with a fake maroon pocket square that fits me almost as well as my tailored jacket and the sexiest silk shirt I've ever seen. "How much is this?"

The spider-thing behind the counter maybe looks me up and down. It's a lot of eyes to keep track of, and I'm not entirely sure where most of them are looking. "Thirty dollars for the shirt." Her voice is surprisingly normal. Though her mandibles move a lot as she talks.

I could wait. I do really need some blood. But this is incredibly nice, and mine is so wrinkled. I pull the two twenties out of my wallet and hand them over, only for her to reach out with an oddly human hand and give me back my change.

"Have a lovely day."

"You too." I grin, admiring the shirt. I feel so much better already. Now I just need a place to change. Are there bathrooms here? Follow-up question, do I want to go to a bathroom in a place like this? Would there even be plumbing?

Sure, I grew up with a chamber pot and no running water, but it's been a long while since I've had to put up with that sort of thing, and I'd rather not force myself back to that life for no reason. I can change my shirt once I find a place to lay my head. And with any luck I'll be out of my old clothes pretty quickly then.

But how am I going to find that?

The sound of someone pouring drinks calls to me as easily as ever. There's a bar here. Would've been nice if hockey lady had mentioned that. I'll have to hope my remaining ten dollars can get me a drink. As sketchy as this place is, I'd expect the drinks to either be around five or thirty, though I'm not too used to the Canadian dollar, so I could be way off.

The bar is in the back corner, and I can almost taste the alcohol and horny fiends. Though the taste of the latter is a bit peculiar. It's an odd scent that really gets in the back of my throat, though not unpleasantly, but I'm not sure which of the myriad oddities drinking in this little bar stuffed into the corner of a mall may have that particularly palpable arousal.

There are two vampires and a snake woman eating nachos at a table that seems to be between this place and some sort of restaurant; there's some pink slinky creature taking up two of the furthest stools at the bar; a few horned people in a booth, laughing and downing a pitcher of beer; and enough other beings that I don't really want to try to track the scent down.

However, there's only one empty stool, and it's next to the pink thing, and the whiff I'm greeted with as I sit confidently answers that it is indeed the owner of that overwhelming scent.

My eyes are watering, but I do my best to ignore it. I too am a little overeager sometimes, but sadly, pink guy things are not my type. I lean against the counter and find a bartender looming over me.

She's nearly nine feet tall, covered in some sort of scales, and looks like she could crush me without even trying. Be still, my already still heart. "Hey there, beautiful. What drink would you recommend? Preferably for under ten dollars."

The giantess chuckles, rewarding me with a small smile. "Vampire, right?"

I flash my fangs. "Why, interested?"

Her expression grows a bit less sympathetic. "I'm married. But I'd always recommend a Bloody Mary."

That is always a novelty. Tomatoes weren't even in Europe when I first started drinking. "Is it less than ten dollars?"

"I can give it for ten."

She pulls something from a fridge behind the bar, and I nearly drool and not at the sexy creature. The scent of blood fills my nostrils, overwhelming even the pink thing's musk. God, I really do need that drink. I must be starving for it to overwhelm me to this degree. I can't believe I didn't just rip into somebody's throat earlier if I'm this bad off. She mixes the drink and slides it over to me, and I promptly pony up the cash and take a deep sip.

There's certainly no tomato in this. Blood and vodka, two of the greatest flavors in the world, together at last. I've died again and gone to heaven.

"Hey, could we get another order of nachos?" a sultry voice asks over my shoulder.

I lick my lips and glance behind me to catch a coy smile matched with emerald eyes. Normally, I'd offer to pay for her food, but that seems to be well past my abilities at this point, so that leaves only one real option. "Hi there," I say, giving my best smile, which has always framed my fangs perfectly and led quite a few women into my bed over the years.

She brushes red hair back behind her ear, her smile coy and playful. That's a good sign. "Hi."

"You know we don't have the grill over here," the giant bartender says.

"There's a long line there," she says, her voice threatening to rise into a full whine. "Can't you at least ask? It's hard to slither past everyone."

"I have a full bar too."

"I could ask," I say, standing, still holding my bloody Mary in one hand and my new shirt in its bag in the other. The woman has a snake tail that has to weave between the tables for her to even be standing before me, so I can hardly imagine how annoying it must be to deal with the hundreds of people in here. "Go sit back down. There's no need to trouble yourself. I'll take care of it."

"Let me at least give you the money."

Right, I don't have that. "If you insist." I smile more, letting my gaze linger on her eyes. They're a deep dark green with flecks of yellow ringing them. They almost match her scales, particularly since they also have black dots, but they have a few more shades and completely different patterns. "I'm Freddie."

She giggles, showing slightly sharper, humanlike teeth. "I'm Phoebe." She fishes in a purse slung from her shoulder and hands me a ten. "You really don't have to."

"I'm hardly going to make a beautiful woman have to figure out her way through all this. That would be cruel."

She bites her lip and looks me up and down, seeming to consider something. "Well..." She takes a breath and meets my eyes again. "I still need to get those nachos back to my friends, but...maybe you and I could get out of here?"

I hadn't expected it that quickly. Normally, I get that from humans who really want me to bite them, but I figured I'd have to work for this. She's ludicrously beautiful and apparently in as bad a way as I am. "That sounds absolutely wonderful."

She gulps, her eyes seeming to fall on the money still in my hand and then to my feet. "I don't usually pick up girls like this."

"Really? Why not? You're not too bad at it."

That same smile returns. I could kiss her. "Not the response I expected. Aren't you supposed to act like it's all new to you too?"

"Oh, no, not at all. I don't play games, at least not like that. I enjoy beautiful women, and I particularly enjoy falling into bed with them and spending a night, or a few nights, maybe a few weeks tangled in bed and absolutely loving life."

Her smile is oddly less flirty but still satisfied. "Okay, yeah, that is exactly what I need right now. There's just..." She groans. "Something you should know."

"That you have a snake tail? I think we can figure something out."

She giggles, and that flirtier smile returns, seeming to light up her face as she toys with a strand of red hair. That kiss is sounding all the more tempting. "That *is* good to know, but, no, I'm trans."

"Oh, super. Thanks for letting me know."

She blinks. Did she think I'd freak out? I don't see what the big deal is. "And have dicks."

Plural? I hadn't expected that part, though I suppose snakes do have that unusual trait. "As long as it's not more than three, 'cause that's two holes and a hand, and I'd want to switch off, and what's even the point if I don't have a hand free to drink or fondle. It sounds like it'd just get exhausting, and neither of us would be satisfied."

She giggles again, her smile only growing as she slides closer, her thumb running along the collar of my shirt. "You surprise me yet again. And it's two. But, yeah, I think you are absolutely what I'm looking for tonight."

I grin at her. "Fun?"

She nods. "I couldn't have put it better myself. Order those nachos and come meet me at my table, and we can get out of here."

A new shirt, blood, alcohol, and a drop-dead gorgeous woman to try to figure out how snake sex works with. The day is already looking up.

# CHAPTER FOUR

## *Phoebe*

That was the best sex I've ever had. This is terrible. I wanted good sex, maybe decent sex, the kind of thing that would get that bitch out of my system and leave me ready to go off and figure out what I want. Even terrible sex wouldn't have been too bad. Amazing sex, though, that's the kind of thing that makes you fall in love with someone. And the best sex I've had in my millennia of life, that's terrifying, and if I don't keep this girl the hell away from me, I'm asking for pain.

Her lips press against my shoulder, and she lets out a soft moan. Her arm is draped over my belly, and my tail is hugging her to me, coiled around us. It's so comfortable, and I can already feel myself ready for another round. I need to ask her to leave, but how can I do that when all I can think is how badly I want to hear her scream again?

"Where the hell did you learn to do that?" I ask. I'm not even sure what I mean exactly. She has a few tricks, but if you took out any one of them, it wouldn't have really made it worse; there was just something about how recklessly she threw herself into it. Or maybe it's just her taste. My mind is still swimming from all those orgasms, and I'm not sure I can conjure a decent analysis.

"Learn to do what?" she asks, fangs grazing my bicep as she kisses down my arm.

Yeah, definitely ready for round two or five or whatever round it would be. That's distracting. "All of it. I've had more than my fair share of practice, and I've never felt like that before."

"I don't think I really did anything special. Though I do have a doctorate in sexology. It's a hundred years out-of-date, but it's possible I picked up a few things."

I giggle, wrapping my tail tighter about us. She murmurs into me, and her hand drifts lower on my belly. Not helping with the distraction. "I don't think that's what sexology is about."

"Is it not? I never really paid attention in class."

"Could you even get a doctorate in it back then? I'm not even sure if you can now."

She chuckles against me, and I'm not at all sure if the degree is a joke. But at least questioning her on that takes my mind off how badly I want to fuck her again.

"How old are you, anyway? Having a degree from a hundred years ago."

She squirms, and I think she may be trying to sit up, but my tail has her pinned. I loosen it, and she sits, her naked body silhouetted against the window as she cups my cheek, blue eyes glinting in the late morning sun drifting in through my curtains. How long were we at it? At least the sun doesn't kill her. That would've been awkward. "Risky, asking a woman her age."

I roll my eyes. "Well, I haven't known too many hundred-year-olds who"—I glance downward—"were quite as under-standing as you. Normally, that tends to mean twenty-somethings and me feeling like a creep."

"I was born in the year of our Lord 1189. I am 833 years old. I did, in fact, study sexology and was a member of the Society for Sexology. However, no, there were not doctorates available at the time in it, and I have a medical degree. However, that was back in 1910, so I can't exactly give you any prescriptions, but if you'd like some leeches or bloodletting—I'm especially good at that one—or for me to see the balance of your humors, I could probably remember that stuff."

I'm reasonably certain that all of that was out of practice by the 1900s, but she's probably joking there. Maybe. She could also just be lying. It certainly wouldn't be the first time I let a liar into my bed. Maybe she's not even a hundred years old. "And what, you're just one of those rare eight-hundred-year-olds who's totally fine with trans people?" She didn't even seem to be fetishizing me. I've gotten that before. Sometimes, if I'm desperate enough, it's worth humoring them for a fun night, but I tend to regret it in the morning and feel like I was just used, but she doesn't make me feel like that. She didn't get excited at the idea; she seemed completely indifferent, and then, unlike every other girl I've ever known who acted like that, she backed it up in the bedroom. She wasn't at all hesitant. Maybe that sexology doctorate really did do something. "I haven't known too many people like that."

"How old are you? I'm sure it feels like it's some big new thing, and acceptance is certainly higher now, but for the most part, there hasn't always been that same hatred for you all, either. Back in the twenties—the last ones, not the ones we're in now—even while it was illegal, there were still procedures in place to get official dispensations to legally live as a different gender. I got to help quite a few people with that. Including..." She trails off, her expression oddly forlorn. "And I think the acceptance is only growing again," she adds, her playful smile coming back.

"I'm about three thousand. It's tough to say. I didn't interact with humans that much, and you all change your calendars so often that it's always made keeping track of that sort of thing rather tedious."

Her eyes widen, and for a second, I think I've finally found a deal-breaker. I hadn't even realized that was what I was looking for. She's too perfect. I need an excuse to get her out of my apartment, and it would be so much easier if I didn't want her to stay in my bed for the next week. "Well, I've always liked older women. I'm just not used to there being any."

This is exactly what I mean. This is what made the sex so amazing. Nothing throws her. Everything seems to only make me more attractive, and seeing that desire, that complete acceptance in those beautiful blue eyes, is not making this easy. "Well, you're just a baby to me. Not even a third of my age."

She grins. "That's a novelty. So what have you been up to all these centuries, other than telling people what sexology actually means?"

Is that a reason to kick her out? I haven't been doing anything for most of my life. Maybe that'll finally make her stop looking at me like I'm perfect. "I ate a bunch of people when I was younger, mostly just living in a cave and staying with my own kind."

"You ate people?" Finally, there's actually judgment there. I just didn't think that was the part that would make a vampire judge me.

I nod. "It's been a long while. And I mean a long, long while." I want to say longer than she's been alive, as that's what I tell most people, but it's not true for her. "It's how I was raised. People were for seducing and food. And…" It's an excuse. If I cared that much about how my family raised me, then I wouldn't be the woman I am. "But I did stop. As for what else I've been doing, well, I couldn't really go out and explore the world." I gesture at my tail, accidentally giving the perfect reason to drag her gaze back to my distraction. "I didn't interact that much with civilization no matter how hard I tried. I met a few people, dated a few women, talked to a couple very drunk philosophers a few times, but if I went into town, it would cause a panic, and I could hardly have that."

"I'm sorry." She still looks a little bothered by the idea that I've eaten people, which must be hypocritical, but she seems genuinely sympathetic. "I can't say I know what it's like to be unable to go outside, but I do know how it feels to have people look at you in utter terror and run. It's not an experience I'd wish on anyone."

I squeeze her with my tail, which is certainly not a gesture that says go away so much as climb back onto me. I need to focus on the conversation. I already have her judging me, so I'm sure I can find a reason why it'd be a bad idea to just pull her onto me and forget that there's anything in the world that I need to do besides feel her. "It's okay. There's the internet now. I can get food delivered, I can work, I can do anything I want. I would've killed to have this thousands of years ago. I'm finally not so sequestered."

"That sounds quite freeing. I've never really thought about it. I've done online gambling, used Tinder and a few other sites, but I dunno, maybe I'm too old. I need that tactile sensation." Her thumb brushes along my hip, and it's all I can do not to grab her. "I hate that you had to miss out."

"I still had tactile sensations. You're far from my first, and you won't be my last." There, that at least says something. I'm not after anything serious, and she needs to know that, even if I should've mentioned it last night.

Her smile remains undeterred. "I'd hate to think I was."

"I ate my first like I was always taught to, but I've had quite a few people who lived, as well." I'm trying so hard to make her want to leave. All I'd have to do is tell her to, but I can't bring myself to say it. Instead, I have to dredge up the one thing that bothered her.

She doesn't look upset in the same way as before, but there's something in those eyes that I'd be able to read so much better if my curtains were a little thinner. It's not quite sadness, but I'm not sure what it is. "Yeah, I did too. Probably for the best. We don't need to linger on the past. The present is far more fun."

Did I touch a sore spot? "The present is indeed quite fun," I concede. I've told her I'm not looking for anything serious, and she seems to be done with all the getting-to-know-you talk. That should be a good sign. I don't have to kick her out. I can enjoy how amazing she feels against me and not have to think about anything else. But can I take that risk? Will I still not want more tomorrow morning?

"I think I need a little more of that chocolate vodka," she says. I move my tail out of the way so she can climb off the bed. She looks around until she finds the bottle on its side on the carpet. "Lid's on!" She cheers, popping it off and taking a swig. "Want any?"

I bite my lip. If I say yes, she'll come back into my bed. I'll drink, and I'll fuck her, and I don't think I'll ever regret that decision. Now she knows what I like, and that most amazing sex in my life may end up in second place. Or third, if we keep at it. "I don't want anything serious," I finally say, just in case telling her she wouldn't be my last wasn't enough of an indication.

"Switch to beer, then?" She chuckles.

"I was more thinking we could have absinthe. If you're okay with—"

"I'm not the dating type."

That shouldn't hurt. And since it does, I certainly shouldn't let her back into my bed. "Why's that?"

"Every time I fall in love with someone, they end up dying. I'm tired of that happening." The words are oddly both bitter and playful.

I could point out that I'm immortal and older than she is. That that's one thing she'd never have to worry about. But that would suggest something that I don't want, and neither does she, so it would be silly to even mention. "The absinthe is in the cabinet over there." I point toward my kitchen. I'm really not going to kick her out, am I? "We should probably order some food too. I don't know about you, but I'd like to have enough energy to make sure I get to keep hearing you make that noise."

Her smile only grows. "All right, pick a place." Her eyes widen. "I don't really have the money to—"

I shake my head. If she can't pay, I can. I'm not going to ask about her financial situation. I'm not going to worry about her. None of that matters. I'm going to enjoy a fun crazy night of sex, drinks, and food, and I'm not going to try to learn anything more about her. "I'll order some blood for you, and we can get Indian food. Do you like—"

"Sounds perfect. I'll get the glasses. Do you have any sugar cubes?"

This is such a mistake. She's too perfect for me. "Yeah, they're in the pantry. I can show you."

She shrugs. "Just order the food. I'll find it. I'm sure I have time before it gets here."

Why is she trying to take care of me? It's tough to get around the Community Center, but I can handle my own apartment.

Maybe she wants to pay me back for being the one to buy food and wants to handle things herself? Or maybe she's planting cameras, and this is all a trick.

I keep an eye on her as I call in the blood order, but she seems to only be looking for sugar cubes. Though she'd probably be doing better if she'd realize the pantry was the big door. I point to it, trying not to laugh as I tell the woman on the other end of the phone that I'd like a couple bags of O positive vegan. I hope that's what she likes. It's what I usually get for Dinah.

By the time she's back in bed and the orders are placed, my fears are starting to subside. She hasn't tried anything weird, and I didn't see any cameras. Maybe I can simply enjoy another night of fun and move on with my life. This really is exactly what I need.

## Chapter Five

### *Elfriede*

"So what brought you to town?" Phoebe asks over eggs and leftover naan.

I smirk. She seemed rather done with trying to get to know me last night. I thought she needed the distance between sex and intimacy to make things easier for her, and I'm always willing to accommodate whatever is necessary to make sure everyone involved is having a good time. "Do you want to know, or are you just trying to make casual conversation over breakfast before you kick me out?" I wince. "Sorry, that sounded harsher than I meant."

"No, it's fair." She sighs. "I don't know. I had a really nice— no, that's selling it short. That was the best sex I've ever had, and it was nearly thirty hours of it. It was amazing. And I really needed it. But I'm not up for anything more than that."

I have practiced a good deal to earn that praise. It probably makes me a bit conceited, but I don't tend to let that get to my head too much, as sex is about the only thing I'm good at. "I'm not either. And I had a phenomenal time as well. I never thought of all the new positions a tail would make possible."

She has the most adorably embarrassed smile on her face. She'd probably be blushing if she wasn't cold-blooded. I don't think anyone has ever made her feel okay with herself before. It's a crime, as she's absolutely perfect. "Well, I'm glad it was fun for you too."

"It very much was." I think that answers the question. We're done here. It's a shame. I'd have loved getting to spend a few more weeks exploring all the possibilities, but I don't want to play with her heart. If she can't handle getting to know me, then a week is definitely too long. Though it could always give her a chance to learn to hate me. I look at my half-eaten breakfast. It's good, but I don't actually need to eat, and it's not so amazing that I'll regret it. "I should probably get out of your hair."

She bites her lip and looks between me and the door. I think she's considering how bad an idea it would be to ask me to stay. I'd do it, I don't mind feeling used, but I don't know that it'd be for the best. "Yeah," she finally says. "You probably should."

Normally, I'd kiss her good-bye, but that look scares me. I doubt she has feelings for me yet. I may know a few fun tricks, but I'm not that desirable. However, given the few hints she let slip, she's probably on the rebound or something similar, and that can make people attach a little too easily. It's best to nip it in the bud, and kissing her again would probably end with us on the bed. Or just on her tail again; that had been interesting. I stand and push my chair in. I'm wearing my new shirt, though I would love a clean pair of pants and underwear.

"I had a great time with you. Take care of yourself." I hesitate. I probably shouldn't say anything more than that. I don't want her to think I'm trying to be romantic, but I can't stop thinking about how shocked she was by me. "And if you don't mind a word of advice, don't settle for people who don't treat you like the beautiful woman you are." I turn and head for the door, knowing that I absolutely said too much.

"Wait."

Shit. I pissed her off. I turn back, but she doesn't look angry. Her eyes are shimmering and not meeting mine, but there's nothing else to suggest that my words bothered her. "There's another blood bag in the fridge. Since you're broke and apparently don't kill people, I thought you might want to take it with you."

I grin, flashing my fangs. "You're the best." I grab the bag from the fridge and lick my lips. I should probably save it. I'm not in need yet, but I've been depriving myself for so long, and I don't have any way to store it. But either way, I should get out of here. I wave, and she waves back, so I let myself out.

Her surprisingly nice loft looks more like a run-down old building from the outside. I barely even noticed it the other day. She was intoxicating and incredibly distracting. Where am I going now anyway?

The Community Center? Not without money. And I'm back to needing a place to stay but with a good deal less energy after all that sex. The blood's probably enough that I could manage mind-controlling a few people, but I need to start looking for a good casino in town.

I didn't even charge my phone since she didn't have an iPhone charger, so it's back to being dead. Well, what's the point of life if you never use superspeed? I don't know exactly where I am, but I can at least find a store or a bank or someplace else where I can make someone give me money. I hurry, leaving the sexy snake girl's house behind until I find myself in something resembling a downtown. I'm not sure if it's the actual one, but there are tall buildings, and I smell coffee from every direction. It's nearly overwhelming, but it's better than the overwhelming scent of human and animal feces, so I'll take industrialization any day.

Coffee doesn't sound terrible, but before I reach a café or a bank, I find a hotel towering over me. Now that's promising. I walk inside, smiling at the women at the counter. "Hi there, I assume whatever company is your biggest client has a card on file?"

Her brow creases, and she glances toward the phone on the desk like she's planning on reporting me.

"Perfect, thank you." I beam at her but find myself hesitating. Normally, I wouldn't question using my powers on someone. So long as they rest and it's not used on them again too soon, they'll be fine, but as I'm learning, this is Toronto. What if someone else has already put their whammy on her, and I end up adding the finishing blow to brain damage? Vampires seem to be immune to venereal disease, so it's been a long time since I was in any real risk of hurting anyone else.

But as she's suspicious and starting to reach for the phone, I should probably act fast. I really hope no one messed with her already. "Put an executive suite on that business card and send up a fruit basket with some champagne. And you have room service, right? Can you get anything other than food? I could use a way to order clothes."

She shakes her head, blinking slowly. It's not an unusual sign. Probably not brain damage. I hope.

"That's a pity. I'll figure that part out later."

She taps a few keys on the computer. "Room 2231 is available. Just give me a moment, and I'll get your keys."

Perfect. She's still forming sentences. That's a wonderful sign. "Thank you. Take your time."

She doesn't call the cops or a supervisor, instead simply putting a couple key cards into a device before handing them to me. "Call the front desk if you need anything. I hope you enjoy your stay. Will you need any help with your bags?"

"I'm good. You have a great day, beautiful."

I sling my dirty shirt over my shoulder and head to the elevator. It takes its sweet time, but it's worth the wait. My room is far from the nicest I've ever stayed in, but it is quite nice. There's a full living room with a huge TV, a couch built more for aesthetics than comfort—but plush enough and surprisingly unstained—a fridge, a microwave, and my basket includes chocolate.

Today started off with amazing morning sex and leads to chocolate and champagne? Only a fool would complain.

I sink onto the couch with a glass of bubbly and a couple chocolate-covered strawberries. It must've been a honeymoon package. I find images of Phoebe drifting into my head, and I can't help but imagine feeding her one of the strawberries, falling into the bed with her, and having a few dozen glasses of champagne.

Damn, it's been too long since I've had sex that good. I look fondly back on every woman I've ever been with, but it's not too often that I'm fantasizing about them the next day. I bite into the strawberry and lay my head on the pillow.

Clothes and money. And I should put the blood in the fridge before I forget.

I eat another strawberry and eye the orange leaning against one of the champagne bottles.

But I need clothes. As much as vampires aren't supposed to sweat, I got plenty gross on that flight as I was nearly dying, and it wasn't like I could borrow a pair of pants from the girl who doesn't have legs.

With a wistful sigh, I drain the glass, get up, refrigerate the blood, and go for a walk.

I'm already downtown, so there has to be a decent place to go. Where would I be if I was a lovely clothing shop? I pull my phone out to check, only to be greeted by that same black screen.

I should add a charger to the list. Three priorities, and I should be able to knock them out in any order and still have time to find the nearest casino. I smell the air out front of the hotel, but as I'm not quite certain what phone chargers smell like, it doesn't help me much.

It does however draw my attention toward a nearby bakery. I'll have to keep them in mind to buy breakfast for whatever woman ends up in my bed. Their muffins smell mouthwatering.

A few blocks farther, someone mutters curses under their breath. "Son of a bitch won't give me my money."

Is someone being robbed? That would work out perfectly. Robbers always have cash on them. I head over to investigate the noise and find someone kicking an ATM. Not quite a robbery. That's going to attract the cops at some point.

"Give me the fucking money," he says louder. "You can't just eat it."

He can't exactly give me money if the ATM isn't working, and I should get out of here before the cops arrive, but I'm curious.

The man stops attacking the machine and seems to finally think to go inside the bank. I could poke around the ATM. If I avoid the camera, he'd take the blame for any damage I cause.

While I'm considering that, a man wearing sunglasses hurries casually over to the ATM and removes something from the bill slot, money falling into his hand.

A criminal! They never complain when you steal their money. This is perfect.

He starts to run away, still trying to act casual as he stuffs the bills in his pockets, and I step in his path. "Hi there," I say.

"Can I help you?" There's fear in his voice as he glances between me and the bank.

"How much did you get?"

I can see him crunch numbers in his head. Obviously, lying is the best choice, but he doesn't know what lie may work. "Is that any of your business?"

"Well, yes, it is. Give me half." I imbue my power into the words, and he blinks and pats his jacket, pulling the money out again and holding it out to me. "A pleasure doing business with you." I take the offered money, but I can hear people moving in the bank to come investigate. It'd be best not to wait here. I grab the guy and move us a few blocks. He's already confused enough that I doubt he'll even notice. "That was a close one," I say, not bothering to control him. "Glad we managed to get away. Great working with you." I wave to him and walk on.

He doesn't give chase or call after me, but I can hear him muttering as he tries to figure out what just happened.

I finally examine what I was given. Three hundred. I can work with three hundred.

It takes me around twenty minutes to find a charger in a questionable electronics store that looks like it must be selling stolen or bootleg goods, but it's fifteen bucks, and I don't care to ask questions. Getting the SIM card is a bit more annoying, but the owner is kind enough to cover the activation fee and the prepaid plan for me, so I thank him and find a nice clothing shop.

I was really hoping to save money for gambling. I glance around the store. None of the clothes have tags. If the owner's in, I prefer to make them give me the clothes, but everyone looks too young for that, and I'd rather not get anyone fired.

I pick out a few pairs of slacks and find a set of tops almost as nice as the one I'm wearing that must be at least three times the price. I'd prefer to try them on first, but if I'm going to steal it all, I'd rather not attract any attention first. I take the clothes and leave the store in the blink of an eye.

Fortunately, the lingerie store has a manager in, so I get all I want for free and am able to return to my hotel utterly exhausted.

I hate using my powers like that. It's so draining, and it takes all the fun out of life, but I left everything I owned back in Berlin, and I'm not up for sleeping in a park. I grab that wonderful gift from my dear snakey friend, pour the blood into a glass, and microwave it, eating another strawberry while I wait.

Grabbing the half-empty bottle of champagne as I head toward the bedroom, I sip my blood and sink into the lush hotel bed alone. That took a lot out of me. Maybe after a nap I can see about a casino and find a new companion there. They never get exciting until nighttime anyway.

# CHAPTER SIX

## *Phoebe*

Someone knocks on my door. "Come in," I call from the bed. I'm not moping anymore, but I don't feel like untangling my tail from the blanket.

It opens to reveal Dinah holding a Styrofoam box. "Hey there."

For a second, I thought it was going to be Freddie. It's good that it's not. I wave to her. "Come here. And don't worry, I already changed the sheets. They were barely even on the bed."

She giggles, looking a little embarrassed. "I take it you had a good time, then? All you texted me yesterday was that you were still busy with her."

I'm so glad I can't blush. It was fun. I shouldn't be awkward about that, especially since there's no way I'd ever let it be anything more. "I did. I really needed that. She was just…wow. I don't think anyone's ever made me feel like that."

She grabs some plates from my cabinet. "That mean there will be a second date?"

"No!" I sit up, trying not to look angry and also to not think about why that bothered me so much. I don't want to dwell on this. I'm on the rebound, and I'm emotional, and that's all. "It means I had a good time. She's not really my type."

"Seemed like your type the other night." She laughs as she sits on the corner of my bed.

"Yeah, and I think every woman is her type. I'm not interested in a relationship with someone like that. I'm not interested in a relationship at all." My last relationship doesn't feel as fresh today. That's a good sign. It means that this really was good for me, but it's still hard not to think about those pictures. I pull myself over to her and find that I'm smiling. I know part of me is just happy to have someone checking up on me, but I may also still be in a good mood from all that crazy sex.

"I don't get how you can feel that way." She opens the Styrofoam, and the smell is nearly overwhelming. God, how am I still so hungry? "I was hanging out with Rachel at work, and she said I should bring you some poutine. It's supposed to be great for hangovers."

"I'm not that hungover, but I am also not going to turn down Rachel's poutine." I take a plastic fork and have a bite. It might be even better than the Indian food last night. I'm having such a good day. I'm happy. I don't even have to force it. I just wish I wasn't still so sad.

"What was it like?"

I chuckle. How would I even describe it? "I don't think I can really put it into words. Even though I knew that there was no real emotion with it, she made me feel loved and wanted in this pure way that I've never really felt before."

"I know what that's like."

I glance at her, gravy dripping from my suspended fork and onto my sheets. "Do you?"

"Well, not the no-feelings part, but, yeah, that's what it's like with Rachel."

I shudder. She should not be comparing my slutty one-night stand to her wife. "Don't tell me that."

"Why? You really don't ever want to see this girl again? She looked pretty into you when I saw her."

It's all I can think about. The way she looked at me with almost worship and need in her eyes. "It was a night of fun. I'm sure she's already giving another girl that same feeling. I needed it. I *really* needed it." I sigh. It had never been like that with Paula. Or with anyone. "And that kind of terrifies me."

"It sounds like you rather liked it, why is that terrifying?"

"Because it was the greatest…it was maybe the happiest I've ever been. The most comfortable. Definitely the best sex. And I knew if I let her stay longer, I was going to end up being hurt, and I still let her stay another day."

Her eyes widen. "Are you in love with her?"

Sometimes, I forget how much of a child Dinah still is. She looks nineteen despite being in her forties, but she never had any real experience in the world beyond a few tragedies. She married her first love and spent twenty-five years in prison. I suppose I shouldn't expect her to understand the complexities of normal relationships. "No. I'm not sure I even like her. How exactly did she have any room to judge me for having eaten people? She's a vampire who uses women!" I take a deep breath, finding myself screaming at a different vampire, one who does not deserve it. "I'm sorry."

"I'm not the biggest fan of vampires. I've had one kill me, one try to kill me, and another one frame me for murder and try to bury me in concrete. Rachel and I may be exceptions, but from what I've seen, they tend to be rather heartless assholes."

Then why can't I see Freddie as a heartless asshole? I'm trying to. I know that she is one. But all I can see is how loving she was, how accepting. Rebounds make people stupid. "Yeah, she's no different. I don't need that."

"Well what *do* you need?"

I eat a nice big forkful and lick my lips. "Right now, this poutine and a good friend." Speaking of, I should call Larissa. She was blowing up my phone too. Or Vanessa. Or Katie. I shouldn't be relying on only the one friend just because she keeps showing up at my door when I need her. "Thank you for, well, being you."

"A bored actress between gigs trying to kill time while her wife's at work?"

"Yeah, exactly."

She grins, her fangs showing. There's no guile in it. No ulterior motive. But I didn't see any in Freddie, either. "I actually have an audition tomorrow I was going to go to, but I can bail if you need me around more."

"What day even is it?"

She giggles. "Tuesday. Or do you mean the audition? 'Cause then, Wednesday."

Heartbreak and two days of sex really throws off a girl's internal calendar. "I'm doing better, Dinah. It's okay."

"Well, yeah, but you're stressing about a new girl. I feel like I should be here for you. We could go back to that bar and try to find you another one-night stand?"

"I'm not hung up on Freddie." There's a little more heat to the words than there probably should be. I don't know why I'm so emotional about it. Right, rebounds. And it's shot day tomorrow too, so that probably isn't helping. "I'm just emotional. But I'm doing better, and I want you to get that part. Okay, actually, I want you to stop getting parts so I don't always have to reschedule weekend games around you, but that's selfish, and I care about you succeeding."

"Well, then, I'm sure you appreciated my bombing my last three auditions."

"No." God, I hope she didn't think I was too serious there. "You know I was teasing. You do know I was teasing, right?"

"Yes. I miss getting to do our games too. I'm sorry I always end up inconveniencing everyone so much."

"It's okay. We can't all make our own schedules." Oh no, that reminds me. I hadn't even thought about working after all that drama. I didn't even post anything more in the server. I'm the worst.

Dinah looks worried. I must've been showing that anguish.

I shake my head. "It's nothing, just realized how little work I've been doing recently."

"Oh." She glances toward my computer in its corner against the wall. "We could fix that? I know I wouldn't have my own avatar or anything, but I could play with you. I'm still trying to get used to computers, and I'd love the practice."

She really can be so sweet. Maybe that's what I need now. I already got the sex out of my system, so I should focus on spending time with my friends. I'll call everyone back, or at least message them and let them know I'm okay. I shouldn't have been worrying them. I have people who care about me, and I know it. "Sure you don't need to practice for your audition?"

Dinah shrugs. "I can do it later."

"What time is it?" I grab my phone from the nightstand, careful not to hit Dinah with my tail, and check. "Sure, we can do a little stream tonight, and I'll make sure I actually announce a bigger one ahead of time for tomorrow." I let everyone on my server know and turn back to Dinah. "Okay, so we have half an hour to figure out something that we could play and to download it, so let's find an indie game or something."

"I know those words probably mean something."

I roll my eyes. How have I left this poor thing so uncultured? I'm so much older than her, and yet, she's the one who doesn't know a thing about the modern world. Rachel has not been doing enough to get her caught up. "So probably not something too hard. That takes out most shmups. There's a beat 'em up I've been wanting to play that I got in a bundle. I'll show you how it works, and we can restart it once I start the stream."

She grins. "Yeah? I don't want to cramp your style or anything."

"No, it'll be fun. I'm sure my fans will be happy to have a change of pace. Better than watching me farm for shitty drops for twelve hours straight like they'll probably get tomorrow."

Dinah nods, her eyes wide. She has no idea what any of that meant and is just playing along. That's fine. I grab one of my controllers and pull up a chair from the kitchen for her and set it next to mine. "You remember the buttons from the last couple times, right?"

"I guess. I played a couple games in prison, but it was nothing as complicated as your stuff."

"This isn't too complicated." Sometime, I'll have to ask her about those prison games, but we need to get ready for the stream.

"If you say so. I just don't want to end up running into a wall while you whine about how I need to control a camera."

I huff. "I wasn't whining."

"If you say so."

I roll my eyes. "Okay, so let me just show you this." I boot up the game and let her get used to the controls before I exit it, load up my avatar, and make sure it's still configured properly. The anime-looking lamia smiles back at me, and I wish I looked that good. They always say to hide in plain sight.

Once it seems to be moving correctly and I've made sure the hot keys are still set up, I start the stream and introduce my invisible friend, as my computer would probably explode if I tried to run two avatars at once while playing video games and running OBS.

After a few seconds' delay, chat greets her. There aren't too many people here today but still a lot more than when I started streaming a decade ago, before Vtubing was even a possibility, so I'll take a few thousand for a slow day. Most streamers would kill for that.

I grab my controller and introduce the game and have to save Dinah's ass from the first boss and nearly get myself killed in the process. At least she seems to be learning; she kept walking off ledges the first time I tried playing a video game with her a few months ago. Maybe in a few decades, she'll even be the one saving me.

# CHAPTER SEVEN

## *Elfriede*

The city is dark when I look out the window. It was early in the afternoon when I went to bed. How long did I sleep? Phoebe took more out of me than I thought.

At least that should mean more action at whatever casino I can find.

I shower and discover that I forgot to buy a hairbrush. I call the front desk. "Hey, do you have like combs or brushes or anything?"

"Yes, ma'am," a woman says. It's not the same one as before, but I suppose that would be a very long shift if it was. "We have both, which would you like?"

"I'll take both and hair gel if you have it. And some nail clippers."

"It's room 2231, correct?"

"Yes, thank you."

"That'll be right up."

I grin at my reflection, eager to finally get my hair back in order as I put on some of my new clothes. The gray slacks look amazing with the matching vest and the plain white button-up. For clothes off the rack, I'm really pleased with these, even if they're not quite as amazing as the shirt that spider made. I should make sure I get more of those. I wonder if it was made from web. I wouldn't think that would feel like silk, but it would explain the price. I'll happily wear spider clothes for the rest of my life if they're all that amazing.

Someone knocks at the door, and I go out to grab my hair care products. "Thank you so much, gorgeous," I say, flashing my best smile.

The woman smiles at me, but as she looks at my outfit, her eyes seem to only be on it, not the body underneath. She's probably straight. That's a shame. "It's no problem."

"Well, thank you again." I smile less lasciviously. "Would you happen to know where a nearby casino is?"

"The nearest is out in Etobicoke. It's pretty nice."

Etobicoke? Why do I know that name? Oh, right, that's where the Community Center is. I could always stop by and buy some more clothes beforehand. Or after, with my winnings. Before is probably for the best. "Thanks again."

She nods, and I give her a ten as a tip and let her be on her way so I can tend to my hair. When I'm done, I finally look like myself again. How would I handle it if I was one of those vampires who can't see their reflection? I'm far too pretty for that.

My hair looks perfect, styled and slanted to the right just past my eye, so I put my sunglasses on and head outside. I could probably run all the way there, especially now that I can use the map on my phone again, but I just fixed my hair, and I don't want to wrinkle my clothes. I hold my thumb up, but after a few minutes of walking with no one bothering to pull over, I'm starting to suspect it won't work. Do people not pick up hitchhikers in Canada? Or do they not use their thumbs? I'll have to ask about that sometime.

I order a cab on my phone and tell it to pick me up by the bakery. Unfortunately, it's closed. The inhumanity. It's only 10:30 at night; they have every reason to expect that people would still want muffins.

The cab pulls up while I'm wishing for a pastry, and I hop in and tell him to take me to the Honeydale Mall.

I let him give me the change for the hundred I didn't give him and tell him to drive off as I head inside and breathe it all in.

It's so unlike anyplace I've ever been. The smells to my inhuman nose are an intoxicating mix of monstrous and delightful, and most importantly, I smell croissants.

There's a strange goat man standing behind a counter with some of the most delectable-looking pastries I've seen in decades. "Do you have coffee?" I ask.

"There's a stand over there." He points. "They have Turkish beans that I really recommend."

"Fantastic. One, no, two croissants." I give him a ten and a smile and move on to buy my coffee and find a place to sit.

There's an area by the bar I met Phoebe at—the restaurant I ordered Phoebe's nachos from—so I take a seat and sip my coffee and enjoy my croissants. It's the simple pleasures in life, really. Though I wouldn't mind some whiskey in the coffee, now that I think about it.

Just as I'm considering making a trip to the bar to turn my dream into reality, I catch a familiar scent.

I turn to find eyes on me, along with a conflicted expression on the face of a cute minotaur. The face isn't quite like a cow's; the eyes are too human, a cool confident brown, and the mouth doesn't protrude quite enough to be a muzzle. I don't remember her making quite that expression before, but I do recall a few lovely nights with that face between my legs.

"Vivi," I say, beaming at her. "It's good to see you."

She shakes her head, and a cloven hoof thuds on the linoleum. "I didn't think you'd ever actually come out here."

"Oh, just because it's utter agony? Sometimes, needs must."

Without asking, she pulls out the seat across from me and sits, the chair groaning under her. That's a good sign. She sounded upset with me, but maybe there is something else on her mind. It's been far too long since I've felt those hands. "How on earth did you end up in Toronto?"

"Well, you always made it sounds so lovely." I gesture at my remaining croissant. "Would you like one?"

Her gaze flits between it and me before finally settling on the croissant. "I'll take half."

I split it and slide the plate over before dunking a piece in my coffee and taking a bite, watching her. There's something in those eyes that I can't quite place. She looks happy to see me, I think, but there's more to it than that. There's curiosity, but what else? "My situation changed, and I heard from you and enough other people—fiends? That this was the place to go. I needed a new start, so I figured I'd give it a try."

"Why did you need a fresh start, Friede? What trouble have you gotten yourself into?"

I sigh but force myself back to smiling. "Vivi, there's nothing to worry about."

She crosses her arms. "I'm not worried about you."

"Good." I take another bite. "You shouldn't be. I am, as ever, untroubled."

"I can see that." Her tone is flat but with a hint of amusement. So the look isn't anger. I can live with that.

"It's the only way to live. Speaking of living, I have a lovely suite back in town if you'd like to help me break in the bed."

She shakes her head, but her lips curl up in a smile that I don't think a normal cow would be capable of. "I think we'd just be breaking the bed. Again. Not so much breaking it in."

"We can be careful this time. And beds are a lot better made than they were when we last met."

"I'm not sure that's true." She shakes her head and chews contemplatively on the croissant. "Friede, what actually brought you here?"

"Right now? You. Entirely you."

That smile only grows, and her eyes don't quite meet mine. "That's what you always say."

"That I'm looking for you? Why wouldn't I be?"

She snorts. "Fine, Friede. But I'm going to keep asking you."

"And I'll keep telling you the truth, as I always do."

She shakes her head. "So where's this hotel?"

Now that's more like it. Today just keeps getting better. "Let me order a cab, and I'll grab a few jackets while we wait."

She sighs and tilts her head.

"Right. I could make sure it's a big car?"

"I don't think it would work."

"Well, how do you get around?"

She smirks. "I have a van."

That would make sense. I'm so used to not having a car that I never expect anyone else to have one, either. "Well, then, let me buy those jackets, and you can take me to my bed. Or yours." She looks amused. Like I'm an entertaining distraction. I'm used to that. I find that spider again and buy more of her clothes, including those jackets, another shirt, a few pairs of slacks, and some socks. I couldn't resist. That's almost all of my money. Easy come, easy go.

Outside, there's a van in the parking lot. It's white and boring-looking and doesn't at all suit the vision leading me to it. I suppose it stays under the radar. She climbs into the driver's seat that seems heavily modified to accommodate her. The hotel is not going to appreciate what we do to the bed.

"And how have you been, beautiful?" I ask as she pulls onto the road. "You were so busy grilling me before that it slipped my mind." Grilling may have been a poor choice of word.

"Ups and downs. It's been twenty years, Friede. I don't know what all you expect me to catch you up on."

I study her supple lips as they seem to sway between amusement and exhaustion. "Are you happy?"

She sighs and doesn't say anything for a long moment. "It's been a while."

Does she mean since she saw me or since she was last happy? "Is there anything I can do?"

She snorts again. "You're doing all you can."

Why did that sound like an insult? Should I ask more about it? I suppose she'd tell me if she wanted. "I have some champagne and chocolate in my room. Maybe that'll cheer you up." I forgot to buy more blood. Goddamn it. Guess I'll have to be careful not to break a hip.

"I'm sure that'll help a lot."

Neither of us says anything for a few minutes, and she turns the radio on. I want to ask her more, but it can all wait for when she's comfortable. She looks like she needs to get laid as badly as I do.

She pulls into the parking garage of my hotel, and I check the elevator to make sure it's empty. The trip goes smoothly, and we don't run into anyone in the hallway, but when we reach my room, I'm reminded of just how much larger she is than the door. "Huh," I say, trying to figure out how to make this work without getting kicked out of the hotel.

"I think I can squeeze in," she says once I open the door, and we've had a chance to look around a few times.

"Perfect, that's exactly what I was hoping you'd do."

She rolls her eyes. "You're incorrigible."

"Would you have me any other way?"

She doesn't say anything as she turns sideways and crouches, moving slowly to the side until she's in the room and able to give an appreciative glance around. "I suppose I wouldn't. It would hardly be you, then, would it?"

"I *am* a sexologist."

That earns an honest guffaw. "Where's this champagne and chocolate I was promised?"

I grab the bottle and basket and lead her to the bedroom. She has to duck to walk in, but the entryway is large enough to take her whole width.

I drop onto the bed and pour us some drinks, and before I can even hand one to her, I feel large hands roaming over me, sliding my vest up. The bed groans as she sinks onto it, but it doesn't break or go through the floor. I knew they made them better these days.

❖

Vivi pants, collapsing onto her back, much to the bed frame's protest. I trail kisses along her neck and take a bite of a strawberry, washing it down with champagne before I say, "As good as you remember?"

She cups my entire head in her hand, her thumb brushing over my cheek. "You are, as ever, magical in bed."

I lean into her touch.

"And now will you tell me why you're in town? Do you expect me to believe it was just for this?"

"What other reason would I need? As you said, this was magical."

She rolls her eyes. She was never much for pillow talk. "Friede, I never got to know you very well, but we're not strangers. Don't pretend you can hide everything." Her hand pulls away, and she sits up. Something pops in the bed, but she stays in place.

I hold very still. "I'm not hiding anything. I'm here because I want to be, and what I want right now is to be with you."

"And what about yesterday? And the day before? What did you want then?"

Phoebe flashes in my head again. She was certainly what I wanted yesterday. And the day before. "I find it best never to dwell on the past. Or the future. Why not just enjoy the moment with me, Vivi?"

"I did. And the moment's over, so now, it's right back to where you move on and forget about me for a few decades."

Oh. Is that what that look was? Did I hurt her? I never hurt people. How did I hurt her? "Why would you think I forgot about you? Look at you. You're unforgettable. You're beautiful, amazing—"

"You don't know anything about me."

"I—"

"I'm sorry, Friede. No, this was fun. I should get out of your hair." She stands, and the bed's groan is even louder.

I reach for her, the room shimmering. "Wait, no, you don't have to go."

Her hoof clops as she turns back toward me. "It was nice taking a break with you and not worrying about…it. But that's all it ever is with you. A break."

"What do you mean?"

She sighs and looks around the room. "It doesn't matter."

"Vivi, please."

She huffs. "I have cancer. It's given me a lot of time to

think. Sometimes, I look back rather fondly on the couple weeks I spent with you over the years. And there have been plenty of other women. I'm not some angry ex who's mad at you for never sharing your heart with me. I know you're not capable of that. But when I thought of all the people who've been there in my life, the people I wanted to tell, that I trusted to be there, you were one of the first I thought of. I almost called. But I tried to think of what I even knew about you, of any actual troubles you've been there for or that you've told me about." She shrugs.

I shake my head, trying to formulate any sort of response. "We were having fun. Where did all this come from?"

"I thought you'd take my mind off things. And you did. For a little while."

"That's what I'm for."

"Why do you say things like that?" Her eyes finally settle on mine, and I have to blink away tears to see there are some in her eyes as well. I don't even remember the last time I cried. "I was hoping that I was wrong, that we hadn't spent that much time together, but that you were someone I could talk to about this. I have friends here, and they've been here for me, but I don't always want to burden them with it. Catching up with you sounded nice, and I knew the sex would be phenomenal, but I was hoping that maybe when we were done, you'd be a friend and listen to me."

"I am. I will. I thought I was."

She doesn't turn to leave or gather her clothes, but she doesn't sit back in the bed, either. "Why are you in Toronto, Friede?"

Is that what this is about? She thinks I'm not really her friend because I won't tell her about my own woes? "Don't you want to talk about your…thing? How did you find out? Are you going to be okay?"

She shakes her head and starts to turn.

"Wait."

She shakes her head again and picks up her bra. "Friede—"

"I'm an idiot. That's why I'm in Toronto. I…I borrowed money from a lot of people. I figured I'd be able to just make them forget. And I did. But their books didn't. And their accountant didn't. And their boss didn't. I found one of my loan sharks dead, missing a few pieces, and I was reasonably confident that even if it wasn't an intentional warning for me, I was soon on the chopping block. I ran. It's all I've ever done, really. I booked a flight to the first place I could think of. You, Helen, Eleanora, you all made it sound like it was so amazing. And I even heard from Helen after she came out here, and she talked about how great it was. I thought maybe I'd have a new chance, and I wouldn't be that stupid this time."

She turns back to look at me but still doesn't say anything.

"It's weird here. It feels like we're everywhere. I tried flirting with a cute girl, and she was already dating a vampire. I'm not even a novelty anymore. It's so strange. I'm used to that being my biggest appeal."

"Friede…" she says again, but she doesn't finish the thought, instead sitting on the edge of the bed.

"I never meant to hurt you."

"You didn't. Well, maybe you did, but I know you didn't mean to."

"You're my friend."

She meets my eyes again, and that sadness tears me apart. "This is the longest conversation I've ever had with you that wasn't about what we should eat off each other."

"It's a very important topic." My voice is as weak as my answer.

"You're a lot older than me. I assume you've had some chances to look back on your life, and maybe you like the way you're living it, but the women you forget about keep existing after you look away."

"I never forget about any of you." Do I? It's been a lot of women over a lot of years. I barely remember my grandchildren's names at this point. I must've forgotten at least a few women by now. "Well, I don't try to, at least. You all matter to me."

"In the moment. Sure. And there's nothing wrong with that, and I never deluded myself into thinking that we were in a relationship, but I suppose I thought we were at least friends."

"We are," I say again, and it sounds so much less true. Maybe

I don't remember what a friend is anymore. "You could've called. I would've come here." God, I hope that's true. Do I even have the same number?

"Maybe. I almost did. A few times. But I kind of thought you'd rather I didn't."

More tears fall. "You're probably right," I admit, hating the words as they come out.

"Why? Why do you do this to yourself?"

I shrug. "I just can't take caring about people anymore. I still do. I care about you, I really do. None of it has been fake. With anyone. And I like being friends with the women I'm with. I try to be as caring as I can and talk to them."

"Then why is it always so shallow?"

"Because if I get attached, I'll have to watch them die." I blink away tears, but they come even more quickly. "Please tell me you're not...it can be treated, right?"

"I start chemo tomorrow."

"I'll go with you!"

I can barely see her face through my tears. Is that a hint of a smile, or is that pain? I rub my eyes, but whatever it was, it's gone by the time they're clear enough to see any detail. "I already have some..." She sighs. "It's at midnight at the veterinary clinic a couple blocks from the Community Center. Can't exactly see a normal doctor. I doubt I'll see you there, but if I do, it would be nice."

"I'll be there. I promise."

That's definitely a smile. It's a pained one, but it's a smile. I'll take it. "I'm terrified. I think it's why I had to talk to you when I saw you. I knew you'd at least take my mind off it for a few minutes."

"You don't have to be alone. You can stay the night."

She doesn't say anything.

"Please, let me be a good friend for once."

"It's okay. I'm not really in the mood anymore."

"We don't have to fuck."

She chuckles. "I wasn't aware you were capable of that."

I have no idea what to say to that.

"I'm going home, but thank you. I needed this."

"I'll see you tomorrow."

That pained smile returns as she picks up the rest of her clothes. "I hope I see you." She walks out and leaves me in bed. Alone again, with thoughts far less friendly than they had been before. I've always tried so hard not to hurt any of the women I spend time with. It's fun, and I make it clear that that's all it is. How many were left feeling like her?

# CHAPTER EIGHT

## *Phoebe*

I raise myself up on my tail to make sure I can see in the whole cupboard. There's nothing that shouldn't be there. Just like there wasn't last night, and there hasn't been in any other part of the house. I'm going insane. Freddie didn't know who I was and clearly doesn't need to spy on me to get pictures of fiends when she can look in a mirror. Can she look in a mirror? I don't even know if she has a reflection. I slept with someone I know nothing about when I'm already regretting sleeping with someone I thought I knew. How did I think that was a good idea?

And how was I right? I keep trying to insist that I was stupid for it, but it did exactly what I needed, and even more than that, she made me feel good about myself in a way that I really haven't in a long time. Maybe ever. I think I'm just scared that if I accept that she didn't do anything wrong, and that I also didn't do anything wrong by sleeping with her, I may start wanting to do it again, and I know that's not an option.

I grab my phone and shoot Dinah a "break a leg," then double-check that I'm still on with everyone else for after my stream.

Everyone already confirmed. They'll be here in five hours, and then Larissa will drop me off at the Community Center for my game tonight. I hope Dinah can still make it to that, at least, and she can tell me how her audition went.

I sigh. It's probably time to stop procrastinating.

This shouldn't be so scary. I did a stream yesterday, but it was a small, last-minute one with a friend. This will be the first time I've done a stream on my own since any of that happened. I banned Paula, and I scrubbed everything from the internet, but I don't know what people may have seen or heard or how much is still out there.

How am I going to face them without someone here?

On the other hand, putting it off isn't going to change anything. This is my job, and at least there's an update in the game. I can focus on that and pretend that I even slightly care. I start up OBS and my avatar. The cute little lamia looks back at me. Was I too foolish to do that? If I hadn't made my avatar actually look like me, would Paula still have come looking for me?

I can't really know, can I? It let me kind of be myself for a couple years, and if I successfully covered this up, it'll let me keep doing so.

I start the stream and wait for people to show up while the game loads.

"Hey, everyone," I say, hearing my voice break. I can't even keep control of my emotions long enough to say hi. This is a terrible idea. "Sorry I haven't been streaming recently. Just a bunch of personal drama. But the dry spell in the game is finally over, so we have some actual content to do and a whole new island to explore."

A few people say hi, a few more spam emotes, and quite a few ask about the personal drama. I probably shouldn't have been venting to chat as often as I have been. It was only encouraging the sort of parasocial bullshit that caused this.

The game finishes loading so I start it up, get my log-in rewards, and start on the daily quests. They're all easy today, so I'm unfortunately able to watch people in chat talking about what's been going on with me.

It takes an entire eight minutes from the start of stream for someone to finally mention them: *Did you see that fanart that got deleted?*

It's not that bad a question. And they think it's fanart, so it's probably at least not going to make them think I'm an actual lamia.

*Were those pictures real? Obviously not the tail part.*

*Is that why DarkWitch got banned?*

I still can't believe that was her. She'd been one of my first subscribers. "Okay, I guess I actually have to address that. As ever, fanart is still fine in the fanart section, but those pictures were some really creepy photoshops with some old pictures of mine that I hadn't wanted out there in the first place. I don't know how DarkWitch found them, but, yes, that is why she got banned, and anyone else sharing them around will also be banned. That shit was creepy." Focus on that. Don't make it sound like she actually took those pictures herself and all of what that would mean.

If I had at least had clothes on my top half, I could say that they were some photoshopped stills from an old stream back before I was a Vtuber, but it's either say they're real nudes that a tail was added to or that my face was shopped onto another body along with a tail, and the former better explains why I'd be so uncomfortable with the subject.

*Those were your actual tits?*

That's an easy ban, at least.

A few people spam me in-game currency, and I'm not sure if it's trying to make up for the creeps or just because people do that sometimes.

"Let's check out this new boss," I say, trying to draw attention away from the pictures. "All right, pick my team. Don't make this too easy for me."

That finally takes over the chat, and I don't see any more mention of my breasts. Though I do see a good bit of discussion of a few of the characters'. I end up with a nearly incompatible party without a decent damage dealer, and the boss—which should probably be taking me a few minutes to farm for parts for the new character—takes the better part of an hour, and we use the rest of stream pulling for the new unit, getting him only two times while seeming to get everyone else, and then testing him in a bunch of content so we can see what he's capable of.

By the time I've started to get a handle on his abilities, my friends are due to arrive any minute, so I let everyone know that we'll play around with him some more tomorrow and end the stream. That went better than I expected. I knew it'd be mentioned, but after no one brought it up yesterday, I was a little hopeful that maybe Dinah's lawyer had managed to keep enough people from seeing those pictures that I could pretend it never happened.

I suppose I could never be that lucky. That could've been so bad. I think they believe me about it being photoshopped. It didn't look like anyone actually thought that I was a real-life lamia. Probably part of the benefit of having it as my avatar.

With a sigh, I put my computer to sleep and slither back to my bed, laying my head on a pillow. They'll be here soon. I should be up, but gods, that was the most stressful stream I've had since I was a newbie.

I really hope no one spreads those pictures around. If someone realizes that they're real, that could be beyond bad.

A knock sounds from the door, so I hurry over and open it to greet Vanessa and Katie. Vanessa throws her arms around me, and I hug her back. "How you doing, babe?" she asks as I let her go.

I nod. I genuinely wish I had an answer to that question. "Better than I thought I would be, not as good as I'd like?" I suppose it's at least an answer, even if it's not a very good one.

"I could always go eat her. The bitch deserves it." She grins, flashing fangs.

She looks mostly human with black hair and a small face, and like Dinah, she's even kind of a vampire, but manananggals are a good deal different from the other ones. If she was to go after Paula, I'd probably have her lower half hanging out in my apartment while her top half flew off to get her, and that sounds incredibly awkward. "It's okay."

Katie holds up a bottle of tequila. She's blond, tall, has dark red skin, and a pair of little horns protrude from her forehead. "You really had us worried."

"I'm surprised you had time to worry about me."

Vanessa's cheeks redden. "We found some. Occasionally."

I snicker. Their characters got together in a game a couple weeks ago, and by the end of the session, they were making out and haven't been able to keep their hands off each other since. I hope I'm in a place where I can handle that. Maybe that's why I didn't want to reach out to them originally. "Larissa said she's on her way, so we might as well get started. You know how she is."

"Probably hasn't left yet and will stop to get us all food?"

"Yeah, I messaged her, making sure it was tacos."

Vanessa grins at me. "So movies, drinks, and tacos?"

"I can't drink too much or watch too many movies."

"Oh, right, you have your Wednesday game."

"I know. I'm tempted to cancel, but we're right about to fight a big bad that I've been building up for weeks, and I'd feel bad making them wait."

Katie sighs forlornly. "Then maybe not tequila. Do you have any wine?"

"I think there's some sake in the fridge."

"That'll do. A little weird with tacos."

"Well, I'm out of all my other wines," I say. "We'll just have to be a little weird."

Katie's tusks show in a jagged smile. "I'll grab the drinks, and you can figure out what we're watching. Or did you want to talk about it?"

I shrug. "What is there left to talk about?"

"You haven't really told me much," Vanessa says.

I guess I've mostly talked to Dinah about everything. But I don't want to go over it twice. "We can just watch a show until Larissa gets here. Let me figure out how to even tell it."

They seem to both accept that, so we gather on my bed with chips, dip, and the not-at-all matching sake and watch that British comedy that Katie has been trying to get us to watch for the last four months.

After the second episode, the lock on the door turns. Larissa has a spare key since she was the only person who drove me any place for years—and we dated for a few months—but my heart still races as I watch it; I'm barely willing to breathe. Paula never had a key, so it's not a realistic fear, but it's hard to trust anything these days. The door opens, revealing Larissa bearing tacos. She's tall for a human, with curly brown hair, sharp blue eyes, and ludicrously perfect makeup skills. I've had three thousand years to learn the art, and I'm still not sure I could ever manage to make my eyeliner so flawless, though at least she doesn't have wings this time. That was just rubbing it in. "I miss anything?" she asks.

I pat the spot next to me on the bed and adjust my tail to try to make more room, causing Katie to have to move to avoid it.

She sits, wraps an arm around me, and kisses my cheek. "What's been going on with you, girlie?"

I sigh. I had time to think about it during the show, but I was busy laughing for most of it. "Paula was a fan who lied to me the entire time we were together. She was actually one of my first fans. She started following my stream almost ten years ago. She took pictures of me and shared them a few places. They showed…everything. I was able to get rid of them quickly, but it was bad."

Vanessa nearly drops her taco. "Holy shit."

Katie gulps. "So they know you're…"

"Yeah. Like I said, everything. I think I managed to convince people that it was fake and just using some old actual pictures of me that had been leaked, but I don't know."

"Do you think people will start…" Larissa bites her lip, looking between the three of us fiends.

I shrug. "I doubt that it was convincing enough to most people. It wouldn't be too hard to fake a snake tail on someone. But I'm scared of that. And I still feel so violated."

"You fucking were," Katie mutters. "I'll rip her goddamn arms off."

What would happen if one of us actually went through with these threats? She'd die, obviously, as she wouldn't stand a chance, but would people find out? Would the photos leak again? She could have a dead man's switch, but I don't think she was expecting me to do anything drastic for some reason. It's weird that she was that cocky. "And then, I kinda rebounded." I stuff a taco into my mouth, but that phrasing does little to take my mind off said rebound. I can't believe I mentioned that part. It was so dumb.

A smile slowly spreads across Larissa's face. "You didn't… you're dating someone?"

"No."

"Just sleeping with them?" Vanessa asks.

I shake my head. "No. It was a fling. It was dumb. I needed someone to take my mind off things."

Larissa's brow creases into a worried expression. "Did she hurt you too?"

"Not really. It was kind of amazing, and I was insane enough to think that letting her stay here for two days was a good idea. But we didn't get close or talk all that much."

"I'm sure your mouths were busy with something else," Katie says.

I roll my eyes, as ever glad that I'm too cold-blooded to blush. "There was something about her. She looked at me like I was the most beautiful woman in the world, and it felt so real. I know it didn't mean anything but…maybe I wasn't made for one-night stands."

"They can be rough," Larissa says.

"Are you speaking from experience?"

At that, she actually blushes. "No. Not really. The one time I tried, I ended up dating them."

"I don't think that's an option with this one."

Vanessa squeezes a lime, spraying some juice on my tail. "Sounds like you want to."

Do I? I remember how comfortable I felt looking into those blue eyes, how amazing everything was, how loved she made me feel. "She's just some sleazebag," I mutter. "It would never work out."

"That's not a no."

"I do not want to date her."

"Also technically not a no," Katie points out.

I glare at her. "No."

Larissa squeezes me. "Probably a good choice. Maybe don't do one-night stands again."

"I've learned my lesson. Fuck, I'm not sure I even want to ever date again. I thought I knew Paula. It had been three months. I was thinking about asking her to move in. And she…how am I supposed to ever trust anyone again? I keep finding myself acting paranoid. I was checking for cameras before my stream, just in case Freddie—my one-night stand—in case she was another creep. There was nothing, and she hadn't done anything to suggest it, but how can I ever know now?"

Vanessa chews her lip, watching her food. "I think that's kind of part of fame. I know you're not exactly that big, but you have over a hundred thousand fans. This is a risk that comes with it."

"Well, I didn't know that when I signed up."

"I know! I'm not saying it's your fault." Her eyes are so wide. She looks terrified.

I sigh. "I'm not upset with you. I'm upset with myself. You're right, I should've known better, but at the time, I didn't have any real friends, the Community Center was tiny, and I'd just gotten out of a relationship. I never make good decisions then, do I? Twitch was new, and I thought it'd be fun. I hid my tail under my desk, and I had people to talk to, and it was almost like I had friends. I'd been in chat rooms for decades and all that, but this was different. And I could play video games during it, which is always a bonus."

Larissa leans her head on my upper arm. "I know. I still remember how much you'd schedule your life around it when we were dating. It was cute. You loved that job."

"I still do. I just didn't ever think it would bite me like this."

"Well, it won't if we just kill her," Katie reminds me.

I laugh, surprised to feel a smile creeping across my face. "I think it's a bit late for that. But thank you. I'm just going to try to move on. And maybe not let any new people in my life for a while."

"That's probably a good idea," Larissa says.

"At least with other fiends, you know we're not gonna show the whole world what you are," Vanessa says.

"Why, do you want to date me?"

Katie puts a possessive arm around her, pulling her close and prompting a giggle from Vanessa.

I roll my eyes. They really are cute together. "Maybe you're right, but it's just not a risk I'm willing to take right now."

"I get it," Larissa says.

Vanessa presses on Katie's arm, pushing it into her neck.

"God, you're insatiable," Katie mutters, doing nothing to move it.

"Get a room, you two," Larissa says.

They both smirk. "Sorry."

I lean back against my tail, eliciting a yelp from Larissa as she loses her pillow, and I check the time on my phone. I still have a few hours until my game. "Well, now we know my answer, so we can stop worrying about my love life. How're you two doing?"

Larissa chuckles. "I think it's pretty obvious how they're doing."

"Yeah, can't complain," Katie says, earning a glare and a kiss.

I glance toward Larissa. She shrugs, but there's a faint smile there. "What happened?"

Another shrug.

"You can tell me. I'm not going to get jealous just because I'm trying to swear off relationships."

She grumbles. "Fine, I just feel weird telling you about it after everything you've been going through. There's a guy at work. So far, it's just flirting, but it's been really nice."

"Aww," Vanessa says.

"I have plenty of time," I say. "Tell me about him."

Honestly, it's nice hearing her go on, all happy, about some guy I've never met. I know for a fact that I don't feel that way about Freddie, and it's nice being reminded of that. I'm not sure I even sounded like this with Paula.

She really does go on about him, though. I am not prepared for quite this much. By the time she's finished telling us everything, I need to ask her for that ride so I can make it in time for my game. It'll be easier to focus on this session now that I've finally handled everything and made up my mind. And at least Dinah's the only cute girl in my game.

# CHAPTER NINE

## *Elfriede*

It's almost eight. I've slept fitfully all throughout the day. I keep having bad dreams and waking up clinging to nothing. It's not like me, and I don't like it.

I have four hours until that appointment, and I'm starving.

Is Vivi right? Do I really do that?

Do I use and hurt women?

I don't; I know I don't. But she certainly looked like I do.

How did I do that to her? And more than that, how did I do it without even knowing?

I pinch the bridge of my nose. I'm fun. That's all I'm supposed to be. I don't do serious. And that means that the people in my life who have serious events going on don't involve me. I've chosen to hide away from the troubles of the world, but I haven't given anyone else a way to avoid them.

I care about the women I spend time with. I want them to be happy, and not just when they're with me. I want to know that they're fulfilled, that their lives are good, and that they have what they want. I talk to them; sometimes, I'll even actually discuss what they're going through if they're up for it.

And then I walk out, and maybe they'll see me years later, and we'll be familiar, have some good times, and catch up, but they don't tell me about what they've been through. They don't tell me when they have cancer or when they're suffering. They tell me about a few fun things that happened and maybe if they did anything particularly interesting. A new painting, a book, an acting gig, modeling, a marriage, and it's all shallow.

Because that's what I want. Because if I let it be anything more, I end up hurt.

And I've been crying and having nightmares because of it. I not only didn't protect myself, I hurt someone I care about.

Vivi was one of my favorite people back in the nineties. I spent so many unforgettable nights with her. We had so many drinks, so many dinners, and we talked about her dreams, about coming here. That was a connection, wasn't it?

I certainly didn't treat it like one. I call her my friend, I call so many people my friends, and they all know that I won't be there for them when anything goes wrong. That I'm not someone they can talk to. That they can get cancer, and I'm not worth telling about it.

More tears well up, and I can't bring myself to fight them.

There's something wrong with me. I knew for a fact that I wasn't like this. That I made people happy, content; that I was good for them. I'm a distraction, I'm a bit of fun, and that's really all I wanted to be.

But I make people think I care, and then I make them think I don't. I show them how wonderful they are, and then I show them how easy they are to toss aside.

Vivi didn't have to tell me all this; all she had to do was look at me with that pain in her eyes. Once I finally realized it was pain.

I really am the worst friend.

I dab my eyes on the rough hotel tissue and put my sunglasses on. I already showered and got ready an hour ago, but I started crying again. I'm never like this. It's been decades since I last cried, and I haven't been able to stop since she chewed me out.

And she was completely right to do so.

What am I going to do? This is who I am. I can't force myself to be more than this. I can't really be there for people. Can I?

If I go to that appointment, I have to watch someone I care about suffer. Again. I don't know what chemo is like, I don't know if she'll survive all of this, and if I want to stop hurting her, I have to commit to finding out.

I don't know if I have that in me.

I'm not sure there's enough of a heart left to survive another breaking.

Great, more crying. I lean back in the chair, looking out over the city. This was her dream. I came here because she made it sound like the exact escape that I needed, but clearly, it didn't save her from her problems.

Or was I the problem? She never did say why she was leaving.

No. I hurt her, but I think what really hurt her was how little of me there was. She isn't some lovestruck kid who ran off here to find a new life without me. She came out here because it was where she wanted to be, and she didn't bother saying good-bye because she didn't think I cared enough to need one.

And she was right. I barely even noticed.

Because I do use women. Not for sex. I think if Vivi was being charitable, even she'd admit that. The sex is quite a fair exchange, and I always make sure of that. If anything, it's uneven. I force a laugh. I can't even pretend to have an ego right now.

I stare at the empty bed, still sagging where she sat. I use women for fleeting intimacy that ends up hurting them. If I really want to be fair to people, I shouldn't stay after we have sex. I shouldn't try to spend days or weeks with them. I shouldn't pretend that I'm their friend, no matter how stupidly I believe it.

All it does is hurt them.

So that's the answer. I can't change who I am, so I can't be a friend. But I can keep my distance.

I can't take my eyes off that empty bed. That's what I'm resigning myself to. I already only let myself have fleeting glimpses of companionship. If I'm to try to stop hurting people, I can't have that either. Sex, drinks, and that's it. I can give them a good time, but I can't pretend I'm their friend. I can't show them how they deserve to be loved and adored, how amazing they can be, or how beautiful they are.

I really thought that was a good thing. I thought I was helping them.

It's almost ten. That's two hours until her appointment. I should stay in the room and let her see that I'm not coming. I shouldn't pretend that I'm capable of being a friend. I can't watch someone go through that. I won't.

The night outside is beautiful. There's no rain, and there's only a scant amount of snow on the ground. The city glistens like it's covered in a thin layer of glitter.

It's eleven. I'd have to leave before much longer, but I won't. Because she'll be suffering, and I don't watch people suffer. I don't sit there idly while people I care about are dying. I don't let myself care about people anymore because that's how it always ends.

I blink, the tears finally abating as a sick realization hits.

That's what I'm doing right now. I haven't stopped myself from caring about people. I've stopped them from feeling like I care. And while, until now, I'd managed to stop myself from knowing they were suffering, it's not true tonight. If I sit here, what will be any different from Paris? My friend will be hurting while I'm wallowing in self-pity.

I need blood. I'll go to the Community Center and buy some, and after that, since I'll be in the neighborhood anyway, maybe I can check on her.

❖

The cabbie pays me and drives off as I head into the run-down old mall and look around. Even in my present state, it's still a wonder, and it's busier than I've ever seen it. There are so many people of so many shapes and forms. And so many beautiful women.

I follow my nose to some blood and buy a couple bags, along with some blood sausage that I had not considered as a possibility until now. That's brilliant. "These look amazing," I say, smiling at the tree person.

His deep voice seems to almost shake the room as he says, "Thank you. I hope you enjoy."

"I can't imagine I won't."

Eleven thirty. I looked the place up. It's a few minutes from here. I doubt Vivi is even there yet. I can kill some more time here. I could look at clothes or—

I hear dice clatter on cloth.

I can gamble.

The sound leads me to a door against the back wall. I hadn't realized there was more than the stands and restaurants. I peek in, seeing a couple poker tables and a roulette table, but there's no one running them. Instead, at one of the tables, there's a fish man, a fuzzy thing, a vampire, and a very familiar form, all talking and rolling dice with papers and books scattered about the table.

Phoebe looks up, and I see expressions war on her face. For an instant, I see that same pain I saw in Vivi's eyes before she finally settles on a smile.

I didn't hurt her. I couldn't have. She's the one who didn't want to talk. She's the one who didn't want to be close. That isn't on me. I make myself smile back. "Sorry, I thought this was a casino."

"It is, usually," she says, glancing between me and the dice. "We borrow it on Wednesdays. Sorry."

I shake my head. "I don't really have time to gamble anyway." Why am I still standing here? Is it because I want to know how I hurt her? Or is it because I haven't stopped thinking about her? I should talk to her. But what would I even say? I check the time. "I'll leave you to your game."

Her gaze lingers on me, and for a second, I think she's going to say something, but the fish guy cuts her off. "You can join if you want. We're just finishing up a story, so it'd be a good time for a new character."

"I wouldn't know how. Besides, I need to meet someone." Phoebe is still looking at me. What's she thinking?

She shrugs, and there's that hurt again. "Then you should go."

I could offer to see her later. But I don't know that I want that. And I know she doesn't. "Yeah. It was nice seeing you again, Phoebe."

I leave her to whatever that game is, and I head outside. 11:45. If I take a cab, I don't know if it'll get there in time.

So I run. It's barely a kilometer, so I make it in just over a minute and try to fix my hair. Do I just go inside? That would probably be weird. I'm not a patient. And why is a vet open at midnight anyway?

I take a shaky breath and smell Vivi and a few other beings. Fuck it. I open the door and walk in. Vivi is standing in the lobby next to a bunch of chairs that would all collapse if she tried to use them, and she's shaking. There's someone next to her in a chair who's decidedly inhuman, but all I can see is that terror on her face. Her gaze turns to me, and the fear almost vanishes for a second. "You came?"

That shouldn't hurt so much. "I told you I would."

# Chapter Ten

## *Phoebe*

I rub my eyes. This game went so far past when I'd normally run it, but I had to make it later so Dinah could come after her audition, and it went on for twice its normal length since it was the conclusion to a huge part of the story, and I wanted it to feel adequately climactic.

Dinah takes a seat at the counter of Rachel's internet café and orders some paninis for us. "All right, I have to give you some credit, I would struggle to tie off quite that many plot threads and weave everything so well together for a big bad."

I wrap myself around the stool next to her and settle into it. "I've been in your Shadowrun game long enough to know that's not true."

She grins. "Yeah? That mean I won our bet as to who's the better GM?"

"Nope, you're right, you could never compete with that."

She rolls her eyes, still grinning, and takes the bloody milkshake Rachel slides her. "You two had fun?" Rachel asks.

Dinah nods. "It was great."

"Well, guess I'll have to see you pull off something that impressive in our game."

Dinah's eyes widen. "Well, I will." She doesn't sound confident. I should be a good friend and reassure her.

"I mean sure, you have a few decades' experience. I'm sure that can compete with my millennia."

She glares at me.

"I'm kidding. You're a great GM. I can't wait to see what you do with that dragon CEO you've been building up. I always use the regular corporations when I run Shadowrun games, so it's nice seeing what you do with the world. You're fantastic at world-building. I have known Homeric bards who would fail to keep up with your storytelling abilities."

She crosses her arms, an eyebrow rising.

"I'm not actually joking. Storytelling back then was a lot like GMing, and abilities were about as varied, and you're definitely up there. Speaking of your epic storytelling skills, how did your audition go?"

Dinah stops sulking and beams at me. "I actually got the lead. It wasn't even one of the parts I was interested in auditioning for, but they really liked the energy I brought to the character, so they're changing a few details in the script to match my version and having me play him, well, now her."

"Holy shit," Rachel mouths. "Why didn't you tell me? That's amazing!"

She shrugs, but her smile could be seen from space. "I just haven't had the chance yet."

"I'm really proud of you," I say.

"You two eat your sandwiches and let me see about closing up, and maybe you and I can celebrate."

I eat and let the two of them flirt while I check my phone. I have a lot of Discord alerts. It's not uncommon, but after all the drama, it's hard not to be a little worried seeing that symbol.

I click on the first one and lose my appetite. The original messages are already deleted, but I can see all the responses and the messages in the mod chat. "She spammed the pictures in every fucking channel."

"She...Paula?"

I look up to see Dinah wide-eyed and staring. She looks as shaken as I feel. "Yeah."

"That fucking bitch," Rachel mutters.

"Yeah," I repeat.

"I've killed before," Dinah says, as if she hasn't spent

decades hating herself for the one time she actually had to kill someone who wasn't actively trying to murder her. "I'll do it. Give me the word, and she is fucking gone. She can't keep doing this if she's—"

I shake my head and stare at my phone. What am I going to do? I thought that once I'd dumped and banned her, she was taken care of, but clearly, that's not true. "You'd never kill anybody, but she doesn't know that."

"I might make an exception for her," Dinah insists.

"I'll kill the bitch." Rachel does not look as hesitant about the idea as Dinah. I knew she was my friend, but I didn't think she was quite to murder-your-enemies levels of friendship. I'll try to remember that.

"I don't want to kill her."

"Are you sure?" Dinah asks. "I could call my parole officer and make sure he's cool with it, and he'd probably help us hide the body. He might even do it himself. You know how he is."

He's in our Shadowrun game and, for a parole officer, is pretty reasonable. He sold me acid once. "At least for now, let's not go with murder. But I do have two scary vampires who want her dead, so let's use that. Rachel, would you be up for paying her a visit?"

"On my own or—"

"Just drive us and maybe threaten to rip her throat out?"

She grins. "Yeah, I can do that. Give me, like, ten minutes to clean up a little and turn off the fryer, and then we can go."

This should make me feel better. Revenge is supposed to be amazing. I've known of so many who cared about nothing else, and many of them even seemed fulfilled by it, but the idea makes me sick. However, if she isn't going to stop, maybe I don't have a choice.

Rachel is good to her word, and in a few short minutes, I have to stuff myself into the back of her car without blocking the rearview mirror. It never gets any easier. I'm dreading the next time I shed my skin and end up even larger. I'm not sure I'll be able to use a normal car then.

She puts the address I give her into her phone, pulls onto the road, and we head off. What will I say when I see her? I haven't since I found out who she was. "Do you think this is all some cry for attention?" I ask.

"You think she's leaking your nudes to try to get you to talk to her?" Rachel asks, venom in her voice, and I can feel her eyes on me in the mirror.

"I blocked her, so it's not like she can message me any other way."

"If you blocked her, how did she do all this?" Dinah asks.

"It looked like a new account. The mods took care of it before I got there. She must've used a VPN, since otherwise, it should ban any accounts with her IP address." I check my phone to see if there's anything that I've missed. I was kind of freaking out when I looked originally, and it was hard to focus.

Of course, even looking at it is already making me freak out again. I look through all my notifications. A few mods messaged me as well, trying to let me know she was doing it. But they're not the only people who messaged me.

*You know no one else will love you the way I do.* It's from an account that's just a series of jumbled characters. She's probably made a bunch of alts already. I could reply and try to talk her down, but in DMs, I wouldn't have two scary vampires at my back or the ability to crush her bones. All I'd have is my words and tears that keep blocking out my ability to read what she's saying.

I stuff my phone back in my purse and take a deep breath, trying to focus on anything but what that bitch keeps trying to do to my life. Why is she doing this? "Does she think I'll get back together with her if she ruins my life?"

"I'm not sure she even knows what she's doing," Rachel says. "When you're going to this level to fuck someone over, I don't see how there can be any real rationality behind it. She's not spreading pictures of you online because she thinks she'll get anything from it. She's doing it because she knows that it hurts you."

Dinah crosses her arms, sinking into the seat. "She pretended to love you for months. I don't understand how she could turn around and do this. Even if it was all a lie, I don't know how that much could have been fake. How she can be in a relationship with someone and then turn around and act like this?"

Rachel groans. "She's a sick stalker. Maybe to her, that's just what love is."

"I wouldn't think someone can be that deluded, but I guess it's hard to argue with the evidence at this point," Dinah says. "She's a monster. A real one. She knows what could happen if people believe those pictures. They'd know that we're real. And they'd probably try to wipe us out."

"They knew we were real when I was younger, and most of us survived it," I say.

"They didn't have guns when you were younger," Rachel points out. "Or missiles. If they know that we exist, I don't think there's much chance of us all surviving. Especially when so many of us live in one place. It would make the vampire hunts of the early 1900s look like child's play. Maybe we'd be able to replenish our numbers in another century since we can spread like a virus, but for the rest of you, I wouldn't count on it." It's always concerning when a Jewish couple starts warning you about genocide.

I cross my arms and watch the buildings fly by. "Maybe the humans will be right to." I hate how it sounds, especially to them, but we actually are the monsters the stories make us sound like. Or maybe seeing Freddie again just keeps making me think about that horror in her eyes at the idea I'd eaten people. Maybe they're right to fear us. "There aren't too many fiends that are that worth saving, lamias least of all."

"Don't say that," Dinah says.

"How many vampires have you been hurt by?" I ask, already knowing the answer. "We're a threat to them. You don't have to look any further than the fucking slave auction that was happening while we were in the middle of our game. Maybe they'd be right to wipe us out."

Rachel looks back over her shoulder, meeting my eyes for

an instant before she turns back to the road. She's often a little more intense than Dinah, but there's something about the way she seemed to look right into me. Paula may piss herself if she looks at her like that. "What's got you saying that?"

I shrug. "Lamias haven't been any better to me than vampires have been to you two."

"I have quite a few vampire friends," Rachel says. "I've only had one attack me and not apologize for it later."

"Kalila still tried to murder us, and Jerome did murder us."

"And they apologized."

I chuckle. I've heard them bicker about this so many times that at a certain point, the horror of it falls away and leaves only sheer absurdity. I never thought it would be that tough deciding on if someone trying to kill you makes them bad. "Maybe that proves my point. Even the good monsters have tried to kill you."

"Dinah's never tried to kill me. You never have. There are monstrous humans far worse than any fiend, and they kill millions and let them suffer when they have so much power to change it. There aren't too many fiends who can reach those levels. There's no such thing as a good genocide, Phoebe."

"I shouldn't have said anything. I wasn't thinking."

"So let me ask you again, what's put this in your head? Is it just because Paula has you terrified? Because that seems more like you should be hating humans."

I squeeze my tail. I don't like thinking about this. "No… it was thousands of years before she was even born. I got to see just how monstrous fiends can be. And fine, maybe humans can be worse, so maybe we don't deserve to be wiped out, but I've only known one other lamia who was at all a decent person, and every other one has treated me like absolute shit my entire life. And they've done so many horrid things. And vampires have committed just as many heinous acts against you. And we see all the time the kind of atrocities other fiends are willing to commit to make some money. So fine, maybe we don't deserve to be wiped out, but can you really blame me for not being too concerned about it?"

Rachel risks another glance, but she looks worried this time. "You don't talk much about other lamias."

"Yeah, other than Jackie, I've never heard you mention any. And he was nice enough."

"He's the one good one." Gods, I sound awful saying this. I'm not usually this self-hating about it, but I suppose I also haven't had to revisit how my parents raised me to be a monster and murder the people I loved. I should make sure Jackie's still coming to my Warhammer 40k night since we'd had to move it to Saturday. We barely talk since he left my Friday game. "It seems like every vampire these days is against killing. I haven't met too many lamias like that." Is this all because of the way Freddie looked at me? I haven't been able to stop thinking about it, but I didn't realize it had gotten to me that badly. "They wanted us to view humans as only food, no matter how I felt on the subject. And gods, some of the other bullshit they pulled…" It's been so long since I last thought of my parents. "Ever since I hatched, my parents had such specific ideas of who I'd be and what all it would entail."

Dinah turns fully in her seat, watching me, looking even more concerned than Rachel. "What do you mean?"

I point out the window, grateful for the reprieve, but at the same time dreading what I'm about to do. It doesn't matter how this goes, I don't like revenge. All I want is peace. "That's her place. We can deal with one problem at a time. Are you ready to go threaten a human?"

"Are you sure you're up for this?" Dinah asks. "I'm worried about you."

I open the door. I don't want to look in those empathetic eyes. "There's not much more to say. My parents wanted a killer. So let's show them how much of a killer I can be. Just this once, maybe they were right. I should've eaten my lover like they taught me. Then none of this would have happened."

The other houses only have a few meager lights shining through their windows, but the converted garage Paula's renting out is fully lit up. There probably won't be any witnesses so long as we don't linger, but it would certainly be ironic if I was caught trying to keep someone from telling the whole world about me.

Car doors close, and soft footsteps fall behind me. They're with me. I can do this. And hopefully, I can manage without making my parents proud.

## CHAPTER ELEVEN

### *Elfriede*

Vivi pulls me into a hug, and heavy tears thud on my jacket. "I didn't think…fuck, I know this shouldn't be that scary."

"It's okay." I hug her back. I shouldn't let her know that I even considered not coming. I can't keep being that person. She's my friend, and she needs me, no matter how terrible a friend I've been the last few decades. "It's big. It's reasonable to be scared."

She finally pulls back, and a smile touches those tear-rimmed eyes. "Thank you."

I shake my head and have to blink away some tears of my own.

"She actually came," a deeper voice says. "I would've bet money."

I turn to smile at whatever being is insulting me. "Had I known there was money on the line, I'd have come earlier. I can never say no to a good bet." I hold my hand out and receive a sneer.

Whatever they are, they're big, gray, and shaggy. "I've heard dreadful things."

"Well, at the very least, I can assure you I'm disease-free, so the evil won't rub off when you shake my hand."

A lip twitches, black eyes twinkle, and finally, a massive paw-like hand is held out to me. "I'm Luca. I've also heard a few nice things."

I take it and am greatly appreciative of my vampire strength; otherwise, my hand would be crushed. "They're all lies. As are the bad things."

"Hmm." They shake and release my hand. "Well, you did come. I appreciate that."

"If you've heard stories, then you know if there's one thing I'm good at, it's coming."

Vivi chuckles, and her hand settles on my shoulder, but she keeps laughing long after the joke deserved. "Thank you," she says again, and I think she may mean for the joke. "I've been... well, I've been overthinking everything. It's kinda nice having someone who doesn't do that."

"I occasionally reach thinking, but I never go overboard." I'm a little more acerbic today. I hope that doesn't last. Even if I'm going to become a new person, I'd hate to get rid of my good qualities in the process. "So who's this?"

"Sorry, this is a friend of mine, Luca. They've gone through this before."

"And you'll be okay," Luca says. "It's not as bad as you're building it up to be. I know I was terrified the first time, but it'll be over before you know it, and you've got me—you've got *us* here with you."

I smile at Luca and don't receive one in return. I smile all the harder and turn back to Vivi. "How're you doing? Do you need anything?"

"I just need to get this over with. I'm not looking forward to losing my hair."

I reach up and run my fingers through the thick cow-fur on her head. "You'll look hot shaved."

She rolls her eyes.

"I'd still fuck you."

She hugs me again, squeezing me tight enough that I may need to drink some of that blood if I want to have bones again. "Fuck, I really needed you here."

"It's all right." I hug back the best I can. She's big enough that my arms don't quite reach around her. "I'm sorry for making you feel like I wouldn't be."

"I'm sorry for saying—"

"No, you were right. I didn't know how bad I'd let myself be. I needed to be chewed out like that."

She frets, shaking and examining the chairs. "I still feel bad. I just kind of sprang it on you after we'd…"

"Yeah, the timing could've been better, but you're going through a lot, and I've considered you a friend for going on three decades. If I was living up to that, I'd have been one of the first people you told."

She rubs her eyes, but there's a glimmer of a smile. "Can the doctor come out already so I'm not just crying in her lobby?"

"It's not even midnight yet," Luca says. "It'll happen soon. Don't worry."

Vivi seems to be growing quite adept at worrying. She glances around the room again and back to me, her lip trembling. I want to take her mind off it, but I feel like offering drinks or a quickie isn't exactly going to help, and that's most of my skill set. I didn't bring any cards, so that takes out about the last thing I know how to do.

I sit by Luca, look up at my friend, and try to accept that there's not much I can do. I have to watch her suffer. It's what it always comes down to. "I'm right here," I say, hoping that it does anything to reassure her.

She nods, crossing her arms, her fingers digging into her biceps as she looks around.

Finally, footsteps and voices echo through the hall. "All right, just take those pills for the next couple weeks, and it should clear right up. Call me if anything changes, and that'll be a hundred bucks, plus thirty for the pills."

A short woman with black hair and a lab coat, who smells like a vampire, is standing next to a weird turtle thing with water in his head. He pulls his wallet from his turtle jeans, hands her the money, and waddles out the door.

Are there just turtle fiends I'm not aware of? How do I not know, like, any of the creatures I'm encountering? I am over eight hundred years old, and I've never met a turtle person.

"Vivienne?" the doctor asks.

Vivi nods.

Her doctor smiles. "Looks like you brought some people with you. They can bring the chairs with them. I've got you set up in this office." She points toward a nearby door. "It'll probably take around five hours, so I hope you don't have anything urgent planned."

Five hours? Shit. "I just bought some blood. Any chance I can use your fridge?"

The woman chuckles. "Depends, you gonna share with the rest of the class?"

"Help yourself."

She points behind the counter. "There's a mini-fridge there."

I put the blood bags away and grab my chair, hurrying after them toward the office. There's a metal table with supports under it that I think is where Vivi's supposed to go. She's studying it but doesn't seem to have quite worked up the nerve to sit.

"Take a seat. I don't want you falling and hurting yourself— or the floor—if you get too tired during it." Vivi climbs onto the table as I set my chair in the corner. "I'm gonna need your arm."

She nods and holds it out.

"This is going to hurt a little, but we should be able to use the line for everything, so I won't need to keep doing this throughout the appointment." She puts a plastic tourniquet on Vivi's arm and starts tapping around the inside of her elbow. She presses a needle to it only for the needle to bend and turn up. "Can't say I'm surprised."

"Sorry."

The doctor shakes her head. "It happens. But it does mean this is going to hurt more than I was hoping." She grabs another needle from the table. "Take a deep breath and hold very still."

Vivi breathes in, but she starts shaking again.

I walk over, getting a glare from Luca as I take Vivi's hand. She turns to me, fear in her eyes, but the shaking slows, and she almost smiles, but it's broken by a whimper.

The needle is protruding from her arm. "Sorry," the doctor mutters. "Had to shove it in really fast. Hopefully, it didn't splinter. Let me see." She watches the needle as blood starts running through the tube on the other end. "Perfect. Great veins." She pulls a bag from the table and hangs it over a rack. "We'll start with your Benadryl drip, then we can move on. I'm Mia, by the way. It was Vivienne, right?"

"Yeah, and this is Friede and Luca." She gestures toward us with her free hand.

Luca waves from their seat in the corner opposite mine.

"Freddie's fine," I say.

Vivi tilts her head, looking at me.

"I have some other appointments, but there's a bell if you need anything. I hope that's not offensive." She laughs, and when no one joins her, she shrugs. "I'll be back in a bit."

"Freddie? Really?" Vivi asks once Mia closes the door.

"I know it doesn't sound that different, but I just don't like how English speakers say Friede. It sounds weird."

"It's the same."

I shrug.

She shakes her head, a slight smirk spreading across her muzzle. "I didn't think you were capable of change."

"I'm here, aren't I?"

She nods. "You are. Sorry."

I shrug again. "I didn't know this was going to be so long. No wonder you were scared."

"You don't have to stay here the whole time."

"Bullshit." I pull my chair over and sit next to her. "You're clearly scared as hell, and Luca's not much help." They glare at me, and I smile back. "You *are* my friend, even if I haven't always acted like it. So I will sit here, and I'll try to keep your mind off things."

"You're not eating me out during chemo."

I chuckle, and Luca's glare only intensifies. "I'd suggest we play cards, but I didn't think to bring any."

"I can start a show on my phone," Luca says. "That's what I did when I was going through it. Just watched TV until it was over. Got caught up on a lot."

They pull their chair over, hand their phone to Vivi, and we all slide in and just hang out and watch television. That's so strange. I can't even think of the last time I did this. I guess I've watched a couple shows with a few women I was fucking, but there was at least some over-the-clothes action going on at the time.

Before too long, Mia changes the bag out for something else and leaves us be to watch another episode.

About fifteen minutes into the fourth episode, Vivi's hand starts to shake so much that I can't see the screen. I grip her wrist. "It's okay."

She shakes her head. "I'm not scared. I just..." Her teeth chatter. "I can't stop shaking."

"Hold on, let me get the doctor." I ring the bell, and it only takes a few minutes for Mia to come.

"What's up?"

I point at Vivi. "She can't stop shaking."

"Yeah, that can be a side effect. Does it hurt?"

"Not really."

"It's probably just another hour or so. I'm sorry it's like this. It probably won't be as bad next time. Though it might be more exhausting since you won't have all the adrenaline pumping like you do when you first start it."

She nods.

Mia looks at the bag. "I'll be back in about fifteen minutes. Do you need a drink or anything?"

"I think I'd just spill it."

Mia looks between us and the bag but nods and heads back into the hallway. "I'm gonna steal one of your blood bags. I'm not getting to sleep tonight, and I need the energy." She calls from the hall.

"I thought we already agreed to that."

"Just letting you know."

I sit back down and glance up at Vivi. "I'm sorry. I thought she might be able to help."

"It's okay. Just can't really watch a show like this. Distract me. Talk to me."

"Okay." I try to think of what I could say. I doubt she wants to hear about the sexy lamia I was with the other day. There she goes on my mind again. I don't like it. "I'm pretty sure this jacket is spider silk. Feel it, it's so crazy soft."

She reaches a trembling hand toward me and barely grazes my shoulder. "That is pretty nice."

I grin. "Right? Um." What else can I talk about? "Uh."

"What's been going on in your life, Friede? Freddie."

"Friede's fine from you. You say it right." I squeeze her hand and feel it shaking against me. This is what I hate seeing. Even if it doesn't hurt, she's losing control of her body while trying to keep a disease from eating her alive. How do you watch people you care about go through that?

"Tell me."

"There's not much to tell."

"It's been twenty years."

"She's probably just been whoring around more," Luca mutters. "You've mentioned her enough. Surely, you don't think she's actually turned over a new leaf."

She talks about me that much? "What do you say about me?"

Vivi huffs. "That is still not telling me anything. But I've complained about you being a shitty friend, an amazing lover, and how you always have the best drugs."

"That reminds me, if you were my patient, I'd definitely recommend some codeine to take the edge off later."

"Isn't that what you prescribed for everything back then?"

"Sometimes it was cocaine. Or vibrators."

She smiles, but her hand only shakes more. "So that's where you get it from. You're just trying to treat people."

"There's so much hysteria going around. They need the practiced hands, and tongue, of a classically trained physician."

She rolls her eyes, but she's still grinning. "And what has this physician been doing for the last twenty years?"

She's not going to let me drop this, is she? I sigh. "The same as ever. So much hysteria to treat. Just drugs, drinking, gambling, beautiful clothes, and beautiful women. Lots and lots of women."

"And pissing off some loan sharks."

"Well, that was to pay for the drugs, drinking, gambling, and clothes."

She gently pulls her hand away, and I let it go. She grips the side of the table and breathes in. I'm not sure if it actually helps the shaking. "Then let me ask you your favorite question."

"'Do you want to fuck a vampire?' Why? Do you think your doctor's interested? She's cute. I wouldn't be against it, but I saw a ring on her finger."

She stares at me, shaking too much to keep eye contact, as if I'm supposed to know what she meant. "No. Are you happy?"

"Oh." Now I'm the one who can't meet her eyes. Am I happy? I ask so many women that. I try to do everything I can to make them happy. For a few days. And then, I'm gone again to more women, cards, drinks, and clothes. Am I happy? "Honestly? Yes. I love my life. I'm free. I do anything and anyone I want, and I enjoy nearly every second of it."

"Really? Huh." That smile returns, and the shaking seems to slow. "I'm glad. I kind of thought…especially with you being here."

"Oh no, don't get me wrong. I'm a mess, and you're completely right. I need to do better. You didn't ask if I was satisfied, you asked if I was happy. And I am. I'm easy to please—"

"Then what do I put in all that effort for?"

I grin. She can be incredibly cute. "I'm lonely." I feel stripped bare in a far less pleasant way than usual. I've never been one for introspection until today. I didn't even realize how true it was until the words came out. "I am happy now, but I was happier a long time ago. I've been so scared of having to sit there and let people I care for suffer and die, and all it's resulted in is that they do it anyway and don't know that I care." I force myself to meet her eyes and find that they're shimmering with tears. "So, yeah, I think I'm going to try to actually…well." I gesture at where we are. "Have friends."

A shaky hand grips me under the arm, and I find myself yanked out of my chair and into a massive hug. My bones creak, but I hug back, tears falling.

Luca grumbles.

Vivi finally lets me go, and I nearly fall and only have my

superhuman reflexes to let me catch myself on the table rather than ending up on my ass. I fix my hair and smile at her. "That mean we're still friends?" I ask.

"You've been sitting with me for four hours of my chemo, and you're still not sure on that?"

"Just wanted to check."

Luca studies me but doesn't say anything.

"How about I hold the phone, and we can watch?" I ask.

"Fine," Luca says. "Just don't go fucking it too."

"How strong is its vibration?"

Vivi snickers. "Luca, please, she's apologized, can you just play nice? She's not the one who broke my heart."

"I've known enough sleazebags."

"Someone broke your heart?"

She slides my chair closer with her foot so she'll be able to see the screen. "Not anytime recently. Just had a bad ex. I was actually engaged a few years ago."

"Oh, wow."

"Luca's been protective ever since they saw how that wrecked me."

And I hadn't known about any of it. I angle the phone, trying to make sure that we can all see it. "You'll be engaged again before too long, I'm sure. Like I said, you'll look sexy with no hair. You'll be beating off the girls with a stick."

She sighs, but it sounds more amused than beleaguered. "Start the show."

I do, and Luca seems to relax a bit, or at least, they really want to see the show and are willing to be closer to me if it lets them do so.

A little while later, Mia pulls the needle from Vivi's arm. "You did great. I'll see you next week. It's a hundred and fifty. I'm sorry, it's a lot of expensive medicine. Oh, and Freddie, I put the blood in a cooler, so try to bring that back next week," she adds, holding out a cooler.

I wish I could offer to pay for it, but apparently, Vivi is able to afford her lifesaving medication, as she hands it over, and I take the cooler. When we get to her van, I ask, "Do you need me to help you get home? I don't want you shaking while trying to drive."

"It's okay. Luca is gonna drive me."

I nod, feeling completely useless.

"Thank you. Again. You don't have to come next week."

"I have a cooler to return."

"Okay. Just…it's okay if you don't." She reaches in her pocket and pulls a business card from her wallet, still shaking a little as she hands it to me. "It has my updated info. I don't think either of us still have the same number."

The card reads *Vivienne Weber, web developer*, and lists her phone number and email. So that's how she's affording her treatment. I put it in my pocket and try to remember to add it to my phone later.

"Thank you." She hugs me again, and the two of them head off and leave me alone and full of emotions. My two least favorite states. I need a drink. Or a game.

# Chapter Twelve

## *Phoebe*

I stop short of the door. Should I knock? That could give her a chance to run, but her apartment only has the one real exit, and if she went out the windows, I'm pretty confident my vampire friends could catch her. I close my eyes and take a deep breath, trying to will myself to do this. I came all this way. I have to make her stop.

Something thuds, and I look up to see the door kicked in and Rachel looking expectantly at me.

Dinah grumbles. "You know I'm on parole."

"Your parole officer is a vampire who helps you cover up murders. I don't think you have to worry."

"Still, though, we can't just break into people's houses."

I sigh. "It's a bit late now. Let's go in."

I let them lead the way so I won't have my tail stepped on, and follow inside the little apartment. Against the far wall of the only room, a brunette with headphones on types furiously at her computer. Did she already make another account to spam my server? I don't even want to check.

She's right there. I can move over to her and...and what? Crush the life out of her?

Dinah taps her shoulder, and Paula spins in her chair, looking confused before she gulps, and her eyes widen in horror. Dinah gives a little wave. "Hi. We were hoping to talk to you." Her voice isn't its usual cheerful self, and she looks different in so many subtle ways. Her jaw is set, and her eyes are locked on Paula, her hand clenching on her shoulder hard enough that Paula winces. This must've been what she looked like in prison. I never could've imagined my bubbly little friend could do this.

"Like about why you're spreading revenge porn of our friend," Rachel adds. "You know that's a crime, don't you?"

"Uh." She looks between the very close vampire and the one already stepping things up to a threat before finally settling on me. "Phoebe...I wasn't...I was just trying to get your attention."

"My attention?" Anger, horror, and sadness have warred so much inside me since she did this, but now, it's only anger. "You're risking a fucking genocide for my attention?"

"You never gave me the chance to explain! I knew if I did this, you'd at least talk to me. You'd blocked me on everything and weren't replying to my messages."

I shake my head. I can barely even comprehend the fucking audacity of this bitch. I jab a finger toward her. "I blocked you because you've been lying to me our entire fucking relationship. You followed me for years, and when I met you, you pretended to be a delivery girl who didn't know who I was. It has been a fucking decade of you, what, deluding yourself into thinking that you knew me, only to go and lie about everything to get in my pants?" That expression probably doesn't make sense coming from me, but I'm too angry to care.

"It wasn't like that!"

"Then what was it like, Paula?" I cross my arms, my breathing ragged and my heart racing in my chest. She did this. She did all of this. And she expects me to fucking talk to her? She wants my fucking attention? Well, she fucking has it. "How do you justify lying to me for months?"

"I really was your delivery girl."

"And did you get that job because you knew where I lived?" Rachel puts her hands on her hips and lets her fangs show.

Paula gulps, her eyes large and firmly on Rachel. "I..."

"Yes or no, Paula?"

"I just needed the chance for you to get to know me. I knew how perfect we would be together."

I grit my teeth. She was a deluded stalker all along. "That's what I thought."

She slides her chair back, but it bumps into the desk and barely moves her any farther from Rachel.

"So you've been sharing private pictures of me on my server and risking my fucking livelihood and letting people know that fiends exist and risking our actual lives to try to get my attention so you can, what, remind me how perfect we were together? It was all a lie, Paula."

"It wasn't!" She stands and steps toward me, and to my shock, Dinah shoves her back into the chair while Rachel steps between us. I suppose she did manage to handle herself for a few decades in maximum security. "Baby, it wasn't like that." She rubs her shoulder.

"We were together for three months. When were you going to tell me the truth?"

Tears shimmer in her eyes, and she doesn't meet mine.

"You were never going to tell me. If you hadn't been a dumbass and donated on the wrong account when you were trying to show that you were a supportive partner, I'd have never known."

She shakes her head. "It didn't matter. You knew the real me anyway. It's not—"

"It's not what? I didn't know you at all. You lied for our entire relationship. You pretended to be getting to know me while using everything you learned about me over ten years of watching my stream."

"No...I didn't have to. Nothing else was a lie. That's the real me. You know how well we get along, how perfect we are for each other. I just had to give you the chance to realize it."

How deluded is she? I assumed this was for revenge for daring to dump her when she was too possessive, and I caught her in this massive lie, but she thinks there's something to salvage here? "Anyone who was perfect for me wouldn't be the kind of person who would share pictures like that."

Tears fall, and she sinks back into her chair. Apparently, even her delusional mind can't come up with a counter to that point.

Rachel leans in until they're eye to eye. "You're going to delete every record of those pictures, apologize to the world about how they were just a sick joke you made, say that you've never even met Phoebe, and leave her alone. Or we can give you the chance to see the Community Center for yourself with no one to protect you."

Her eyes bulge even more, and she looks pleadingly in my direction, tears streaming down her face. "No. I—Phoebe, I love you. I know you love me too."

"I knew you for four months, and maybe a month of it even seemed okay. I never came close to loving you. You were just a liar trying to use me."

"I wasn't," she insists. "Please, Phoebe. Let me prove it to you. Give me another chance. I can be better."

"You risked killing millions of people to get my attention. No, fuck you."

"Phoe—"

"She gave you an answer," Rachel says. "Now it's your turn to give us one. Delete the pictures, or you'll wish we'd killed you."

Dinah stares at Rachel before matching her posture and nodding. "Yeah." She does not sound confident. "You don't know the kind of horrible stuff they do there. So delete everything now, and apologize or..." She glances at Rachel again. This must be too much for her. I knew actual violence never came easy to her. At least she's able to be scary.

I glare at Paula. I can't believe I trusted this woman. I let her share my bed. I let her take those fucking pictures of me in the first place. I thought it was real, but there wasn't anything real to it. She was a creepy fucking stalker, and that's it. "*Now*, Paula."

"I didn't think it would hurt anyone," she mutters.

"You knew it would hurt me."

She doesn't try to meet my eyes, finally turning back to her computer. "I'll delete them."

"And every backup."

She hesitates but grabs her mouse and starts deleting things. "No one thinks they're real."

"You're still going to apologize for it, and we don't know that no one thinks they're real. We only know that *most* people don't."

Paula pulls up Discord, starts typing, stops, and looks back toward me. Tears stream down her cheeks. "Phoebe—"

"Apologize for spamming this shit. Say you're just a creepy fan who shopped my face onto weird fetish porn."

She nods. "Okay." She turns back to the computer and starts typing. I move closer to make sure she's not pulling something else, but she's basically saying exactly what I told her to. She's been a fan for years but got banned for creepy messages and started sharing these weird pictures to try to get revenge. It's all just a photoshop from some fantasy porn movie.

I'm probably going to have to deal with people trying to find the movie for the next few months, but I'll make sure anyone posting about it gets deleted. "Thank you. Now make sure you actually deleted every copy. You did the ones in Dropbox?"

"They were the first ones I deleted."

"And cleared out your recycle bin?"

She huffs and does so.

"And your phone?"

She winces. Fucking sicko. She grabs her phone from her desk and deletes the pictures. I snatch it from her hand and make sure they're all gone. The naked ones are, but there are other photos of me. I start deleting them. "Every photo of me. I don't trust you with them. Delete everything."

"Phoebe, please—"

"No. You did all of this yourself. Delete them."

She deletes more pictures, and I make sure that she actually got all of her backups since the accounts are on her phone too. She did. I'm a little surprised. At least when the alternative is being eaten alive or sold into slavery, she can almost be honest.

"All done?"

She nods. "I'm sorry."

"It's too little, too late." I wrap my tail around her computer. This is probably going too far. I'd die if anyone did it to me, but she's more than earned it. I tighten my grip, the metal groaning, until I get a crunch and the pleasant tingle of electricity running harmlessly along my tail. "I want to make sure I got rid of everything. You've lied to me too many times. If you come near me again, I will fucking kill you."

"Phoe—"

"I'm letting you live. You can go right back to your life. And you can leave me the fuck alone. Or else."

More tears come, but I'm not sure if they're over me or the computer. I'd probably have cried more if she'd broken mine than I did when I found out she was lying to me. I toss the phone to Rachel since I can't break things with my hands near as easily as she can and turn my back on Paula. If she tries to pull anything stupid, I know they'll stop her.

She screams after me, but I ignore her. I don't have it in me to care anymore about what she has to say. She's a miserable, lying, monstrous asshole, and she deserves whatever is coming to her, just so long as it's as far away from me as possible.

I head out onto the street, hoping that the screaming doesn't attract any attention. The car is still unlocked, so I slither in and hug my tail. It's only a few second before Dinah and Rachel climb in and speed off. There's no blood on them, so Paula is probably still alive, unfortunately.

"I'm sorry," Dinah says. "That was awful."

"It went better than I'd hoped."

"Hopefully, she'll really go away this time," Rachel says. "I'm sorry you had to deal with all that. I can't believe how far she went."

I nod, hugging tighter to myself.

"Why would she do that?" Dinah asks. "I just can't understand. If she loves you, why would she try to hurt you? It didn't make any sense with my old roommate either, but she was at least consistently insane. Paula had never seemed to be any of the times I'd met her."

"She wasn't in love with me. She was obsessed with me. There's a huge difference."

"Obsession seems like putting it mildly," Rachel says. "I didn't know she'd done all of that. You had a terrifying stalker."

"I'm lucky she was human," I mutter. "But it's over now. I don't think I'll be seeing her again."

"If you do, just let me know," Dinah says. "I'll be there." She doesn't say she'll kill her or anything, but I suppose I appreciate the offer from someone with superspeed. I'm just not sure what she'd be able to do. I guess help me clean up the blood after I kill her.

I nod. "I appreciate that."

"Are you going to be okay on your own tonight?" Rachel asks. I'm not sure it can even still count as night. "We have a guest room. You could stay at our place."

"I just need a drink." I feel bad saying it, but it's true. "Just drop me at the Community Center. I don't want to go home right now, but I can't exactly do that with you guys."

"Well..." Rachel and Dinah exchange glances.

I chuckle. "It's fine. I get it. I don't want to make you relapse. I just need..." What do I need? Am I even sad? Angry? I feel a million emotions, and yet, I'm so numb. "Just drop me off there. I'll figure out a way home." Where she stalked me. She knows where I live.

But she's not coming back. I don't need to worry anymore.

"Okay," Rachel says. "But I can come pick you up when you're done. I don't need that much sleep. Just call me."

At this point, I'm not surprised. Rachel has more than proven that she's a good friend. "Thank you."

They double-check on me a few more times before we get there, say that I'm still welcome to their guest bed, and hug me super tightly when they drop me off, but I really just want to forget about everything. I thank them and promise to call if I need a ride and head back into the Community Center. I may as well spend all that money Paula gave me over the years. I can probably buy out the whole bar.

## CHAPTER THIRTEEN

### *Elfriede*

This time, the casino has gamblers in it rather than whatever Phoebe and her friends were doing. I don't like how disappointed I feel at that. Was I seriously hoping to find her here? She made her needs clear, and I can respect that. I take a seat at the table by a man in a suit who smells like brimstone but in a nice way. I didn't know it was possible for brimstone to smell nice, but I'm going to guess he's a demon. I've never actually met any, but I had a friend tell me about a wonderful night she had with a succubus.

The other people at the table are a rock-like creature and an absolutely stunning woman who smells faintly of trees. I smile at her and receive an amused expression back. Normally, I'd already be offering her all the pleasures I can bring, but Vivi has me second-guessing myself. I know that even by the standards of a fair one, I can ensure an incredibly fun night, but is that what I'm after, or am I just scared of going home to an empty hotel room and an empty bed?

"What's the minimum bet?" I ask.

The fair one chuckles. From what I've heard, that's never a good sign. "I'll stake you."

People aren't this nice to me unless I'm mind-controlling them. "And why's that?" I've heard weird things about fair ones with deals.

"I owe you."

"No…"

She chuckles again.

The demon grins. "I love it when a game gets entertaining. I'll stake you too, which is probably a rude thing to say to a vampire now that I think about it. I need the story."

The rock being grumbles. "Just once, can we have a normal game without one of you trying to turn it into a soap opera?"

"We have them all the time," he insists.

"Bringing your ex-boyfriend around last time was a little soap opera-y," the fair one says.

He snickers and rolls his eyes, I think. They're solid red, and it's difficult to tell. He pulls a hundred from his wallet and tosses it on the table.

The fair one also tosses out a hundred, but I'm not sure where it came from. "You are Elfriede, are you not?"

Should I admit to that? I still don't know fair one rules. "I am."

"I have a lover, Gwen, who learned a lot from you. As I said, I was in your debt. Now, I am not. Though perhaps you'd like to fix that."

I grin at her. So my skills are still good for something. And I'm glad to know another old friend made it here safely. People do *not* make it easy for me to hate myself. Then again, neither do I. I'm just so pretty. "We'll see how the game goes." That's not like me. I'm turning down the opportunity to fuck a ludicrously gorgeous ethereal woman? How much did Vivi get in my head?

"Oh, come now," the demon says. "That's everything you're going to give us? What did she teach her?"

"Would you care for a demonstration, James? I thought you'd renounced such vices."

He grumbles, crossing his arms.

"Great, so we can play." The rock guy slides a pile of chips over to me.

"I will simply say that I did not know that a dragon's tongue was capable of doing those things until I met her, and for that, I am quite grateful."

See? How could anyone not be happy when they can cause these sorts of stories? Even demons are impressed. "She was a quick learner."

"Okay, that's entertaining enough to be worth the price," the demon—James—says. "I bet you have more stories you could gamble with, Elfie."

"I prefer Freddie."

His expression looks even more amused. "You can call me James, and this is—"

"Louise." The fair one holds her hand out, and I can hardly resist the chance to be at least a little flirty, so I take it and kiss her knuckle. "A pleasure."

Her hand lingers for a long moment before she finally drags it away, her fingers tracing along mine. I can imagine all the wonderful things they could do. And I like the idea. But I don't really want to see it come to fruition right now. Am I...not in the mood? That's a thing? "The pleasure is all mine, beautiful."

She giggles. I made a fair one giggle. At least my charm's still working. I ante up, and rock guy deals. I still haven't caught his name, but he seems a lot more focused on the game than anyone else.

"I like the outfit," James says, gesturing at my shirt and jacket as he takes my money back with a goddamn full house.

"I bought it here," I say, admiring the fitted jacket he's wearing. "I could introduce you to the spider who made it if you don't already know her. Yours is outstanding. Where'd you get it?"

"Oh, I have a tailor."

I miss my tailor. I probably knew him better than most of my friends, though apparently, that's not saying much. I didn't even have the chance to say good-bye when I left. "I'm planning on staying in town for a while. I'd love to have one here if you wouldn't mind introducing me."

"Afraid I can't. They're back home."

Louise chuckles and raises on a hand I haven't bothered to look at yet.

Okay, I have a pair; it's at least worth staying in for. I call. "Where's home?"

His red eyes blaze.

"Ah." Hell.

"Don't think you're too likely to go there."

"Well, at least I can have you introduce me when I'm dead." His smile is oddly playful. "Not too likely then, either, by the smell of you." What does he mean by that? Why wouldn't I go to Hell? Mirth dances in those crimson eyes. "But I do know our mutual spider friend, Sybil. She'll tailor for certain clients. I'll see if I can convince her for you. It's a crime to have to buy off the rack, isn't it?"

"It certainly feels it sometimes." The flop is another jack. I have three of a kind. That's much better. I raise.

James folds, but Louise stays in the game, and I get to take her money yet again. I do enjoy doing that. "So why are you playing with us at six in the morning?" James asks. "I'm sure a vampire of your pedigree can find someone more entertaining to occupy your time."

Louise smiles at me again. It does sound tempting. Any other day, I'd do it. "Normally, yes, I would be." Do I open up to a demon, a fair one, and a rock I still don't know the name of after half an hour of playing? "I went with a friend of mine for her cancer treatment. I needed something to take my mind off it."

"Ah, mortality is always heartbreaking," Louise says. "I've had a few human toys with whom I had to learn that."

"Yeah." I shouldn't have brought it up. Now I'm having to fight back tears just to focus on the game. "And what about all of you?"

"Is there a good reason to be here?" the rock asks, sipping a beer. Why didn't I think to bring a drink? I suppose I have blood in a cooler, but that's hardly the right sort of beverage. "There's nothing else to do."

"You make it sound so sad," Louise says. "I have someone tied up at home, waiting for me, but I never resist a chance to take James's money. Not that he ever seems to mind."

He smirks. "It's better than being back home on your own, isn't it?" His eyes lock on mine like he's reading my mind. I don't know if he's looking for a kindred soul or reflecting my own feelings back at me. He does have my spectacular fashion sense, so maybe we're just that similar.

"I've never been one to have to spend a night alone."

Louise's foot settles confidently in my lap, and I idly rub it. I should just go home with her. It'd be so easy. And she's one of the most beautiful women I've ever seen. I'd love it. I wasn't lying when I said this makes me happy. But right now, it's hard to think of anything other than how fleeting the lives of those I care about are and how poorly I've insulated myself from it.

Even if Vivi's treatment goes perfectly, she has, what, another thirty years? Fifty? Eighty? Minotaurs can last a while, but they're not immortal. This fair one is. I could go home with her, and even if I let myself care, she'd still be around for millennia, right alongside me. I wouldn't have to worry about how fleeting her life could be.

Or I could do the same with Phoebe.

My eyes widen, prompting rock guy to fold. I successfully bluffed for once, even if it was unintentional. Do I have a crush on the snake girl? I keep finding her in my mind. I wanted to share my honeymoon fruit basket with her, and I was disappointed when she wasn't in the casino. If I just wanted to gamble, I'd have gone to the actual casino in town, wouldn't I? I was hoping she was here.

That's concerning. I don't like that thought at all. I raise on nothing, and everybody folds.

"I'd say penny for your thoughts, but I think you already took it," James says. "That was quite a little journey in your eyes."

I dig my thumb into the arch of Louise's foot and earn a quiet moan. She can't possibly have any soreness or callouses in her flawless feet, but I've had time to notice what spots she likes. "Just concentrating on what I'm good at," I say, checking my new cards. Could get a straight, but it's not likely.

"Of course," James says. "That was a concentrating face and not some horrific realization."

"Is there something you'd like to share?" I ask. What is his deal? Is he reading my mind? Why is he being so weird about it? If he's trying to get under my skin to win at poker, he didn't need to give me the money in the first place.

He laughs, and it's unreasonably perfect. The same way Quinn had described that succubus. So he's an incubus? But he balked at sex earlier, didn't he?

"James, do you have to torment every new player?" Louise asks. "You're distracting her when I have far better uses for a woman of her talents."

He shrugs, smirking and leaning back as he studies his cards. "I have to get my thrills somewhere, Louise. Untangling the twisted desires of the lost lambs who come here is about all I have these days."

"What about that boy toy of yours?"

His eyes narrow, and he leans toward her, meeting her gaze. "He's not…" He straightens his tie and shakes his head. "MJ isn't part of this. I'm interested in her story, and that's all."

Louise adds a second foot. "I only have the two hands, and one of them is busy with cards."

"I guess I'll have to win all your money, then."

This is what I like. Gambling, flirting, fun. Any other day, this would be perfection. It would even take my mind off Vivi shaking in my arms as the medication went into her. Or that look in Phoebe's eyes as she realized that she shouldn't be asking me questions about my life. "Tomorrow," I say, gently moving her feet off me. "I think I'm still processing. I need a drink. I'll be back. I can never stay away from a casino. Could you cash me out?"

The rock guy does so, but there's something in his eyes that almost looks like concern. If even the one person who wasn't messing with me is worried, then something must be wrong with me. I'm not myself.

"Thank you. It's been a pleasure. I'll be back soon."

I can feel Louise's eyes on me as I walk out. I still don't understand why I'm leaving. What do I want? I was gambling. I've been looking for a game ever since I got to town. And they're my idea of perfect company. Especially with a few drinks. A beautiful woman in my lap and interesting people to play with. So why do I want to be anywhere else?

I head to the bar. At least I finally have money. That same beautiful ogre woman looks my way once she finishes the fifth of the other customers vying for her attention. "What can I get you?"

"Do you have anything that can get a vampire drunk?"

She grins. "Yeah, we do. It's not cheap, though. Blood of a drunk person, so we have to get them very drunk first."

"Sounds heavenly. Please, and add some vodka and simple syrup to it."

"It'll be four hundred."

Shit. I check my winnings to see if I have enough.

"I'll pay for it." The voice is familiar but oddly slurred.

I turn to find Phoebe with a half-empty bottle of a whiskey that would've been a few thousand euros back home. How did I miss her? She takes up a quarter of the bar. Where is my mind? She moves her tail out of the way and gestures toward an empty stool.

"I'll get started on your drink," the bartender says as I take the seat.

Phoebe smiles, but it's faltering, and her eyes are red and puffy. "Hi, Freddie."

"Thanks for the drink."

"Trying to spend..." She looks at a cocktail napkin with numbers scribbled out below each other. "Thirty thousand more dollars."

"Jesus. Why?"

She shrugs and looks around the bar. "Want anything more to drink? I'm probably getting a few more bottles of this."

This is not the same woman I went home with a few days ago. There had been a sadness to that Phoebe, but she wasn't this intense. What happened? "Sure, I can always drink."

She waves another bartender over and points at her bottle. "A couple more of this."

Maybe I shouldn't press. She didn't want to get close. "Why are you trying to spend thirty thousand dollars?"

"Well, it's twenty-two thousand now."

I should drop it. She's clearly dealing with something. As am I. There's no reason to make her talk about it. "A friend of mine has cancer and didn't tell me because she thought I wouldn't be there for her."

Her eyes widen, and she spins in the stool, swinging too far and having to catch herself with her tail. "I'm sorry?"

"Thought you might be more open to talking if I shared first." The second bartender sets bottles and glasses in front of us, and by the time he's done pouring, the first one is out with my blood cocktail. She slides it over to me, and I take a sip.

Good God. I can feel it. It's so uncommon for me to really be drunk. I drain half the glass before I look back to Phoebe.

She sighs. "My ex was trying to get my attention. She got it. But I don't feel any better. Maybe I would if I'd just killed her like I wanted to."

"I've never known killing to solve too many problems." I take another sip of my drink. Is that true? I've avoided killing most of my life, but I can certainly think of a few times where my problems would've been fixed if I'd been more willing to do it. "Or maybe you should've. Fuck, I don't know."

She tilts her head. "You seemed so bothered by my killing before."

"I hadn't meant to come off like that." I hurt her. How many people have I hurt and never even knew because I never bothered to see them again? "I just really don't like it, but I know that sometimes it's necessary. I'm not sure I regret my first kill."

"Who was it?"

I can't dodge that question, can I? She's hurting, and I apparently want to be there for her. And she clearly isn't comfortable venting to me without at least getting something back. "My husband. My parents had married me off. Got two goats for me too. I'm still not sure if that was a good deal. I was miserable with him, and he was a miserable person."

"They didn't know you were gay?"

"Did your parents support you?" That sounds defensive. I'm not good at this. "I'm sorry."

"No...they didn't. But mostly because I didn't want to kill people. They weren't too keen on me being a woman, but my not wanting to carry on the family business hurt them a lot more. I was kind of kicked out. I had to find my own cave and..." She shakes her head and throws back a shot of whiskey that does not deserve such treatment. "So I guess I can see how your parents knowing wouldn't have changed much."

"Yeah, they needed the goats more than I needed to be happy. He was an angry drunk, and I was fifteen. When I died, I felt powerful for the first time in my life. And I took it from him. His power and his life. I thought I'd take our kids and run, that we'd finally be free. But they didn't see it that way. They thought I was a monster. And they ran from me." I haven't told anyone that story. Ever. What is in this drink?

Her eyes widen, and she drops the glass. It shatters on the ground by her tail. "Shit."

I stare at the wasted whiskey and finish my blood. "Yeah."

"So is that why you're..." She shakes her head. "Sorry." Her words sound even more slurred, and as she grabs the bottle and starts drinking straight from it, they're probably not going to get any better. "I just, I don't know how you do it, how you just sleep around without getting attached."

"Maybe I don't." How drunk did he get this blood's owner first? I only had a glass.

She nearly drops the bottle, and I reach to catch it, but she manages to right it in time, leaving me holding my hand out with nothing to grab. "What do you mean?"

I should shut up and leave. We're drunk and stupid, and I don't know what I'm doing. I need to figure out what I want before I go and do whatever I think I'm doing here. "I always get attached. Usually, it's just as friends, but sometimes it's more.

I…" I can still leave. I haven't said anything stupid. I bet Louise would love to take my drunk ass home. "Sometimes, I find I keep thinking about them."

"Yeah? Anyone do that to you recently?" Is she leaning closer to me, or am I falling out of my chair?

I nod.

Her smile is coy, but a forked tongue barely flicks out, and she looks nervous as she asks, "Do you want to get out of here?"

Maybe I was too quick to decide I wasn't in the mood. "Yeah."

She unwraps her tail from the stool, puts the bottles she bought in her purse, and holds her hand out to me. I grab my cooler and take her hand.

We walk out of the bar, mostly in a straight line, but as we grow closer to the door, she stumbles, and I have to catch her. She's drunker than I thought she was. Snakes have slow digestions, so it probably takes longer to set in, while with my blood, it goes right into my veins.

I help her get outside, and she leans her head against me, instantly falling asleep. She's way too drunk. I should get her home. Except I don't remember her address.

She can take my bed. I fish my phone from my pocket while her tail wraps around me, and I call for a cab.

The sun is low in the sky. It's early in the morning. People could start passing by any moment, and I have a giant snake woman wrapped around me. I should get her back inside, but I don't want to risk hurting her.

So I wait until the cab finally pulls up. The driver's eyes are wide as he looks between us.

And he looks familiar.

Shit. I've mind-controlled him before. That's not good. This could really hurt him, but he also just saw a lamia, and at this point, I have to do something. "We're two normal human customers, and you're to take us to the garage of my hotel. We already paid." He blinks and looks foggier than they usually do. I try not to think about how much damage I may have done as I open the door.

I help her in and have a tail wrapped around me and a head pressed against my shoulder. Hopefully, she'll forget everything I told her by morning. It was stupid of me to open up. But at least I can look after her tonight. She didn't tell me much, but she probably needs the sleep.

# CHAPTER FOURTEEN

## *Phoebe*

My head feels like it's on fire. I blink and stretch, only for my tail to fall off the bed. Did I move over to the corner?

I look around and find that I'm not in my room. The bed is too small, and there's no computer. Where am I? The last thing I remember is...Freddie! I roll over, only to find the bed empty. Did she already leave? I start to climb out of bed, only for the motion to feel like a cannonball was just fired into my head. I groan, falling back against the pillow.

There's a blur in the corner of my eye, and I see Freddie at the door to the room. She didn't leave. "Good morning, beautiful. I got you some aspirin, and I was just about to order breakfast. Lots of bacon might help with that hangover."

"Some of us can't just drink blood to heal," I mutter, sounding meaner than I meant to.

Her steps ring out in my head, and she holds the pills and a cup of water out to me. "I'll order from the phone in the other room." Her voice is quieter now.

I take the pills and drain the water. "Fuck."

"I think your metabolism might have betrayed you."

"Most of my stomach is in my human half," I mutter. But then it goes through my snake half and gets reprocessed and gets me more drunk. Right. I know how my body works. Until I'm too drunk to think about it. "Did we..." I bite my lip. I don't know which answer I want.

"Have wild, incredible sex again? No, I wasn't so fortunate. You were very drunk, and you needed the sleep. I slept on the couch."

"You didn't have to do that."

She chuckles. "Well, if you're still feeling that way once you can handle moving, then maybe we can revisit that idea. I'll go order that breakfast. Take your time."

She's gone before I can say anything. I rub my temple. Why is she being so nice? Then again, she was about that nice last time too. That may just be what she's like. I grab one of the pillows and hold it over my head. Why does it have to hurt so much?

Why did I go home with Freddie? And why do I want her to come to bed with me? The answer to both those questions seems pretty obvious, but I'm going to assume that's just my hangover, and the answer is actually something totally different. It was two days of crazy sex with a woman who clearly isn't interested in anything more than that, and that's all.

Or did I just never give her the chance to be interested in anything more? She's not acting like she only wants sex. She's taking care of me and buying me breakfast. And she seemed rather concerned about me last time too. Did I misjudge her?

I'm not sure if I fall back asleep or if the medicine just kicked in, but I take the pillow off, and I feel a little better.

And something smells amazing.

"Food's here if you want it," she calls from the other room. She appears at the door. "Sorry, that too loud?"

"It's fine. I need the food. Can you hear every time I move in here?"

She chuckles. "I can hear every time anyone moves on this floor or the one above or below. Sometimes even farther."

"How does that not drive you crazy?"

"I've had quite a few centuries to get used to blocking it out." She wheels in a cart from the other room, and the smell redoubles. Bacon. Crepes. Waffles. Eggs. I lick my lips and pull off one of the lids, finding a pile of bacon waiting for me. "Does this really help with hangovers?"

"Always seemed to." She's still standing there, watching

me. It doesn't feel like she's trying to keep me here or anything, just that she's... I stare at her. She looks nervous.

"Sit down." I make sure my tail is out of the way and pat the bed. "You're making me nervous."

She nods and sits next to me, keeping a bit of distance between us.

Did she say something last night that she regrets? I try to remember what we talked about. Before we came here, she'd... "Oh."

She stops in the middle of sliding the table between us and looks at me.

"I know why you're acting like this."

Her eyes widen. "I was just—"

"Thinking about me?"

She gulps. "It doesn't happen often."

"Thinking about me or confessing it to people?"

"I've thought of you a few times since we last saw each other, and, no, I never confess anything to anyone."

I came here with her for a reason. Do I still want that? She's absurdly pretty, nice, and now she's got this awkwardness that's making her seem adorable. She's scared. It's so strange to see on that cocky vampire who rocked my world. "I've thought about you too."

"Yeah?" There's that cocky smile. Much better.

I take a bite of bacon, and it really does take a bit more of the edge off my headache. "Last night, before I saw you, I'd confronted my ex for stalking and lying to me. I really don't think I'm up for anything right now."

"Okay." She doesn't even look hurt. "The day before yesterday, I had a very strong reminder of the fact that I try to keep myself distant from the people I care about, and that rather than it preventing anyone from being hurt, as I still have to go through all the same loss, all it means is that they don't know when I care about them. I enjoyed spending time with you, and I'd like to spend more, if you decide you'd like to. It doesn't have to be sex."

"It'll probably be at least some sex."

Her smile only grows. "Thought you weren't ready for anything."

"I'm not ready for a relationship, but the only way I'm resisting pulling you to me and kissing you right now is that I'm slightly hungrier than I am horny. I have a lot of emotions going on right now, and you're hot and sweet, and you make me feel better."

She leans in and runs her fingers through my hair and gazes into my eyes. She's not wearing her ludicrous sunglasses right now, so I can appreciate how bright and blue her eyes are. "Friends, then. That's about how I know how to have friends."

I chuckle. God, how did she get so cute? "You have an interesting idea of friendship." I've certainly had the same a few times.

"You're the one who specified it wasn't a relationship. Not that I'm after that either. I just…I keep forcing myself to be alone, and I'm finally realizing that I hate it."

The bacon is becoming an increasingly less compelling distraction. I wrap my tail around her and pull her to me, managing to make her yelp, and I kiss her, hard. She shudders against me, her hands running down my back.

Am I sure this is what I want right now? I just got out of a terrible relationship, but I clearly have something with this girl. Do I want to risk this being a lie too?

I break the kiss, panting and very distracted. "You didn't know who I was before we met, right?"

"Are you famous? I haven't fucked a celebrity since the queen."

"Which queen? Wait, no, so you didn't…really?"

"I am a terrible liar. All I know is that you're a very beautiful lamia, your name is Phoebe, and that there was some drama with your ex. And I guess I know about your vampire friends. You didn't tell me much."

I believe her. I may just be naive, but I do. I'm not ready for anything more, but crazy sex and a friend sounds about perfect. I kiss her again and guide her back on the bed, trailing more kisses down her neck.

This is probably a terrible idea, but Aphrodite, I really do want it. How does she do this to me?

Her moan as I nip her throat answers that question very adequately, and I move my attention to unbuttoning her shirt. I know why I want this: she's ungodly hot and makes me feel amazing. It doesn't have to be any more complicated than that.

❖

I chew on cold bacon and pour cold syrup on a cold waffle. It's still good.

Freddie fixes her hair and kisses my tail before prying herself free from it. "I can order fresh food if you're hungry."

"It's fine." The waffle tastes amazing. It's so fluffy. I'd say I regret missing it when it was hot, but I was busy eating something even more delicious. "Come have some."

She climbs over and sits on my tail, nipping my shoulder. "You're right, it is delicious."

I roll my eyes, trying not to focus on how amazing she feels there and that I'd rather just move her up a bit and have my way with her again. God, how am I going to keep things to just being friendly, even if sex is allowed? Did I really just think that? I just got out of a relationship. I'm smarter than this.

She grabs the plate of strawberry crepes and a fork, helping herself to a bite. "Oh God, this really is good. I usually don't wake up early enough for their breakfast."

I let out a nervous breath. "Tell me something about yourself."

Her mouth is too full of crepe to answer.

"Please? 'Cause otherwise, I'm pretty sure I'm just gonna fuck you again."

"Can I eat the crepes during 'cause that sounds like a win-win."

I could lick syrup off her. That's tempting. But sticky. "We're trying to be friends, right? So we should, like, actually talk and get to know each other."

"Oh, I certainly had some getting to know you in mind." She

chuckles. "But, yeah, you're right. Okay, fine, something about me. Like what?"

This would be so much easier if she wasn't sitting on me, but the last thing I want is for her to get off. Well, it's also one of the first things, but with a rather different meaning. "Have you always been from Germany, or is that just where you lived last? That's the accent, right?"

"I'm from Berlin most recently, but I was born and raised in Heidelberg. I went to university there, one of the times I went." She stares at me, and I'm not sure if she's considering fucking me or if she's trying to decide if she wants to say the next part. Maybe both. "I had gone back there for uni because I wanted to check up on my grandchildren. After I fled town, my kids came back to the house and lived there for a while. They grew up and had kids of their own, and I knew I couldn't really be in their life, but I wanted to at least keep an eye on them."

"Wow. I know you mentioned having kids, but I hadn't really thought that all the way through. I never had any myself. It needs to be another lamia to actually reproduce, and they weren't too big on me."

"Well, it was their loss."

I shrug. "I didn't really want kids anyway. Except maybe to try to raise them better than I had been. All lamia look…well, not too dissimilar to me, but we still have some pretty strict gender ideas, and between that and my not wanting to eat every woman I fucked, my family didn't much approve of me, and neither did any other lamia. So I had to leave. I found my own cave. Appropriately enough, in Lesbos."

"Did you meet Sappho?"

"I did, actually." Pleasant memories dance through my head. She was a lot like Freddie. "She claimed to have written a poem about me, but I'm not sure that it really was."

"That's some bragging rights."

I eat my waffle, grateful I can't blush. It had still been weird with Sappho too. And she wasn't as understanding about a few things, but if I tell Freddie that she's a better lover than Sappho, her ego will only grow more insufferable. "Do you still check up on your great-great-great-however many times grandkids?"

Her fork clinks on the plate, and her hand falls to my tail. For a second, it seems like she's going to get up, but she stops and shakes her head. "The last one of them died in the war to end all wars. And then we just kept having them. It was all for nothing. So many deaths all because someone killed a duke. Nearly every country got involved, and millions of people had to die. Including three of my grandchildren."

"Is that what…" How do I ask this without being an ass? "Is that what made you so scared of getting close to people?"

"No." She lets out a shuddering breath.

"You don't have to tell me what was if you don't want to."

She nods, setting the plate back on the table and taking a swig of orange juice. Or maybe it's a screwdriver. "That was the next one."

"The next…" Oh shit. She was in Germany during World War II. "What did you even do?" I don't want to ask her if she was a Nazi. God, I hope I didn't fuck a Nazi. No, obviously she wasn't. That wouldn't make sense with anything I know about her.

"I was working at the Institut fur Sexualwissenschaft at the time. We were one of the first places to ever research trans and gay people. I gave several people the legal ability to live as their actual gender. I was even dating one of my patients at the time, Hertha. Not exactly professional, I know, but I couldn't resist."

"I can't imagine you as a doctor."

"Well, medicine was different back then." She laughs, but her expression stays somber. "When the brown shirts came to ask me for my files on—well, they said degenerates—I wanted to kill them. I have so rarely felt that in my life. But I told the fascist pricks to write down the names of every one of the brown shirts that they knew and return that as my list of patients. I don't know if it worked, but they left my office with it, thinking they'd done their job.

"They'd had time to start up…well, I'm sure you know. It

wasn't a genocide yet, but the general direction was already clear. I took all the notes I could fit in a couple briefcases, as many of my patients as I could find and as many Jewish and Roma people as I could convince to come with me, and hijacked a train. It was full of gold they had stolen. It bought us a decent life in Paris."

Oh gods. "Paris?"

"I didn't see a hole in that plan. Until it was too late."

So she rescued dozens of people from the Holocaust and kept them free for at least a year, only for the place she'd run to be taken over as well. That is the worst luck I've ever heard of. "Wow."

She nods. "Some of them had moved on from Paris, but it was a beautiful place. Good drinks, amazing food, outstanding fashion. A lot of them stayed with me. Even the ones I'd barely known had become my friends. And Hertha and I…we were engaged. And then, they invaded. And everyone decided to fight. But I…I don't kill people. I don't hurt people. It's not who I am. I was a fucking doctor. And I sat there, getting as drunk as I could manage, not raising a finger to help them while everyone I cared about died."

I pull her to me, rubbing her back as I wrap my tail around her. "I'm so sorry."

She shakes her head, but she doesn't say anything else.

That explains so much about her. No wonder she's even more terrified of commitment than I am. "It wasn't your fault. You saved them."

Tears fall on my chest, so I simply hold her and let her cry. She's probably been repressing that for a very long time. I wonder if she's ever told anyone before. I lie back, and she clings to me, sobbing. I think she needed this. And I think I trust her. And that terrifies me.

## CHAPTER FIFTEEN

### *Elfriede*

How am I supposed to even face her after confessing that? She knows that I did nothing while the woman I loved threw her life away. She knows that I'm a coward. She can say all she wants that it's not my fault, but we both know it's not true.

I try to pull away, but she's holding me quite firmly. Tails are fun.

Her tail slowly unwinds from me until I can pull back. I feel her eyes on me, but I can't bring myself to look. There's no way there could be any affection left after she heard that.

"You've never told anybody that before, have you?"

I shake my head.

"It isn't your fault," she says for the dozenth time, as if it makes it any truer.

"If I'd fought, they could've lived." My gaze is locked firmly on her chest. It's a very nice image to be stuck on, though it's wet from my tears.

Her tail presses under my chin, guiding my head up. I don't resist, but I still can't meet her gaze. "Freddie." She cups my cheek and leans in until there's no place else I can look. She pulls away enough that I have a clear view into those yellow-flecked green eyes. They don't look disgusted. Or even disappointed. They look almost loving. "You're a hero. You saved so many people. Even if you only bought them a year, it was a year of freedom."

Is that what I did? I suppose it kept them from camps and ghettos, and it did let us enjoy Paris. And a few got away. But it's not enough. "I know how important freedom is, but being alive means more, and I could've given them that too."

"You did. Were they civilian casualties, or did they join the resistance?"

I don't like where this is going. "They joined the resistance."

"Then they chose to die like that, didn't they?"

I have to blink away tears again. "Hertha tried to convince me to join her."

"But she still joined without you. That isn't your fault."

I shrug. It certainly feels like it was my fault. "I swore, after my husband, that I'd never let anyone control me like that again. And that I'd never kill like that again. The horror in the faces of my sons and daughter still haunts me, and I couldn't do that again."

"And you'd have given up both of those by fighting. You did enough."

"Yeah, good job not fighting the Nazis. I'm sure so many have shared that sentiment."

She huffs. "Good job saving people from the Holocaust."

I open my mouth to reply but come up short. It's hard to think of a way to say how that was awful of me.

"I never thought I'd say this, but you have a rather low opinion of yourself."

"The hell I do. I'm fantastic."

She grins. Goddamn it, she just won. All she had to do was play to my ego. Her lips catch mine in a quick kiss, and she pulls away, grinning. "Then you admit it."

"Fine. I guess I did something good."

"Yes, you did. And you did a lot of good for me too. I was in a terrible place when we met, and you made me feel amazing. And not just because of the sex, but because of…well, everything. I don't think I've ever had anyone look at me that way before. And I don't think I've ever had anyone open up to me the way you just did."

I shrug.

"I trust you, Freddie."

Why does that hurt so much? "I don't know that I deserve that."

"I don't think either of us have much of a choice there. I wasn't sure I could ever trust anyone after what my ex did. She was a stalker who lied to me, watching my stream for a decade and using it to try to get close to me while pretending to have no idea who I was."

I vaguely know what streaming is, but I don't want to interrupt her to ask for clarification.

"And then she used my pictures to tell the whole world we were real and show exactly what I was like. She broke my trust so fundamentally that I wasn't sure I'd ever be able to trust anyone again. But I had friends there for me. And I had you."

So that's what she's been working through. That's why she hadn't wanted a relationship and why she wanted to make sure I didn't know who she was. "I don't know that I did much."

"You did a lot." She kisses me again, gentler this time. "Though I probably shouldn't be kissing my friend quite this much."

I climb off her, and she looks forlorn, like the loss of my touch pains her. I've had quite a few friends with whom I spent dozens of nights tangled together in breathless lovemaking, but I've never had one look at me like they didn't want to stop touching me, as if their life depended on it. "Do you want me to stay on you?"

"Kind of."

I lie on the bed, pressing close to her. "This better?"

Her tails wraps around me again. "Yes."

Should I ask her if she wants to make this not simply a friendship? Is that what I want? I haven't even considered dating anyone since Hertha died. Or since she chewed me out for not joining the cause and threw my ring in my face.

I lay my head on her chest and wrap my arm around her. It would be so easy to just say the words, but I don't know that I want it yet. No, that's not true. I do want it, but I don't know that I'm ready for it. The idea of a relationship terrifies me, and

I've always been a coward. I don't want to run away and hurt her when things get too serious.

She toys with my hair and sighs contentedly. "I'm still probably not ready for a relationship."

"Yeah, I was thinking the same thing."

"We're not very good at this, are we?"

I trace a circle along her hip, barely grazing her scales. "I think we're pretty good at sex."

"Not that part."

"I know. No, we don't seem to be good at not getting emotional and fucking."

Her lips press against the top of my head. "Should we stop cuddling?"

Obviously, the answer is yes. Normally, it's not too much of an issue, but I also don't normally have a crush on someone. Or feelings. I don't know what she's done to me, but it's hard to call this merely a crush. "What are we going to do?"

"Try to take it slow? Get to know each other?"

"You know more about me than anyone has in nearly a century."

"Well, we have centuries' worth of stuff to know."

If we were going about this practically, we could spend years getting to know each other and still be too much strangers for a real relationship. "Yeah, that's true. So definitely have to take things slow."

"And we might want to do that taking it slow in public. Otherwise, we'll end up naked and preoccupied. But that only leaves one real place I can go."

I can't imagine how hard it must be to have to worry so much about where she can go. I can pass for a human, and if anyone suspects anything, I can make them know for a fact that I'm human. She can't do any of that. I want to find a way to give that to her, to let her have a normal life, but I'm not sure how I'd do it. "That's starting to sound an awful lot like dating."

"Shit." Her tail uncoils from me, but she doesn't move away. "It kinda does, doesn't it?"

"Well, that's still not a relationship."

"I suppose not."

All right. I guess I'm going to say it. I sit up, meeting those beautiful eyes, and I gently scratch the back of her tail. "Phoebe, let me take you out for dinner. Let me take you out for a proper date." It's not a relationship, but I suppose it's not just a friendship, either. It's taking things slowly.

She bites her lip and slowly nods. "Okay."

"It's been a long time since I've been on one."

"Yeah...well, not really for me, but I get it."

"I don't really know what I'm doing anymore."

She smiles at me, and it makes it a lot harder to be so scared. "Well, I trust you with it."

I know how much that means coming from her. "Tomorrow. Friday. I guess at the Community Center. We'll get dinner." What else do you do on a date? And what could I take her to?

"Okay. Then, I guess we should stop fucking in the meantime."

I give a lingering glance along her body. It takes a while, as there's around six meters of it. "Yeah, just let me commit this to memory first."

She lies back, letting me enjoy the view. Her long red hair with the slightest curl, splayed around her head; her dark nipples, still wet from my tongue; her belly, smooth and just plump enough to squeeze; her tail stretching off my bed, its scales shimmering; and those compelling parts I just had inside me. She's even more beautiful than Louise. I hadn't given her enough credit. I want to kiss all the way along her, to feel her, to straddle her, but we're trying to be good. It's not something I'm used to being.

"Does that mean we're putting clothes on?" I ask.

"Yeah, we probably should. I'll...I should go stream anyway. I can get a friend to pick me up. You don't have a car, right?"

"I don't."

"Then, yeah, I'll ask Larissa. She's usually free around now. She works nights. A cab is too much of a risk."

"I could make them think you're human."

She shakes her head. "It's okay. Thank you, though. So…" She trails off, reaching for her discarded clothes. "I'll see you tomorrow?"

"You will."

Her smile is so cute. And makes her look all the more kissable. She grabs her phone from her purse and calls her friend, and I put my shirt back on and finish my crepes.

How the hell do you go on a date?

## CHAPTER SIXTEEN

### *Phoebe*

Larissa's car pulls into the parking lot, and I slither out from hiding behind an SUV. I didn't want anyone to see me, but I knew if I waited in Freddie's hotel room, my clothes wouldn't be staying on.

She pulls to a stop in front of me, and I hurry into the passenger seat, letting my tail snake through the back. "Are you going to tell me what you were doing here?" she asks as she pulls back onto the street.

I grumble. I've told her so little about Freddie, and almost none of it was good. "You remember that girl I slept with the other day?"

"The psychopath who uses women?"

"I don't think that's quite how I described her."

"It was implied."

I shrink in my seat.

"What did you do, Phoebe?" Her tone is so harsh.

I don't think I quite deserve this. I can feel her eyes on me. What can I say that will convince her that this isn't as bad of an idea as it sounds? "She's not like you think she is."

"So she didn't just use you for another one-night stand and leave you all torn up inside, wishing for more from a woman who can clearly not provide it?"

That makes things easier. I can assuage her fears there a lot more effectively than with any other complaint about her. "No. She asked me out. We're going on a date tomorrow."

She slams on the brakes right in front of the hotel and turns to stare at me, but I don't meet her gaze. "She what? Are you even ready for a relationship? I saw those posts on your server. Clearly, the Paula drama is still pretty fresh."

I shrug. "She hurt me. A lot. Freddie hasn't."

The car starts moving again. "Do you know what you're doing? This girl could hurt you just as badly as Paula. And unlike Paula, you can't hide from her in the Community Center."

It's so strange having a human lecture me on the Community Center. I told her about it all back when we first met, before we were even dating, but it doesn't make it any less unsettling. "I really like her, Larissa. She's...she's incredibly sweet, and she makes me feel..." I sigh, and it's wistful rather than exasperated. That's a new feeling. "She makes me feel so beautiful, Larissa. And don't get me wrong, I don't have that low a self-esteem. I've lured lovers to their death as well as to years-long, loving relationships. Lamias are literally made to be beautiful to the point that even our men look like beautiful women. I was blessed, and it made my transition easy, but I've still never had anyone who seems to so easily accept me. It felt like she loved me from the first time we touched. And I'm not saying she's in love with me or that I'm in love with her, but that's how amazing it felt."

She sighs. "Okay. I can understand that. You were the first person I dated as a girl, so I definitely get how important being accepted as yourself can be."

"But it was more than that." I don't know how to explain it so that it doesn't sound hokey. It's simply magical. "She's amazing. And maybe that's just how badly I'm crushing on her talking, but I think I was wrong about her."

"You think she doesn't use women?"

I grumble. "She might still do that, but she's not using me, at least. I'm sure of that. And I've learned about her past. I know the kind of person she is."

"And what kind of person is that? Was she a fucking saint? I don't see how it was enough to turn your views on her so quickly. Are you sure this isn't just post-orgasm stupidity? I've been okay with some pretty bad relationships just because the sex was good."

"I hope I wasn't one of those."

"You weren't. The sex was pretty great, though," she adds, lightening up her tone.

I take a deep breath. It feels like a secret that I shouldn't be telling people. It was such a big deal to her. But I can at least say part. "Over a hundred years ago, she was a doctor for trans people, back when it was still illegal in most of the world, and she snuck a bunch of those trans people out of Germany before the Holocaust started."

Larissa is silent for a long moment. "Okay, fuck, that is pretty compelling."

"Yeah, now maybe you understand what I mean."

"And you're sure it's true? That's a pretty big story. It would make sense to be a lie. Maybe she was actually one of those Nazis."

"She wasn't. I was scared of that for a moment, but I saw the look in her eyes. She was being completely honest, and the revelation nearly broke her. She lost people. People she loved. It seems to be the source of a lot of her issues."

Larissa groans. It's very difficult to hate someone who did something that heroic, and I'm not sure that she can manage to figure out a way. "I still don't trust her."

"Well, maybe you can meet her sometime."

She huffs and turns at a light onto the road to my apartment. "You're sure this is what you want? That you're ready for a relationship?"

I sigh. "I'm sure this is what I want. I don't think I'm ready for a relationship, but that's why we're taking things slow. We're going to have a proper date, out in public, or as public as I can be, and just try to get to know each other better. If we don't make it a date, we'll just end up in bed the whole time and not learn anything except what makes the other scream."

"Damn, that's an enticing picture, at least."

"And you don't know how good she is at it." I try not to dwell on any of the numerous images of our time together. They're so crystal clear in my head, and she looks so beautiful, so perfect. I can still hear her moans. "So I really need help. I need to both keep from fucking her in the middle of the Community Center and to get ready for a date. It's gonna be big. I think I really like this girl, and I just want to make it all go right. She doesn't really know me that well yet, and I want to impress her."

Larissa pulls into my driveway and stares at me. "You're sure about all this?"

"I keep telling you that I am."

She sighs. "Okay. We have our game night tomorrow, so we can—"

"Shit!" How did I forget about that? It's every week. How did I schedule a date at the same time? Larissa was right about post-orgasm stupidity. "Can we make it earlier? Also, since I have to go stream, can you ask everyone about it?"

"I'm pretty sure you still have time to ask."

I shake my head. "Nope, definitely need you to."

She rolls her eyes. "Fine, we'll come over early, do our games, and help you get ready for your date."

I have a date with Freddie. It still feels so surreal. I wasn't sure I'd ever date again. "Thank you."

"You better thank me. I still can't believe you're dating the same woman you were complaining about the other day after she used you for meaningless sex."

There's one thing I've learned for certain. "I don't think it was meaningless sex. It was casual, yes, but based on everything she's said, I think it meant as much to her as it did to me. She hasn't been able to stop thinking about me since."

"Sounds like a pickup line."

I pull on the door handle and pause halfway through opening it, turning to Larissa. "I know it does, but she's real. I have a date with her, and even after everything with Paula, I trust her. I really like this girl, Larissa. Can you please be happy for me?"

She nods, but she looks sad. "Of course I'm happy for you,

Phoebe. I'm just scared. I don't want to see you hurt again. Especially so soon."

"I get that. And I appreciate it. But I'm a big girl. I'm three thousand years old. I know what I'm doing. And I'll be okay."

"All right." She sighs and pulls the car into reverse. "I'll see you tomorrow. Just take care."

I smile at her and drag the rest of my tail out of her car and close the door behind me. I wave as she drives off, and I head back into my apartment. My upstairs neighbor is stomping around, and I can already feel the ground threatening to tremor. I tap on the ceiling with a broom to get her to stop, and I head over to my computer.

There are no worrying Discord alerts. The server has been busy, and the mods confirm that a few people have still been talking about what happened, but there seems to be a general understanding that DarkWitch was insane and just being a total creep making weird snake porn.

I need to photoshop a picture of me with actual legs to post to kill off any doubts she may have caused. I have a few old ones, but I feel like that would be less convincing. I'm probably overthinking things, though. No one thinks I'm really a lamia.

After all, what lamia would be crazy enough to use a lamia for her avatar? I start up OBS and my avatar and get the game set up.

As soon as stream starts, thousands of people flood in. That drama must have attracted a lot of attention. Or apparently, a streamer I'm friends with just ended her stream right when I started mine. "Thanks for the raid," I say to her followers. Whitney is the only other fiend I know who does this. She's not even in Toronto, but we've tried to support each other the best we could.

I start the game and do my dailies. I've barely touched the new content between all the drama and the cute vampire, so I at least still have a good deal to show for my stream. And I have plenty of people talking in chat.

A little of it is about the pictures and how bad the photoshop was, which makes me a little self-conscious. Does my tail not look natural? I'm pretty sure my hips lead into it rather organically. I've never had anyone accuse me of looking fake. But I know it's a good thing that they think that.

Freddie's loving gaze from last night reminds me of just how perfect my body looks. It's not a thought I've ever had before. I know most other trans women would kill to look as easily feminine as I do, but I can still see all the minor differences between me and other women lamias, even if humans can't.

Maybe Freddie can't tell the difference either, but she makes me know that it doesn't matter. Three thousand years of being myself should've given me the confidence that I need, and for the most part, it has, but nothing quite gives the same boost as the way she looks at me. God, I really am already crazy for her. I hope I can keep it together for our date.

## CHAPTER SEVENTEEN

### *Elfriede*

I have a date. I have a date? I have a date. Not a word of that sounds right.

And yet, at the same time, I can't imagine canceling it.

What does Phoebe do to me? Well, she does quite a few things to me that I rather enjoy, but none of that would normally be enough to make me want to date anyone. And she doesn't at all remind me of Hertha or anything that would suggest it's some weird displacement. So what's causing this? Why do I feel this way about her when we know so little about each other?

Except she knows so much about me. She knows what I never tell anyone. And rather than looking at me like the despicable monster I am for sitting idly by while people died, she acted like I was a hero. She's wrong, obviously, I'm nothing of the sort, but that probably isn't helping with the whole wanting to date her thing.

I've never met anyone quite like her. And the fact that she's in the top dozen or so sexual partners I've had is a pretty big point in her favor. And of the people around there, there's only one other who was actually likable outside of the bedroom.

Shit. Speaking of, I didn't check up on Vivi.

I'm trying to be a good friend for once, and I didn't even think to see if she was okay after her chemotherapy. I had a lot of other things filling my mind, and a few other places, but that doesn't excuse my lapse. I grab my phone from my pants on the floor. It's at about thirty percent battery. That should be enough.

Her business card is in another pocket, so I type in the number and sit in the chair while I wait.

She answers on the third ring. "Hello?"

"Hey, Vivi. It's me."

"Well, I only know one German girl who calls me Vivi, and I don't think she'd ever call me unless it was for a booty call, so I have no idea who 'me' could be."

It would be nice to relieve the stress, and I'm not in a relationship just yet, but for some reason, I don't really want to suggest that it's a booty call. "It's Friede."

"What's up, Friede?"

I bite my lip. It's still a little tempting, but I need to be a friend first and foremost. "How're you doing? I meant to call and check in earlier, but…"

"You were busy having meaningless sex with the first woman to look at you?"

She knows me too well. "No, actually. I was busy having very meaningful sex with the second woman who looked at me. I only gave the first one a foot rub before I turned her down. I…I'm trying to ask if you're okay, Vivi."

"I'm fine. I was a little sick when I woke up, and my stomach isn't exactly doing great, but I'm pretty okay now. I'm just trying to take it easy. I'm only doing a little work and trying to baby myself."

"I could bring you food if you want?"

She's silent for a moment, and I'm not quite sure what's going through her head. "Yeah, okay. I'll text you my address. Are you okay? Am I supposed to believe this is simply you checking on me?"

I sigh. I wish she could trust that I was a better friend, but I haven't done much to earn it. "I am legitimately worried about you and want to take care of my friend. You are very dear to me, and I'm sorry I never showed that. But I also kinda wanted your advice on something."

"We talking ties or jackets?"

"I wouldn't mind your input on my outfit, but it's more about my date tomorrow."

She's silent again, but this time, I'm pretty confident as to what's going through her mind. *What do you mean you have a date?* I just have to wait for her to say it. "I'm sorry, I must have the wrong Friede. This is very confusing as you called me, but somehow, I must have the wrong person. There is certainly no way that my Friede has a date."

"Well, I wasn't aware I was your Friede, but yeah."

She's silent for another beat, no doubt processing this insanity. "All right, fine. Come bring food, something easy to keep down, and I will teach you what dates are so you can realize how out of character this is."

"It's a kind of fruit, right?"

"It's probably in that basket with all your strawberries."

There isn't anything left in the basket now, and there had decidedly not been any dates in it. "I'll get you some soup. Maybe some grilled cheese if you think you can handle that."

"Thank you. I know I'm lashing out, I just...I'm sorry."

"I thought you were ribbing me."

"I was. But I was being harsher than I should've been. You've already shown you're being a better friend. I should stop giving you a hard time for it."

I sigh and rub my eye. I'm not quite tearing up, but I'm not far from it. "I haven't done near enough. I'll be there soon. Just get some rest."

I take a quick shower and brush my hair, then throw on spider-silk boxers, slacks, socks, bra, and a shirt, and rather than debating any of my jackets, I head out. It's already getting late, and I don't want to risk the place closing before I have a chance to get her food. Even if the gray slacks and teal shirt would look a lot better with a jacket. I should've just grabbed one.

❖

The line at the drive-thru is way too long and would've substantially added to my bill if I was paying my cab driver, but

I arrive at Vivi's house just under an hour after I called. I wasn't expecting a house. Back home, even fiends had apartments. And Phoebe lives in one. Does she make this much in web development? No wonder she wasn't bothered by her chemo fees.

I knock on the door and have to wait a few minutes for Vivi to meet me. She doesn't look as bad as I'd feared, and she still has her fur, but she looks more tired than I've ever seen her. She hugs me. "Thank you for coming."

"It's nothing. Let's get inside so you can sit down." It's probably too cold out for her in her condition. Even with fur.

"I'm not that fragile."

"Well, you can always prove that later." I'm not sure I'll ever be able to not flirt with Vivi. "But for now, let's get some food in you." We sit at an old table with a plastic tablecloth over it, and I set the food and drinks in front of us.

She seems slower than usual unwrapping her sandwich, but that may be my imagination. As nice as her massive hands can be, they don't always have the easiest time with fine tasks.

"Do you need any help?"

"I'm not a baby, Friede." She sighs and gives me an apologetic look. "I appreciate it, I really do, and I know you're trying to make up for everything, but you being here is enough."

"Okay." I never looked anyone in the eye as they died back in Paris. I don't think Vivi is going to die, but I can't shake the fear that she will. I sat in bars and in my apartment, and I drank while they fought. Hertha never came back after I refused to join the resistance, and I don't think anyone else I'd brought did either. I had a few French women from time to time, but that was it. No one who was in any real danger unless their escapades with me got out. But I look Vivi in the eye. I can be better. She's suffering, and there's nothing I can do about it, but I can be there for her.

"So tell me about this girl. Who finally managed to convince you that you should date someone?"

"You did, Vivi. And I don't mean that in my normal way, where you're all I'm thinking of because I'm looking at you. Though you do look as lovely as ever, and I'd be lucky to be fucked against your wall."

She rolls her eyes but smirks around a bite of grilled cheese. "You made me realize that I need connections, and that made me see how badly I was already starting to feel one. That lamia I was with the other day, Phoebe, she's something special. She made it clear that she didn't want anything more, and I thought I didn't either, but we started talking, and well, you know me, it went where it always does. But she's still not ready for a relationship, and I'm probably not either, but we're going to take some time and see if this can really be something. So I'm taking her out tomorrow night, and I'm fucking terrified. I haven't dated anyone new since the '20s."

She nods, setting the rest of her sandwich back down in her wrapper. I'm not sure if it's because she wants to talk or because she's about to throw up, as it looks like it could be either. "I don't know that I'm really capable of offering much advice. I haven't dated all that much in my life, and I don't know much about this girl."

Hadn't she been engaged a few years back? Clearly, she's at least dated some. "She's in the community here too. Are you sure you don't know her?"

"I think I'd remember a lamia. I've maybe seen her once or twice, but that's about it. There are so many of us here. It's not like Berlin where we knew every other fiend."

I sigh. "I'm starting to see that."

"But we can practice, and we can figure out what you want to wear, and we can get you trained so that you don't go and sleep with the waitress in the middle of the date."

I want to look offended, but I have slept with a waitress in the middle of having dinner with Vivi, so I may deserve that. "I probably wouldn't."

"You're nervous for this date, right?"

"Obviously."

She smirks, and I realize what she's getting at. She really thinks I'm gonna go fuck that waitress. "And what do you do when you're nervous?"

I open my mouth and hold out my hand, pointing vaguely, wanting to insist that I'm not going to fuck someone else just because I'm nervous, but it's hard to think of much to say in my defense. I haven't done a lot in my life to suggest I have healthy coping mechanisms. "Just because I've drunk, used drugs, gambled, and fucked to deal with every emotion for the past eight hundred years does not mean that's what I'm going to do this time. I didn't fuck that fair one yesterday, and she wanted it badly."

"Not making a great case for yourself, are you?"

I groan, my head falling back as I sink in my chair. What am I thinking, trying to have a normal relationship? This isn't who I am. I have no idea how to do it. "I think I really like her, Vivi," I whine. "I don't want to fuck this up."

"Then don't. You're already making changes. Just keep doing it."

I sit up and meet her eyes. They still look tired, but they're as lovely as always. She looks rather kissable. Wait, no, that's one of the impulses I'm trying to avoid. "What did you mean about practicing?"

"Just pretend I'm her. We'll talk, and you can figure out how to act like a normal human for once."

"Then we'll end up fucking."

She chuckles. "Well, you're not in a relationship yet, so if it happens, I suppose we'll just have to enjoy it, but given that you're so into this girl that you're wrinkling your shirt on my chair, I feel like there's a good chance you might be able to do better than you're giving yourself credit for."

I jump to my feet and adjust my shirt. Good God, she's right, I was. How could I ever be so cruel to my clothes? "She's made a mess of me."

"Apparently. So let's get you to the point where you're not going to act like this in front of her. And it'll take my mind off things."

I turn back to her. "Have you heard from the doctor?"

"There's not much to hear. We got the biopsy back before I started chemo, and it's non-Hodgkin's lymphoma, but as big as I am, that gives it a lot of room to spread, and there are already growths in…well, a few places they really shouldn't be."

"I'm so sorry, Vivi."

"It's okay." She's still smiling. I don't know if I'd be able to smile if I had something like that going on. "Mia thinks there's a really good chance that the chemo will take care of it. Obviously, she could be wrong, and I'm not quite sure what I'll do then, but I'll probably be fine. Other than the fur."

"I could make you a vampire. Please. You'd be immune to diseases. It's probably the only thing that's kept me from inventing a few new ones." I'm not sure it would actually work. I've never heard of a minotaur vampire, but I'm desperate enough to try anything.

She shakes her head. "If the chemo doesn't work, I'll think about it, but let's at least wait and see how this goes, okay? But I really appreciate how concerned you are."

I sink back into my chair and toy with my sandwich. "Okay."

"Now come on. I'm Phoebe, and you're you."

"Can I be Phoebe? That sounds more fun than being me."

She rolls her eyes.

"Fine, fine, I'm me. Damn, it would've been a nice break." I'm so much more self-effacing now, it's strange. "Can I ask you something? You Vivi, not Phoebe. Before we start."

She nods.

"I told her about what I thought was the worst thing I'd ever done, and she acted like I was a hero. I've hated myself for it for so long, and she insists that I not only didn't do anything wrong but that it was amazing of me, and I just kind of want your opinion on it."

She dunks her grilled cheese in her soup. "You have to actually say it, Friede."

I take a deep breath. She'll be the second person I've ever told, but I have to do it. I go into my story, the whole thing, just like I told Phoebe, and I watch her face, expecting the horror that I've always known I deserved, but it never appears. She only looks more tired.

"Jesus...no wonder you're so fucked-up."

"Thanks?"

She snorts. "Sorry. I...wow. I knew you'd been in Germany

at the time, but I'd never really wanted to ask what you were doing. I doubted you worked with them since you'd joked a few times about having worked at the Institut fur Sexualwissenschaft and being a sexologist, but I didn't know to what degree. Fuck... yeah, I can see why she thinks you're a hero."

"I let them die."

"You did. And you let them live. Do I think you should have gone and fought with them? Yes, you could've made a huge difference, you're a vampire, but by that same standard, I could be out there using my strength to fight neo-Nazis right now. Maybe not right now, as I'm very tired, but in general. Do you think it's terrible of me to not be doing so?"

I shake my head. "Of course not."

"You saved dozens of people, Friede. You could've done more. We can all always do more, but quite frankly, if I'd known you'd gone through that, I probably wouldn't have been as hurt by how distant you'd sometimes get. How hot and cold you always were in our friendship. I never knew how much you lost."

I don't know what to say to that.

"You already told her this, and that says a lot. I'm glad I was able to help you make such a difference in yourself. I think that you can really start being a much better friend and that you'll be an amazing partner to her."

"You really don't think it was awful of me?"

"Do I need to keep saying it? I thought I was supposed to be the one with a thick skull. You can be a real piece of shit, Friede, but you were a hero then, and I think you're finally starting to be a real person again, so maybe you can get to the point where you can be a hero again. From what you're saying, it sounds like that's the woman Phoebe deserves."

I think about her, and I can't deny it. "She does."

Vivi nods. "Then let's get you to be something resembling a decent date, even if I have to work all night to transform this wreckage of a canvas."

I roll my eyes. "You need your sleep, Vivi."

"I guess you'd better put a lot of effort in. I'm not going to bed until I'm confident in you."

She sure knows how to hold things over my head. But it works. We practice walking through how to behave, what I should do, and what to expect, and she helps me pick out my outfit. I had pictures saved, and they made it a lot easier than simply describing the clothes.

By the time we're done, I feel a lot more prepared, but she looks ready to fall asleep on her feet, so I help her into bed, despite a great deal of protest, thank her, and tell her to let me know if anything gets worse, and I'll turn her into a vampire.

She grumbles about how weird a vampire minotaur would be, and it's probably not even possible, but she doesn't fight me on it. I don't know if she's as scared as I am, or if she's only too tired to fight and placating me, but I appreciate it.

I call a cab and head back to the hotel, and for once, I'm not so bothered to be sleeping alone.

# CHAPTER EIGHTEEN

## *Phoebe*

Dinah's demigod manages to successfully steal the throne from her siblings, and all it took was betraying every last alliance she'd forged and literally stabbing Larissa's character in the back while laughing evilly. She's been putting that acting experience to good use.

"I can*not* believe that worked." She grins.

Katie shakes her head. "You're just so innocent. No one ever expected you to be a manipulative genius."

"Beginner's luck. I'd never done a Throne War before, so I just watched what you all were doing and tried to copy it."

"Jesus," Vanessa mutters. "I'm almost more upset now. I had my fleet working against Larissa's to keep her forces busy so we could take her out of the running, only for it to allow you to trap me. I'd assumed you'd at least planned it ahead of time."

She shrugs. "I just had the idea when you proposed it."

She grumbles, flopping back in my bed. "That's some serious beginner's luck you've got there. Can we do this again next week instead of switching games?"

I giggle. "It's a lot of work to run."

"I'll run it," Dinah says. "I have some downtime during rehearsal, and now that I know how it works, I can start on some plans to set things up for you all."

I never get to play in our Friday one-shots. I've always wanted to try a Throne War. "All right, I'm up for it if you all are." I look around the room, and everyone nods. "Awesome, I can't wait. You're in charge."

Dinah grins. "I'll try not to let you down. I have to leave for rehearsal in an hour, so do you want to get your freaking out done with?"

I didn't know I could schedule that. She's right, though. The game was a good distraction, but I've been agonizing over it all day, until I finally got into the various coups and scheming of my friends. "I picked out a cute blouse to wear, but I'm still scared and second-guessing it. And I think I really like her, and holy shit, is she ever cool, but that doesn't mean that she's ready for a relationship, either. And this is only a date, and we're not, like, getting together yet, but we've already had sex a bunch, and I don't know if I know how to separate that from everything else." I sigh. "Yeah, I think I'm ready to freak out."

"Thought you might be." Dinah sits next to me and puts her arm around my shoulders. "You're sure you want to be dating this girl?"

Even with all my doubts, I'm not sure I could convince myself to say no to that. "I'm pretty sure. She's a bit of a mess, and I was really scared after I first fucked her, and she seemed like she was really flighty and everything, but…she makes me feel good, and I love spending time with her."

"That's a pretty good sign," Vanessa says, climbing into Katie's lap.

"I'm still mad at you for murdering me."

"Yeah, but you love me."

Katie rolls her eyes and wraps an arm around Vanessa, squeezing her hard enough that I hope her top half doesn't pop off again. "I don't know much about this girl of yours, but if she makes you happy, it sounds like it's worth it. See what happens and try not to get too invested too early. I know how scared you still are after Paula."

Larissa looks worried, but she's been oddly silent on this whole thing today. Maybe learning about Freddie's past really got to her.

I nod. I keep switching back and forth between barely remembering Paula ever existed and being convinced that Freddie is somehow going to be just as bad. I guess everything Freddie told me could be a lie too, but it's so hard to believe it with the pain and sorrow I saw in her eyes as she told her story. But I didn't think Paula would lie to me, either. "I should be cautious. I know I should. I don't know Freddie very well, and I don't want to be hurt like that again, but I'm fairly confident that I want to take a chance."

Dinah kisses my temple. "All right, it sounds like you're sure."

I take a deep breath. Am I sure? I was getting there. No, I can't imagine backing out. "I am. I really like her. There's something special about her, this energy. Not, like, in a magical way or anything, but I've never known anybody who makes me feel like she does."

"Yes, she's good in bed, you've made it clear," Vanessa says.

I throw a pillow at her, but it mostly hits Katie and earns me an annoyed groan. I expect it to be thrown back, but she sets it to her side. "It's not just about the sex. I like being around her."

"I get that," Katie says, sounding a little annoyed. "But you need better aim."

"I'll try."

Vanessa leans back against her. "Are you all done freaking out?"

"No...I don't know. I don't know what to expect. It's not like relationships are new to me, hell, I just got out of one, but they seem very new to her, and I'm not sure what it'll mean. But also that's skipping a lot of steps. We're just trying to get to know each other right now."

"And you're scared that you're going to leap into a relationship before you're ready?" Larissa asks.

"I practically am already." I groan. "If she'd asked me to be her girlfriend, I might've said yes. I know I shouldn't, but I'm crushing so hard on this girl. And considering just how not relationship material she is, that's really scary. I get that relationships don't always work out, and I'm willing to put up with that risk, but after Paula, I second-guess everything, and I'm scared."

Dinah pulls away to look in my eyes. "Because you're second-guessing her, or because you're not?"

I stare at the bed. "Kind of both somehow. I'm scared that she's not ready, but I keep having to remind myself not to trust her. I had my heart ripped out and stomped on by a lying stalker, and I'm terrified at all times that I'm being watched now, and instead of taking all of that out on Freddie and being convinced that she's doing the same thing, I think I trust her. I *know* I trust her. And that's scary as all hell. I barely know her, and I'm already trusting her…"

"I get it," Larissa says. "She opened up to you." I'm glad she doesn't tell the whole story.

"Love can make people kinda dumb," Dinah says.

"I'm not in love with her." I glare at Dinah, and she smiles innocently, her mouth closed to hide her fangs.

Katie's booming chuckle draws my ire. "I'm sure you're not in love with her yet, but it's still the honeymoon period. When we were like that, Vanessa didn't annoy me at all."

"Hey!"

She chuckles and plays with her hair. "It doesn't always make you rational. And it can cause stupid mistakes. But it can also feel amazing."

"Yeah." I hug my tail, emotions warring inside me to the point that I'm not even sure what I'm feeling. "So what, you're saying just enjoy the moment?"

"Pretty much. You're getting to know each other. So date, have fun, have some more of that crazy sex you won't shut up about."

"I haven't said it that many times."

She quirks an eyebrow. Ogres have very impressive stares. "You're overthinking things. As you probably should be, no matter what we say, but try to relax and enjoy it. And if she's lying to you, I can rip her head off."

"Thanks." Everyone always offers to kill people for me, but

I don't think any of them would actually do it. They're almost as non-murderous as Freddie. And great, I'm already comparing everything in my life to her.

"What? It kills vampires, right?"

"It does," Dinah confirms. "And on that note, I should probably get going. I love you all, and I hope doing it this early still works for everyone, 'cause I always miss these games when I have plays."

I hug her tight. "Well, if you're gonna be running them, I think we'll manage."

She rolls her eyes, but she's grinning adorably. "Let me know how your date goes. Don't get up to anything too crazy without me."

Rachel is probably going to chew her out for using super-speed in public instead of just asking for a ride or taking her own damn car. "So," I say. "Now what do we do to help me not panic until my date? I probably shouldn't show up completely wasted."

"Board games?" Katie asks.

I blink. "Well, if you're going to twist my arm. That would work." I climb out of bed and head to my closet, looking through the game options for something that can reasonably kill the next five hours and will take enough focus that I won't be worrying. "And, Larissa, you'll still drop me off?"

"I always do."

"I'm sorry. I really do take advantage of you there."

She shakes her head, smiling at me. "You think I'm going to let you just wal—slither everywhere? You'd be seen. And you can't take a cab for the same reason. I'm not leaving you here to be a little agoraphobe. You live in Toronto so you can be around other people. What kind of friend would I be if I didn't help out with that?"

"Well, when you put it like that…" I still feel like I rely on her too much for it, but I don't want to keep pushing.

"And I can give you rides sometimes too," Vanessa says. "I know I'm not great about it, but I have before."

"You have. Thank you. Ah, this will do." I grab the Call of Cthulhu board game and set it up on my kitchen table. Hopefully, focusing on existential horror will take my mind off first-date jitters. Does it even count as a first date when we've already had sex so many times? I shouldn't even be nervous. How can I be nervous to see a girl when I already know what she tastes like? But it doesn't matter what I say or how much I already trust her, the first date is always scary, and I don't know if I'm hoping that we can succeed at taking things slowly or that she ends up in my bed again tonight.

We play and talk, and it helps. It doesn't actually make me stop thinking about her, not anywhere near as much as GMing had, and as it gets closer, I'm so nervous, my tail nearly knocks over a chair, but at least it manages to pass the time.

Everyone approves my blouse, and I get in the car with Larissa, ready to try to have a normal date with a woman who I'm not sure even knows what a date is.

## CHAPTER NINETEEN

### *Elfriede*

Who convinced me of this idea again? Oh, right, me. Shit, when has that bitch ever had a good idea?

Oh. I see her tail first, winding its way around a table in the corner, and above it, she's wearing a black blouse with fake gems as the buttons and enough of a window to her breasts that I can't help but take a moment to appreciate them. Her red hair has a single braid in it, tucked behind her ear. I've never felt underdressed in my life, but I am quite glad that I made sure I looked perfect.

I make sure my tie is properly aligned with the buttons of my shirt and that there's no dust or cow fur on my jacket. I'm nervous. I'm not used to being nervous, especially when all I have to do is talk to a beautiful woman. That's second nature to me.

But this isn't just that. This is…I don't quite know what it is.

Her eyes settle on me, and her face lights up, though her smile stays coy. She's nervous too. She reaches a hand up to tuck her hair behind her ear, but it's already there, so her hand only brushes against it.

I take the seat across from her. "Hey there, beautiful. I hope I didn't keep you waiting."

She shakes her head but doesn't say anything. I'm glad I can still leave her speechless.

I want to take her hand and kiss it, tease her wrist with my fangs, and do everything I can to show exactly how badly I want her, but this isn't that kind of date. I'm not trying to get her back to my bedroom for days of acrobatic lovemaking. I'm here to get to know the woman I can't stop thinking about. So I can behave. Probably.

"I got here early," she finally says. "I wanted to make sure I could get a table for us. You know how busy they always are. Or I guess you don't really know. You're new in town."

"I am." This is why we need to be in public, so we can actually learn about each other rather than ending up with our mouths full. But it may be a lot easier if I could think of anything other than how badly I want to be on top of her. "How long have you lived here?"

"Toronto or Canada?"

I blink. "It wasn't the same time? From everything I've heard, fiends always came to Canada because they wanted to be in Toronto."

"Sure, after they built this place in the 1800s."

She's been here longer than the Community Center? "Then, why'd you come here?"

"It was the new world. I…" She sighs, and I'm not sure if it's more wistful or melancholy. "I'd had to struggle for a long time. As the world modernized, it grew so very difficult to hide, and I only kept growing larger. When society wasn't so densely packed, I wasn't even a few meters long, and I could easily hide from them and even fit in normal human areas without much issue. But then as time went on, that kept growing more difficult, and I wanted a chance at a new life."

So like any other snake, she just keeps growing. I hadn't thought of that.

"How did you manage to get here if you couldn't hide anymore?" I hope she didn't have to eat the whole crew or something. I know she's better about killing people than other lamias, but she can't make people forget she's there. I'm sure she's had to kill to defend herself before. I can't blame her, but I'm certainly not comfortable with it.

"The same way I managed to do most things. I knew a lot of homeless people. Well, I guess I kind of was one sometimes, but I'd usually manage to hang on to a house for a few decades or centuries. I'd hire one of them to act as my envoy. He'd handle my money, do business transactions, make excuses for why I was never seen. It was simpler when I had time to set up a more convincing noble cover, but once big successful businessmen with international dealings were a more common concept, it became easier to manage my affairs without being seen."

"Oh, wow. I didn't think you were that well-off."

"Oh, I'm not now." She sighs. "The big issue with having to always rely on people to handle your money is that no matter how well you pay them, eventually, they likely realize that they don't really need you. It happened a few times. They'd take everything and leave me having to figure it all out again. I tried coming up with alternatives, but if you add more people, it's more potential weak links. But when I had one who was reliable, I had him help me book a ship to the New World. No one was allowed to look in my cabin, and I was able to relax and try to deal with my seasickness." She chuckles.

"So you were, what, one of the first colonists?"

"Not quite that early. I came here in the 1600s. There were still a lot of people here, whole civilizations that have been wiped out, but it wasn't as dense, especially up north. I was able to hide. I'm cold-blooded, so I had to be careful, but fire is easy enough to make, and I found caves to shelter in. It wasn't too different from what it was like when I was younger. I never liked caves, but I'm used to them, and it was nice not having to deal with so many people."

"Wow. I was partying eternity away in Rome while you were…stuck living in caves." I've had a few reminders over the years of how much easier it is being a vampire than most other kinds of fiends, but it always hits hard. We can pass as human and can recover from nearly anything, so it makes life a good deal simpler than one where humans will run or try to kill you the second you show your face. Or your tail.

She shrugs. "It doesn't sound like you exactly had an easy time."

"I suppose."

"What were you doing in Rome? I figured you'd stayed in Germany for most of your life."

I shouldn't have brought that up. This story makes me sound so much worse. "There had been rumors about me for a while. I moved around to try to keep people from realizing that I was a vampire, but it'd happen sometimes, especially since I tried to stay close enough to keep an eye on my family. Then the Black Death came back. The first time was shortly after I died, and I was away from my family, though most of them were lucky enough to survive, but this time, they all noticed that that same mysterious, un-aging woman was around again. And they blamed me. Thought I was a witch, funnily enough. So I decided to get out of town. I stowed away on a ship, which was absolute agony, days of feeling like my body was falling apart and the worst pain you can imagine, only to find myself in Naples. They'd gotten over their own outbreak just a few decades earlier. People still bore the scars. I stayed there for a few months, in a few beds, as I headed toward Rome. I grew up in the Holy Roman Empire, so I'd always wondered what the real place was like. I made it there, and it was beautiful, and I spent the next few years partying while my grandchildren back home were dying."

Her expression isn't quite horror; if anything, she's sympathetic, but she does at least seem put off. I'm glad she hasn't completely fooled herself into thinking I'm some hero. "I was still in Europe for the first two bubonic plagues, but I missed that one. I'm sorry you didn't."

"Two? I thought that was the second time. My medical knowledge is out-of-date, but I didn't think it was that bad."

"It happened in the 500s too. Right around where I was. But I was still living in caves, so it mostly just meant I had to be careful with my food." She stiffens up. "Sorry, I know you hate that kind of talk. I was joking. I wasn't really eating people then…that often…but when the second plague hit, I'd been living as a noble lady, and all I really had to do was keep hiding from people. I did lose the guy I was using to run my errands and deal with the bank, but most people had to go through far worse than that. I'm sorry you were one of them."

"I'm not the one who went through much. It was my family suffering."

She sighs. "And I know how much you care about them. Besides, you suffered plenty on that ship. I didn't know you couldn't cross running water. I've never known any vampires who actually had that problem, and Dinah and Rachel are really fragile for vampires, so that's saying something."

"Yeah, it's not fun. I've heard people say that bringing dirt makes a difference, but I've tried it, and it never seemed to. The big thing that tends to help is getting very, very drunk, which was easier in the days of sailors. Find someone who traded their dinner for some extra beer and is nearly falling over, and just help yourself to a sip of them. Then you can suffer in peace."

Phoebe chuckles, and her tail brushes my foot. "It's nice to know you're not completely invincible."

"What suggested I was?"

She shrugs. "You can't catch illnesses, you don't get hungover—"

"I do, I can just fix it immediately."

"Right, like there's a difference there." She shakes her head and sighs exasperatedly, but she's grinning. "I'm sorry you have to suffer for it, but it humanizes you a bit more to know that there actually is something that can hurt you."

"Getting stabbed hurts plenty. Had enough jealous husbands do that, like it was my fault their wives weren't into them."

She covers her mouth, laughing into her hand. "Hera, have you always been like this?"

I shrug. "Kind of? Is that so bad?"

"If it was, I wouldn't be here. I just didn't expect it. I figured it was a more recent thing."

That's surprising to hear. How can she still want me after all she knows about me? "I enjoyed precisely none of my life.

My sister and my brothers were all better workers and actually well-liked in our community and attracted far more promising spouses. I was the good-for-nothing layabout and treated like it. And my husband was even worse. So once I died, I wasn't willing to be miserable another second. I wanted to be free, to not let anyone treat me like that again. And after eight hundred years of relishing my time, partying, having fun, I can honestly say that I'm not tired of it. I was stupid to stop letting myself get attached to people, but the rest, I stand by. I hope that's not a deal-breaker."

She shakes her head. "I think I'm the same way. I never died, but my family was terrible to me, and I spent so many years struggling to even have a life in a world that so clearly wasn't made for me. But now I have friends, and with the internet, I can do so much more, and I love it. I play games, I spend time with friends, and my job is basically just doing more of that. All I wanted was to actually enjoy my life for once, and for the last couple decades, I mostly have."

"Huh." I take her hand, gently trailing my thumb along her knuckles. I want to do so much more, but it's more than that. I've never had anyone who really understood me before, and I think she does, or at least could. "I didn't know anybody else felt the same way. So many people seem to enjoy or at least know how to make themselves live a normal life. I've enjoyed working before. I liked being a doctor. I've been a carpenter, and I was a nun for a little while. They can all be fun, but I don't think I could ever spend my entire life devoting it to work. I can enjoy those breaks because I know I have eternity. If I only had the one life, I don't think I'd be able to stomach it."

She nods, her smile only growing. "Exactly. All the drudgery and hardship we've been through would've ruined any normal life, but we were able to keep going because we have so long, and it's let us reach this point, at this time, where not only can we have each other...er, well, enjoy each other's company." She giggles and pulls her hand away, fidgeting with her hair. "But we've gotten to see so much advancement and had so many opportunities for fun we couldn't have imagined as children. Three thousand years ago, I never would've even considered the idea that a video game could exist, and now I get paid to play them and talk at people for a living. And I love it."

God, I want to kiss her. "Yeah…"

She bites her lip, her slightly sharper than human teeth leaving the barest imprint. "So what about you? What's your favorite video game?"

"Really? That's the part we're focusing on? Fuck." I sigh. I was not prepared for this question. "I spent a few weeks in a condo with this couple in Munich, and they had, I think it was on a Nintendo 64, or maybe it was with a weird attachment, but I spent a lot of that time, sometimes even while doing…" I never know how explicit to be with these stories. "Other stuff, playing this Pokémon card game on it?"

She actually guffaws, taking wheezing breaths trying to stop herself. "No way. I will not believe that's your favorite game."

"Why, is it bad?"

"No. It's a cute little Gameboy game, it's fun, but just…so much that I learn about you is a surprise."

I shrug.

"Gods, you're adorable."

I tilt my head. I'm not sure I've ever been called adorable before. "Thank you? I more go for stylish, gorgeous, handsome, sexy, beautiful."

"You are. And you're adorable."

The plan was to not pin her onto the table and ride her, right? I'm trying to remind myself. "Did you want to tell me yours too? I doubt I'll know it."

"Like, half the Super Nintendo library. Probably an exaggeration. but it sure feels like it. Maybe Castlevania 4. Or I could reveal just how bad my taste is and say 2." She sighs. "But okay, you said something a bit ago that I've been dying to ask about, but we got caught up on all that life philosophy stuff."

"Oh?" What did I let slip now?

"You were a nun?"

Shit. I grumble. "Yes."

"Tell me more about that. How did that happen? Can you handle churches okay?"

"It would've been a lot harder if I couldn't." I chuckle. "But they're fine. I was never very religious, much to my parents' chagrin, but I'd been wooing this woman in a village a little outside of Frankfurt and, well, her family didn't approve. They sent her off to the convent, and being the romantic little lesbian I was at the time, I followed her. You would not believe some of the fun those, well, us nuns got up to. It was practically a feast." This story does *not* make me sound good, does it? "After a few years there, I left with Sisters Agnes and Christine, and we got a nice little cottage out in the country. God didn't seem to mind, if he is real."

She shakes her head. "Have you just lived out every lesbian movie?"

"Probably. Who'd they cast as me?"

Her grin is so adorable. "There are a few movies like that, though usually, it's monogamous, so I think you were a composite character."

"That's a shame. But fine, when did you end up in Toronto? You only said about your being in Canada."

"No, your life is so much more interesting." She toys with her hair, letting the braid rest on her shoulder.

"Please."

She nods, biting her lip again, I think she may also be considering that riding her on the table idea. "I heard about the Community Center. It was just an idea at the time. Some people— well, some demons from what I've heard—had wanted to set up a place where fiends—though it was still 'monsters' at the time— could try to live normal lives. As I'd been struggling with that for a long time, I jumped at the chance. Back then, it was basically a cottage, but they'd help you find a place to live or build one there, and for a little while, it was almost like a real life. Then the city kept getting bigger, and it was right back to hiding. But at least we had the Community Center."

"Wow." I knew how important this place was to so many

people, but I never realized it was intentional. I figured enough fiends had gathered here that it just came about naturally. No wonder Vivi was so set on this place; it was literally made to give people like us a real life. "I'm glad it was able to help you."

"It was. I had so many resources that I wouldn't have had until the internet. I didn't have to rely on humans to handle everything for me. It was like a miracle."

We have so many years of life to explore. I want to know so much more about her, and I feel like I've barely scratched the surface. "Had you ever found any place before then? Like when you were younger, was there any place else that felt like home or where you could be yourself?"

Her head tilts to either side. "Not exactly. Not to the degree it is here. But I'd met a few other fiends who weren't so beloved by their people. A couple other trans people, long before we ever had the word for it, whose communities hadn't accepted them, and some other fiends who weren't as bloodthirsty as their families wanted them to be, but we were always hiding, and it made it hard to have a real life. And unlike me, they'd die eventually. Unless someone actually kills me, I just keep shedding my skin and getting bigger."

"I think I could handle having more of you."

She giggles, focusing on the table. "There was a brief while, before I went to Lesbos, where I found some other fiends who had put together a little shantytown. I became fast friends with a cyclops there, Agapetus, who didn't like eating people. I was never as strongly anti-cannibalism as him, as I know you hate. I just didn't like having to eat my lovers, but he was hardcore about it. And maybe it kinda brushed off on me, made me realize how awful what my family wanted me to do was, even more than I already had. But he was a good friend, and he was the first person to really accept me as myself, even after he knew." She shrugs. "It was nice."

"And what happened?"

"People found out there were monsters there. And they attacked. I was lucky to get away. I never saw him again. I don't know if they killed him or if he found someplace else."

I sink in my seat. "They never let us live in peace, do they?" She shakes her head.

Before long, it'll probably happen here. I hate that thought. Toronto has been a sanctuary for so long and for so many. "Tell me something happier."

She chuckles, her tail coiling along my leg, settling on my knee, occasionally creeping toward my thigh, only to stop and go back a bit. "I don't know...uh..." She sighs, lightly squeezing me. "I made a bunch of friends once the internet was around, and I could start talking to people who had similar interests. I found D&D here at the Community Center. Well, a different one. Oh!" She beams. "I thought of something fun. Not sure if it's quite what you were wanting."

"Tell me."

"I was Homer."

I blink.

"I was one of the storytellers for *The Odyssey*. It changed a lot over time. But it was one of the few times I was able to try to have a life. I was small enough that I could pretend to be human. I just acted like my legs didn't work, and I'd keep my tail covered with a blanket. And I'd join in stories, just like I do now. I played a big part in crafting what ended up being *The Odyssey*. That happy enough for you?"

I nod, feeling myself grin. "That's amazing."

"I've written since then too. I never ended up near as famous as that story should've made me, but I had a few poems and stories that were pretty well received. Even wrote a few queer stories that seemed to resonate with people and were shared in secret and that there were only a few copies of before the printing press was invented."

"That's wonderful. I can't imagine doing something so meaningful to so many people."

"Says the doctor who literally helped make transitioning possible."

I shrug. "I guess."

Her tail tugs, pulling me closer until my belly presses into the table. "You're amazing, Freddie. I know that you are completely convinced of this and think you're awful and deserve to suffer, but let me just tell you that you are absolutely wonderful."

"Yeah?" I'm not sure I've ever had anyone say that to me. "Let's go back to my place. We can get delivery instead of eventually looking at these menus we haven't even touched. I just don't want to not be able to touch every inch of you."

"I thought we were taking things slowly."

"I know." She stares at the table. "And we probably should. I just..." She sighs.

I stand, her tail unwinding from me without a word as I round the table slowly and hold my hand out.

She looks up but hesitantly takes it.

"I would love nothing more than to go home with you and kiss you and do everything else to you until long after the sun comes up."

She giggles, and I help her stand. "All right, then. Let's get out of here."

## CHAPTER TWENTY

### *Phoebe*

I open my eyes to see a beautiful woman sleeping in my bed. Her hair is so messed up, she'll probably lose her mind when she sees it, but she kept making cute sounds whenever I pulled it. I hug her to me, wrapping my tail around her. This is so terrifying. How do I already want this so badly? I was ready to swear off relationships a few days ago, and now...

She murmurs sleepily, and eyelashes flutter against my chest. "Sorry, did I wake you?"

Freddie nods slowly, barely making a noise.

I run my fingers through her hair. "I'm sorry. I just needed to feel you."

"Not complaining," she murmurs. Her fang grazes my tit.

"Did you just bite me?" I release her and find her grinning as she pulls away.

She chuckles. "It was barely a nip."

I kiss her. How am I so hopeless? I shouldn't already want this so badly, but I couldn't even manage to go a whole date without feeling her against me.

Her hand rests on my hip. It's always nice having people give my scales attention. I'm not used to it. Other than some idle petting, people always seem a little worried about what to do with my tail. She licks her lips when she finally breaks the kiss. "Good morning, beautiful."

My heart flutters in my chest. I feel like a teenage girl. This is so silly. I know better. I don't know her well enough. "Good morning. A girl could get used to waking up like this."

She seems to take a moment, her gaze trailing appreciatively over me. "Yeah...I think I really could too."

Shit. "I probably shouldn't ask this. I know it's dumb."

"Don't worry, I think it's adorable that you hiss when you come."

I hit her with a pillow.

She grins back at me, undeterred. "Then what was the actual question?"

"It wasn't..." I take a deep breath. "I...what if maybe I *am* ready?"

It seems to take a second, then she blinks, and her eyes widen. "Oh. Like..."

"Like I said, it was dumb. We shouldn't rush things." I turn from her, trying to calm down. I can't think straight when I'm looking into her eyes. She's too beautiful, it's not fair. They're so blue and deep and perfect, and...I just want to keep kissing her for a century.

She takes my hand and pulls me back to her, those damn eyes locking on mine. "You want to be with me?"

I barely resist nodding. I think. I may have inclined my head a little. I'm insane. No one should ever want to jump in like this. Especially after everything I just went through.

"Are you sure? You know a lot about me, and not much of it is good. I'm a mess, and I'm not sure I can give you what you deserve."

"Well, you can certainly give me what I want." I did not just say that. Curse Aphrodite for doing this to me.

She purses her lip, her fang scraping it. "Fuck. Yes."

"What?"

Freddie pulls me to her, sending a shiver along my spine, and that's a lot to shiver. "I don't really know how to do it. I don't know that I'm any good at it. It's been almost a century since the last time I was in a relationship, and you know how that ended. But I haven't been able to get you out of my head since we met and..." She sighs. "Maybe I'm finally ready for something normal. Not like it's boring or mundane. Like, I've never met anyone like you, and I really...I want to. Be with you."

Fuck. Maybe we're both dumb. I should tell her we need to wait, that I still need more time, that there's too much going on, but all I can do is kiss her and throw my arms around her. I want this crazy, messed-up vampire to be my girlfriend, no matter how little sense it makes.

Her hand trails along my hips, her nails lightly scratching my scales until she settles on the front and drifts farther. I take in a sharp breath, kissing her again, moaning into her mouth as I feel her touch.

I could *really* get used to this.

❖

"So how'd the date go?" a voice says, and I hear the door close. Larissa is standing there by my kitchen, her eyes widening as she looks at the tangle of Freddie, me, and the sheets. "I guess that answers my question." She giggles, grinning, her gaze decidedly on Freddie.

Freddie, for her part, smirks. "Did you want to join us?"

I roll my eyes and squeeze her to me. "What's up, Larissa? There a reason you're in my kitchen?"

"Well, you weren't answering your calls, I wanted to see how your date had been, and we have Warhammer in half an hour. I always show up early to help you set up."

Oh shit. I forgot I'd agreed to that. My normal Sunday Warhammer night had to be moved to Saturday since one of our players has his anniversary Sunday. "I..." I don't want to reschedule, especially when some people are probably already on their way, but I also want nothing less than getting out of bed any time in the next decade.

"I can see you're rather distracted."

"So who's this?" Freddie asks, looking between the two of us and not at all bothering to cover herself. "She smells human. I didn't know you had human friends."

I sigh. "This is Larissa. She's a good friend of mine. And my ex, not trying to keep that a secret."

Larissa attempts a curtsy.

"I'm not the jealous sort," Freddie says. "She could actively be your girlfriend, and I'd still be fine so long as I was too."

"I'm sorry, she's your what?" Larissa asks.

Of course she focuses on that part. Why couldn't she just take Freddie up on the threesome? Then at least her mouth would be preoccupied, and I wouldn't have to answer any questions. "Uh…my girlfriend?"

"What happened to taking things slow?"

Freddie grins. She's so proud of getting me to repeatedly go back on what I said, isn't she?

I glower at her, but she only looks cuter rather than showing any shame. "We…I like her, okay?"

"I can see that."

I make sure the sheet is adequately covering me. Not like it's anything Larissa hasn't seen. "I didn't plan on it. I only asked her a few minutes…" The sun is much lower outside my window than it had been when I'd last woken up. "Well, hours ago."

"So you asked her? After you were just going on about how not ready for a relationship you are?"

"I'm irresistible," Freddie says. "I mean, have you seen me?"

"I have." Larissa continues to unabashedly admire my girlfriend. "I can see what she meant. You are indeed very pretty."

"Aw, she called me pretty."

I roll my eyes. "Did your ego need the boost?"

Her arm wraps around me, pulling me close. "Always."

I laugh into her shoulder, hugging her back. "You're pretty. Gorgeous. Sexy. Beautiful. Handsome."

"You can keep going."

I roll my eyes.

"She forgot stunning," Larissa adds.

Freddie nods. "Everyone always does."

"Do you two need a room?" I ask.

Larissa smirks, but she shakes her head. "I'm just teasing

and window shopping. I don't want to try to steal your girlfriend. I'm happy for you. Even if I am a little worried."

"Yeah, I'm dangerous too. And dashing."

"Very Han Solo."

That's not going to help her ego. Freddie nips my ear. "I should probably let you get to your game. I could…come back here tonight? Maybe with takeaways from someplace?"

"It's a date."

She beams, taking my chin and guiding me into another kiss. Gods, she can be smooth sometimes. She pulls away, and there's not a hint of showboating in her smile. She looks ecstatic, loving, maybe even worshipful. It makes me feel so warm.

She stands and finds her clothes, making Larissa turn bright red by the time she finally waves good-bye and blows me a kiss.

"So," Larissa says.

"Yeah."

"You didn't say how hot she was."

"I did."

She slides one of my kitchen chairs closer to the bed. "Well, you didn't adequately tell me, then. Wow."

"What, think she's out of my league?"

"You know you're beautiful too."

I smirk. I have to give her a bit of a hard time after all that. "So are you busy memorizing her for later, or do you want to give me a warning lecture?"

"Probably both. Just…be careful, Phoebe. I don't want to see your heart broken again. After Paula…it was scary. I knew I'd hurt you before, but it was nothing like that, and I don't ever want to see that again. You know I love you."

"I love you too." I sit up, the sheet still draped about me. "Do I have time to shower?"

"I'm sure you need it."

Probably best not to spend game night smelling like sex. "Yeah. Give me a few minutes. Help yourself to some cereal." I slither out of bed and to the bathroom, throwing the sheet onto my bed as I close the door behind me.

It's hard not to think about last night. And this morning. But

I need to not get caught up in wonderful fantasies and just get clean, get dressed, and get ready for the game.

Maybe I could text Freddie once I'm all set up. Or I could send her an after-shower message.

Shit. Or not. I still don't actually have her number. I asked her to be my girlfriend before I even asked for her phone number! This is what happens when you don't take things slow. You don't bother to think about anything.

She'll be here tonight. I can ask then. But I can't even tell her when I'll be free. Fuck. I swear, I don't have a brain when she's around.

But I know I'll see her, and it'll be okay. I may not be thinking anything through, but clearly she isn't either, so we'll figure it all out together. I only have to wait until tonight.

## CHAPTER TWENTY-ONE

### *Elfriede*

I'm...not single. That's a disturbing thought. I chuckle to myself as I walk through the lobby of my hotel, some fresh cash in my pocket from the latest cab driver. I never thought I'd reach this point again. Sometimes, I felt like I wasn't worthy of love, but what it really came down to was cowardice. I thought that I was protecting myself by not allowing any real connections, but I was wrong. I was only hurting everyone more, me included. I can have friends. I can have a partner. I can have a real life, and I can still be happy, and even if I do lose some of them, it only hurts that much because I cared about them in the first place, and that's so much better than just numbing myself for another century.

The elevator chimes as it opens, and I step inside and hit the button for my floor. I just hope that I can remember how to be a partner. I wasn't a great one to Hertha, or at least, she would say I wasn't. I know Phoebe would insist that saving her from a genocide was a pretty good step, but Hertha would insist I was a coward, and she'd be right. I don't kill people. I can't. I won't. But fortunately, that doesn't tend to come up too often in relationships. It's only all my other flaws that make them difficult.

I sigh and shake my head as the elevator stops and the doors open. I step out, almost sad to be home, if this even counts as home. I can hear people bickering, fucking, and watching television in the rooms throughout the floor, but there's something else, and it grows louder as I move closer to my room. There's someone tearing through bags, cutting something, maybe a mattress? They're muttering about how they can't find what they're looking for.

There's enough blood in me for it to run cold. This doesn't feel real. I fled across the fucking ocean, and it's only been a week. But they found me. It's the only explanation. There's someone tearing apart my hotel room and looking for me or the money they think I still have.

They'd have better luck searching every casino in Berlin.

What do I do? They smell human. I could confront them and tell them to tell their boss that they killed me. Or I could run.

I'm good at running. It's what's gotten me this far. It makes sense. I should do it. All I need to do is turn around and never come back. And they'll keep chasing me. Apparently, far quicker than I'd expected. I thought I'd have years. Or at least months.

I slide my keycard into the lock of my door, but there's a loud bang and a splitting pain in my chest. And again.

I look down to see bullet holes. They fucking shot me. God, it hurts. It's like it's spiraling out through my body from the holes now ruining my shirt. What if I'd been a maid? I open the door and find a man in a cheap suit aiming a gun right at me. He pulls the trigger again, and I barely manage to move to the side in time. There's only one man I can see, but he's all the way across the room and still pointing a gun at me.

Fighting is not something I do. I've been shot at a few times, mostly by jealous lovers, twice by Nazis. Once when I was stealing a train and once in a bar in Paris. I talked my way out of most of those. "Stop shooting me."

He pulls the trigger, and the air is knocked out of me as a twisting pain tears through my belly. What the fuck?

I wince, tearing up, trying to focus, but there are three bullets in me.

I could run?

But I can't. He could shoot me when I turn my back.

His finger tightens on the trigger.

I've hurt very few people in my life who were not literally asking for it. And usually, that's only some light slapping. Or biting. I killed my husband. And I punched one of the people who shot me. It was enough to collapse one of his lungs. I don't think I'll ever forget that wretched sound as he tried to take a breath. He was a monster, but in that moment, so was I.

I knock the gun out of his hands with a backhanded slap. I hear bone crunch and feel sick to my stomach. He gasps, clutching his hand. "Tell your boss that I'm dead."

He whines, tearing up.

Why can't I compel him?

I grab him by his collar and lift him. It's a good way to woo a lot of women, so long as I'm careful. I'm not careful this time, and his shirt digs into his throat hard enough that I can hear the blood slow. I want to sink my fangs in, to drink him, to make these stupid holes in my chest stop hurting.

"What the fuck are you?" he asks.

I look the man up and down. He's confused, terrified, his hazel eyes all but consumed by his pupils, like he's seen a creature walk out of his nightmares. "They didn't tell you?" I ask. "I'd assumed they'd put it all together."

He doesn't answer; it doesn't even look like the question registers.

He can't hear me, can he? I tilt him in my hand to look at his ear. There's an earplug in. I reach up and grab it as he squirms, kicking at me, but I take it out and drop him on his ass. "So, now we can talk," I say. It's what an intimidating person would say. Especially if they hadn't just ruined an exquisite shirt and my favorite of the spider silk jackets. I wonder if she could patch them up? It wouldn't be the same. I should just buy new ones.

"What the hell are you?" He gasps, scrambling to his feet, looking around, likely for his gun.

"They didn't tell you?"

"They said you're some kind of witch. That you can get in people's heads."

That's very interesting. I haven't been accused of that in centuries. I could rock a witchy look. I should try that sometime.

I bet Phoebe would enjoy it; she loves all that fantasy stuff. It'd be like her Dungeons and Dragons games. "So they told you to wear earplugs?"

He nods, looking around the floor. Maybe it's not for his gun. He wants his earplug.

"Got it right here, buddy. What'd they say to do? Kill me and send back a picture as proof?" There are three bullet holes in me, and blood is already dripping down to the point that it's staining my slacks too. I'd make a convincing corpse if we sent a picture in.

He shakes his head.

"Why'd you shoot me if I'm not supposed to be killed?"

"You are. But they don't want just a photo." He isn't German. That's a surprise. He sounds like everyone else here. Except Phoebe. Just another Toronton—Torontoan? Canadian. "They said we had to bring back your head or the two million. We don't get paid until then."

Well, so much for faking my death. I can't survive losing my head like I can everything else. At least I know what they're after, but he's being oddly cooperative. Is it because I scared him that much? Wait. "We?"

Footsteps thud from the other room. I'd heard someone cutting into my mattress. This guy was in my living room. There are two of them. This is why I don't do the big action hero shit. I'm not a fighter. I don't have the brains for it. I need a drink.

I turn to find a man raising his gun. I'm about out of options, aren't I?

I can kill them. Or I can run.

So I take the only real choice. I run.

The gun barks, and I hear the bullet sailing through the air, but I make it to the door and out into the hallway. There's no time for the elevators, so I take the stairs. Every single step is agony, sending waves of pain through my torn-up insides.

At the bottom of the stairs, I nearly collapse. I need blood. If I don't drink…

I don't actually know what will happen. I've never not drunk.

But my blood is up in my room, and so are the guys with guns.

I take a deep breath, trying to steady my steps, but the adrenaline is wearing off. I shove open the door to the lobby and stumble past the desk. One of the receptionists calls toward me, but I don't want to risk them seeing the condition I'm in. I push open the door and head outside, the same afternoon sun shining down on me as when I left Phoebe's.

I can barely believe it's the same day.

People are all around. They don't seem to be looking at me yet, but I can smell them. They're food. I need it. I need it more than I've needed it since…since I killed my husband. The bastard deserved it, but I can't. I won't feed on people like that. If it's given freely, I'm more than happy to take it, but right now, I'm not sure I could keep from killing the person.

So I need blood, and I need a way out of town.

The bus station is an obvious choice. I could easily drink someone there. But I won't be that monster. I saw the terror in that killer's face as I threatened him. It wasn't quite like my children's, but it wasn't far enough away for my comfort.

I don't think I can manage to run. I'm barely stumbling as it is.

They could be right behind me. If I stop, I may die.

I find myself at an intersection with cars waiting at the light. I step in front of one, looking the driver up and down. She looks like food. No, she looks like a harmless woman in her forties who could use a good screw, but that's not what I'm here for. I move as quickly as I can with the wounds and open the passenger door.

She stares at me in shock, not even screaming.

"Drive me to the Honeydale Mall," I say, putting all the will I have left into the words as the world goes black.

❖

"We're here," a terrified voice says.

I blink, trying to remember what anything is, and find a

woman staring at me. Her eyes are wide, and she keeps looking between me and the mall. I've never stuck around to see how anyone I compel feels afterward. I can see why it'd be upsetting. She has no idea why she's here. "Thank you."

"Are you sure you shouldn't be going to a hospital?" Or is she worried about me? Did I even actually make her come here, or did she just fulfill what probably sounded like my last request? "You don't look so good."

"My doctor's here. I'm a doctor." Shit, I'm delirious. "You should go home, or go back to whatever you were doing." I wince. Making words is starting to hurt. How much damage did they do?

I open the door and fall on the cement with a terrifying crunch.

I pull myself up and find the world cracked. My sunglasses are broken. This is the worst thing to happen to me today. I look so good in them.

And they're so hard to find.

My feet are shaky, but I manage to stand, and when I look over, I see the woman next to me. "Are you okay?" she asks.

"I said go home. I'm fine." Maybe I can get the lenses replaced inside.

"You need to go to the hospital."

If I compel her again, it may scramble her brain. "I assure you, I'm okay. It's just stage makeup. I tripped on your seat belt. Please, go home."

Her gaze falls to my wounds.

I shrug and limp toward the building.

"At least let me help you," she says.

"No." If I let her inside, people will eat her. She's too nice to be eaten. "I don't want to bring you any danger. This is a mob operation, and I'm seeing a black-market doctor." Mia will probably be happy to be a cover. "You'd only be putting yourself in danger. I'm a criminal."

She looks skeptical, but she steps away from me.

"Get in your car and go. If they think you're a witness, they might shoot you."

She looks between me and her car and finally seems to settle on fleeing. She climbs in and drives away and leaves me hobbling across the parking lot until I can finally manage to open the door.

I sink onto the floor inside. There are other fiends milling about, but no one seems to particularly care.

I lean against the wall for support and try to walk through the room.

Finally, I attract someone's attention. "Blood," I say. "Just get me the blood guy."

I'm not sure if I pass out or if somebody else used their superspeed, but I blink, and there's a bag of blood in front of my face.

I snatch it from their hand and bite into it, moaning in pain and pleasure as I feel it run through me, knitting my wounds back together. I slump against the floor.

"It's twenty bucks," a voice says.

My eyes are closed. God, I used up too much energy. I look up at a vampire who looks more amused than anything else. I grab the money from my pocket and stuff it into his hand. "Do you have any glasses lenses?"

He chuckles. "No."

"Damn. Well, thanks for the blood." I stumble back to my feet and look around. I need a change of clothes, or at the very least, a shirt. I have enough money left for another spider silk button-up, so I buy one and change into it in the middle of the Community Center. He didn't shoot my bra, and I don't care if anyone sees.

I finger the holes in the back of my jacket. "Can you fix this?"

The spider woman snorts. "Not with those bloodstains."

Great. "Thanks anyway. I love your work. I'll try to come back sometime." I toss the jacket and shirt in the trash and walk back outside.

I have to get out of town before they find me again.

# CHAPTER TWENTY-TWO

## *Phoebe*

Who invited James again? I glower at him after he kills my last space marine. I knew I should've played Chaos. "Good game," I mutter. "Didn't you not even know how to play last month?" He grins. "Yeah, I'm amazing at everything I do."

I'm only a little annoyed. Losses happen, but he's either ludicrously lucky or the quickest learner in the world as he hasn't lost a game all day. I glance over toward Jackie and MJ's game. At least *a* lamia is winning at Warhammer 40k. I'll take that.

Larissa taps my shoulder. "My turn."

I slide off my chair, letting her take it. James has already beaten her once, but maybe she figured something out. I wish Dinah had been up for spending a fortune collecting pieces and using all of her non-acting time painting them so she could join us. Five players makes it so difficult.

Jackie lands the final blow on MJ's army, and MJ chuckles. "Damn, I really thought I could still make a comeback."

"That's because you underestimate orks."

"Clearly." MJ stands, stretching, as if vampires actually need to. But I suppose he's only been one for a few months, and it probably takes some getting used to. He slides his chair over, and I squeeze in. "I see James did a number on you."

"Have you been teaching him?" I ask. "He didn't even know what Warhammer was when you first brought him."

He shrugs. "I've learned by now not to underestimate him."

I shake my head. I shouldn't be annoyed. Especially as happy as I am today. I have a girlfriend. Or maybe I should be annoyed but at myself for jumping into that after promising myself I wouldn't. "All right, Jackie, let's see what you can do."

We set up our armies and start the game. I was so glad Jackie messaged me a couple months ago with this idea. I'd wanted to start up a war gaming group for ages, but it was hard enough to find people for D&D at the Community Center, let alone something this niche. Apparently, he's missed me since he'd left my Friday game.

I look him up and down, trying to get into his head, to figure out what his plan may be. He has long black hair that's as perfect as mine, a tail a couple meters shorter, and is wearing a loose-fitting shirt. People tend to assume a lot about lamias, mostly that we're all women, and I've seen how much it gets to him. It's why I bought him a binder for his birthday.

He goes first, but I play aggressively, not wanting to let him have the time to pull off anything like James did. But before I can clinch my victory, someone knocks at my door.

Is it Freddie? She said she'd be back tonight, but it's only been a few hours. I guess she can't stay away from me. She can be so shockingly adorable. I've missed her too. "Let me let her in." I hurry over to the door and open it only to find two men in ill-fitting suits.

And I just opened the door, showing off my snake tail and all the other fiends in my apartment. I slam it in their face, terrified by how much they could've just seen.

"Uh." I turn toward my friends, who are all looking at me, and gesture toward the door. "Someone with feet answer. They look like cops."

MJ sighs and stands. "Everyone else get out of view." Once we're all safely sequestered in the kitchen, he walks over and opens it again. "Hi there, something I can help you with?"

I can't see what the humans are doing outside. I hope they don't try to pull anything. They must've seen me and maybe even Jackie. That was so stupid, but I was sure it was Freddie.

I've been so excited to see her again. "We're looking for a Ms. Elfriede Bauer. We pinged her phone here earlier. Thought you might know something."

Are they not going to ask about the scary snake monsters they saw? Elfriede? Is that Freddie's name? The last name is German, so it would make sense. Aphrodite, how do I know so little about my girlfriend? I knew I was rushing into things, but it didn't occur to me that I didn't even know her name. "I'm afraid I don't know an Elfriede."

"What about the girl who answered before?"

"That was Phoebe. I can see how the names sound a little similar, but they're definitely different people."

The guy groans. "I know they're different people. I just saw Elfriede a few minutes ago. But she ran away, so I thought I'd look here. I'm Officer Hancock. She's wanted for a string of thefts. If you could cooperate, I can bring her in safe and sound. I don't want anyone to be hurt."

That's a weird way to put it. Almost like it's supposed to be a threat. "Well, none of us know an Elfriede."

"This isn't a joke, Mr...."

"Officer, actually." I can hear MJ grinning. "It's Officer Michael Jefferson." He's a parole officer, not a cop, but I doubt they realize that. I hear him pull something from his jacket, likely a badge. "What did you say your name was? Officer Spatchcock? From what precinct?"

"The 53rd." I think he produces his own badge. "And it's Hancock. So now that we've established you're only a parole officer, how about you answer a few questions before I take you in for impersonating an officer?"

MJ sighs. Is he going to cooperate with them? "No, you see, a normal cop would be a bit more concerned about the snake girl that he saw. Neither of you seem to be, which makes me think you already saw something you probably shouldn't have. So you're going to tell me everything you know, and then once we're done, you're going to forget everything that happened today."

Shit. MJ's using his powers for evil. I love it. I try to get a better look. They're going to forget me now, so there's not any real risk. I slither closer until I see the men in their suits again and the edges of a gun visible under the nearer one's jacket. I really hope he's human, or MJ's thing won't have any effect.

"We were sent to her hotel," he says, sounding confused by his own confession. "She owes someone a lot of money. We weren't told names, but we have to bring her head or the money back to Berlin. The reward was more than enough for it to be worth it. The room was empty when we got there, so we searched it, hoping we'd be able to find our payday and get out of there."

The other one cuts in, leaning forward. "She walked in on us. I managed to shoot her, but she grabbed me by my shirt and picked me up like it was nothing."

"You did what?" I snap, moving closer.

He doesn't seem to even notice me. "She took out my earplug and started asking me questions. I knew I couldn't resist, but…" He trails off, his eyes fuzzing up. "She ran. I'm waiting to hear back with a new location on her phone, but I can't rely on the precinct too much without raising questions." He blinks, shaking his head, like he's not sure why he's doing all this.

"Any of this mean anything to you?" MJ asks, turning toward me. "I'd assume they were lying about everything if I hadn't compelled them. It sounds like they're corrupt cops on someone's payroll. Not exactly rare for Toronto. I've had a few fiends offer to pay me off."

"You ever take the money?"

James chuckles. "Never ask a man about his bribes. It's just rude."

MJ sighs. "A couple times, when it's something I would've covered up anyway to avoid drawing attention to fiends and didn't mind getting paid extra for it. Why, are you offering?"

I shake my head. "No. But they're after my girlfriend."

"Your girlfriend?" He smirks. "When did this happen?"

"Ah, young love." James's voice is nostalgic and full of whimsy.

"I'm three thousand."

"A mere child." He sighs, his red eyes glowing dreamily. "Well, if they're trying to go after my dear friend's lover, I suggest we butcher them and dissolve them in acid."

He's probably joking. I think. At the very least, I doubt I'm his dear friend, as I've known him for about two months, ever since MJ invited him to our weekly Shadowrun game. I was shocked when an incubus showed up with a character sheet for a street samurai instead of a face, but I suppose that teaches me to profile. "If we were to do that, I'd just eat them. I don't want to damage my tub."

James flashes a flawless, glinting smile and laughs his melodious, perfect laugh. "Well, this is a war gaming group, isn't it? Let's think tactically. Your darling lover is apparently in a good deal of debt. And there are people out for her head, literally. Which likely means they know she's not human." It would suggest that, wouldn't it? "So have them feed misinformation to their companions, call your boo, tell her to run, and then I can resume my game."

I never understand him. "I can't."

"Because you're too worried? Then run with her. Leave me the keys, and I'll lock up when we're done."

I groan. "Larissa already has her own keys, so she'd lock up, but no." Do I really want to confess to the weird incubus that I don't have my girlfriend's phone number? "It's all been such a flurry of romance and feelings and stuff, and…I never actually got her phone number."

"I'm sorry?" Jackie asks, staring at me from his spot safely in the corner of my room. "You have a girlfriend, who is apparently a different one from the one you had last week, and you don't have her phone number?"

It sounds a lot worse when he says it condescendingly. "Are we just gonna leave mind-controlled cops outside my door?"

"Don't dodge the question," James says. "This is amazing. Young love truly is magical. I remember the shenanigans I was embroiling myself in when I was your age." His brow furrows. "Oh wow, I really do. I might have been even dumber."

Larissa clears her throat. "Can we stop picking on Phoebe long enough to deal with the issue of the people trying to murder her girlfriend? The people with guns who just came to her apartment?"

"They're humans," James says. "Hardly a real threat."

"I'm not bulletproof," she says. "And for that matter, I don't think Phoebe is, either."

"Nope," I say. "I'm long-lived, so long as I can keep shedding my skin, but if I get shot, I could die. So I'm rather focused on the people trying to kill my girlfriend, as that seems like the pressing part."

"But I'm just about to win," James whines.

Larissa glares at him. "The hell you are."

"Gods, you two," I say.

MJ chuckles. "Okay, how about I tell them to tell their boss that they cut her head off, and she turned into dust. That plays on some vampire stereotypes if he knows as much he seems to, so the response should tell us something."

"What makes you think it's a he?" Larissa asks.

MJ doesn't bother answering for his crimes. "So, men, officers, my brothers in blue, Hancock specifically, message the guy who sent you saying that you cut her head off, and she turned into dust."

The cop twitches weirdly. I've never seen anyone react like that. Did he fry his brain? "I…" He blinks and shakes his head, then stares blankly ahead.

"Well, shit," MJ mutters. "Other guy, do you have your employer's contact information?"

"No, we were only given a dead drop location in Germany and the promise of three hundred thousand dollars."

How much money does she owe?

James's perfect laugh annoys me yet again. "So you're not the only person too dumb to get someone's phone number. I bet you feel better now."

I sigh, pinching the bridge of my nose. "Make them forget everything." And then what? They said she ran. Is she still going to come here? I don't have any way to contact her. She wouldn't...would she up and leave without a word? "And send them home." I sink onto a chair, my mind racing. I don't know where she would've run, and I can't call her—

Wait, can I? "Before they go, could you see if their brains are working well enough to get me something?" They were pinging her phone. They must have her number.

## CHAPTER TWENTY-THREE

### *Elfriede*

The bus station is so full of people that I'm nearly salivating. So much blood, and someone must've cut themselves, or there was a fight I just missed, as the sweet scent of it wafts in the air. I could track down its source and have a drink, but I've had enough. It's not worth focusing on, no matter how good it smells.

I need to get out of town. There are people trying to kill me, and I'm not going to stay in one place and wait for them. I don't know how they found me, but maybe the next city will be better. The soonest bus is going to Quebec City. It's not exactly a booming metropolis, but it'll have to do.

Surely, there's something worth seeing there. Or experiencing. A few beautiful women—

Shit.

I'm in a relationship.

Not only that, I'm with someone who just had a partner horribly betray them, and I'm thinking of leaving town without a word?

The line moves up a person, and I pull my phone from my pocket and stare at the screen. I've never gotten her number. What the fuck? How did I miss something that important?

There must be another option. I can call Vivi and have her find Phoebe at the Community Center and let her know. How will she feel about that? "Hi, you don't know me, but your girlfriend is a friend of mine, and she just left the city without a word because she's in massive debt to loan sharks and doesn't want to get murdered."

Even assuming that Vivi would portray me that favorably, it doesn't seem like the kind of message Phoebe would appreciate. Sure, Vivi could give her my number, but by the time they run into each other, it will have been days after I stood her up for our date tonight. If I leave, I probably don't have a girlfriend anymore.

That's fine. I should still do it. If anything, I'm keeping her safe this way. Not only from the people trying to kill me but from me. I'm not a person anyone should be with. I'm too much of a coward. At the first sign of trouble, I'm in line to buy a ticket to Quebec City.

And I'm sure I'll hurt her in other ways. There's no way being in a relationship with me is a good bet. Buying this bus ticket isn't me hurting her; it's me keeping her safe. This is me doing the right thing. There's no way that I could possibly go back and tell her everything.

Not only would it be exceedingly out of character, but all it would do is doom her to a life on the run with the least responsible person in the world, who will let her down again and again until finally she realizes that she deserves better and leaves me, just like Hertha did.

And Hertha died because I was too much of a coward to do anything.

But the situation is different here. No one is after Phoebe, and she's not joining any war effort. People are after me, and I'd be putting her in danger, so being a coward is the noble choice for once. The line moves again, and I realize I'm out of cash, so I just tell the guy behind the counter to give me a ticket.

I move to stand in line for the bus. It should be here any minute. I'm doing the right thing. This is the noble option. I'm protecting the people I care about.

It's just that it's a noble option that involves breaking my word to a woman who has already had far too many people lie to her.

I stare straight ahead. The bus is already pulling up. A woman in uniform opens the door, and the couple in front of me head outside. It's my turn. I'm holding up the line. I have to go. I have to get on the bus. I have to leave Toronto if I don't want to die. And I've spent this entire time looking for excuses to stay. For once, I don't want to run. My girlfriend and my only real friend are in this city, and I'd be leaving them behind for what I'm quite certain is a hellhole with no nightlife to speak of. "Sorry, I just wanted to admire that smile," I say and turn around, walking back toward the entrance. I hand my ticket to someone in line as I pass.

What the hell am I doing?

I open the door and step outside into the still sunny afternoon. Where am I going? What am I going to do? I've been to Phoebe's a couple times now, and I know the address. I'll get a cab and head there. I can explain everything to her.

I call one up and wait, so close to my escape. All I need to do is walk right back into that bus station, grab that ticket back, and I can be on my way to safety. No one has to get hurt. It's the best option. The bus pulls away, driving down the street. I could still catch up to it. It wouldn't be difficult.

But I've made my choice.

The car pulls up in front of me, and I get in and give them Phoebe's address.

My phone buzzes in my pocket. It's a number I don't recognize. Could it be the loan shark? What if they're trying to trace my phone or however that works? I shouldn't answer, right? Curiosity gets the better of me. "Hello?"

"Oh, thank the gods. You're okay."

I feel myself smiling the second I hear her voice. It's Phoebe. "I wasn't a few minutes ago. I...there's some stuff I need to explain to you. I'm on my way there."

"You..." She gulps, and I swear I hear a sob. "You are? I thought...I heard that you'd run away?"

"Who told you that?"

She takes a deep breath. "The guy who shot you."

I blink and wish she was here to stare at in shock. "I'm sorry, what?"

"The cops who went to your hotel. They came over here asking about you."

"Are you okay? Wait, they were cops? But you're okay?"

She chuckles. "Yes, I'm okay. I managed to get your number from them. They were using your phone to track you."

"Son of a bitch. That's how they knew where I was so quickly. The rat fucker at the electronics store who helped me set up my phone must have sold me out. I guess I can't exactly blame him, but still, I'd certainly never sell anyone out to a cop. That's low."

"It is."

"Wait, so…I'm gonna throw my phone out the window, and I'll see you in a few minutes?"

She's silent for a long second. "Yeah, that's probably a good plan."

I roll down the window and wait until I'm certain I won't hit a pedestrian, then fling my phone as hard as I can, cracking a chunk of sidewalk as it explodes into shards. I probably didn't need to throw it that hard. I was panicking a bit.

"Just keep driving and don't worry about that, and give me all the money you have," I tell the cabbie. I have a feeling I'm going to need it.

## CHAPTER TWENTY-FOUR

### *Phoebe*

Another knock sounds at my door. She really came. I knew she would. She said she would. She was on her way. There's no reason I should've doubted her.

I open it, and this time, Freddie is actually standing there, looking, for the first time ever, worse for wear. Her hair is mussed, her glasses are gone, and there's a bloodstain down the front of her pants.

She throws her arms around me, and I yelp, hugging back. "Fuck." She collapses against me, and I hold her, looking around as I close the door. My friends are still here, and no one is presently trying to shoot us, so I'm not sure what to do.

"Sorry." She sighs, pulling away, looking a bit guilty.

"I didn't mind."

"No." Another sigh. "I wasn't trying to keep anything from you. This wasn't some big secret. We've just been talking about so many other parts of my life that it slipped my mind. I'm so sorry. I didn't think they'd come to your apartment looking for me."

MJ chuckles. "Well, it wasn't exactly difficult to handle them."

Her eyes widen, and she finally turns from me. "I didn't know there were people here. Hey, you're that demon from the poker game."

James waves. "Nice seeing you again too. So this is why you didn't want to keep the fair Louise company. You have good taste."

I want to know more about that, but I feel like there are more pressing issues, so I try my best to ignore it. "How much money do you owe these people?"

"A lot," she mutters. "I didn't think I'd ever have to pay it. I was mind-controlling them, but apparently, their bosses still noticed. One of the people I borrowed money from turned up dead a few days ago. It's why I ran to Toronto. I had a few friends tell me how amazing it was, so I figured I'd try for a new chance at life."

That explains a lot. From everything I know about her, I'm not certain she's capable of thinking beyond one step ahead. They wouldn't know she stole the money, so obviously, it would be fine. Until someone else realized how much money was missing. "Maybe I can pay them?" The second I say the words, dread creeps up my tail. *Relax, Phoebe. This isn't a con. She's not using you for your money. She doesn't know how much you have.* There were real police here, and I'm honestly not sure she is capable of planning something this intricate.

"Not unless you have a few million lying around."

I cough. "I'm sorry. Millions?"

She laughs nervously. "Yeah."

"How are you so broke, then?"

The laugh only grows more uncomfortable, and she scratches the back of her head. "It was over a decade or so and a lot of gambling. And a decent bit is tied up in my flat back home. I just left everything and ran."

"Fuck." I shake my head, trying to think of what we could possibly do.

"Have you considered killing them?" James asks.

MJ shoots him a glare before shrugging and asking, "Are they human or fiends?"

Larissa gives both of them a bug-eyed look, her hand still on her chaos marine. Jackie seems focused on his game against her.

"Everyone I met was human," Freddie says.

That makes things easier. "Well, the police they sent after you were too, and they didn't seem to know that much about how fiends work."

"I came here to…" She shakes her head, looking around the room. "I don't know. I'm tired of always running, and I want to be able to actually have a relationship with you. But I'm not killing anyone. I won't."

"Just almost kill them," James says. "They'll usually leave you alone if you break all their bones and promise to do it again if they ever come back. Hell, it even worked on my bestie."

I would also like more information on that, but I am beginning to suspect that James has no useful answers and a lot of distracting anecdotes. "Let's go there and compel them."

Freddie shakes her head. "They—I can't. They know to wear earplugs. And I can't just run back to Berlin. They'll be expecting me. They'll be ready for me."

"They know you're in Toronto, and they know that you ran last time anything happened," I say.

"Yeah, they'll never expect you to come for them," James says.

Larissa shrugs. "Are we really plotting to murder someone in Germany next to a law enforcement officer?"

"That's well outside of my jurisdiction."

James does his perfect laugh. "He's a parole officer, and you're not on parole. I don't think he's under any obligation to report you. Otherwise, I'd be really concerned about the cocaine I did at his place last weekend."

MJ rubs his nose, though I'm unsure if this is over annoyance from James's usual bullshit or because he's remembering how much the cocaine itched.

"Do you have any left?" Jackie asks.

James grins. "Finally, a man with some discerning tastes. I always make sure to have anything I could need in an emergency on me."

"I wouldn't say no," Freddie says.

"We're planning something important!" How is everyone I know like this? Except Dinah, she's actually straitlaced and probably feels that I'm like this in comparison. "Cocaine is only going to make you jittery and not help us figure out what to do." James laughs again. "I think you've already got it figured out. Just kill the boss, maybe a few others, all good. Or compel. Whichever works."

Freddie looks all the more terrified. I should've just let her snort coke. "This is insane. All of you are insane. Phoebe, you know this is ridiculous, right? They want me dead. I'm not running into their territory and…"

"Using your superhuman abilities to make them stop trying to kill you so you can be safe and actually have that relationship with me?"

She huffs. "It's—"

"Sometimes, you have to fight. I know you're not comfortable with that, and I'll do what I can to help you, but there isn't always another option."

She looks between all of us.

"I think it's crazy too," Larissa says.

"Thank you."

"But I also think you're a bunch of fiends who could probably handle this in, like, five minutes if you wanted to."

"Leave me out of your *A-Team* fantasies," James says. "Or don't. I would make an amazing Hannibal. But I'm not being dragged into fighting loan sharks that any normal vampire could handle. This isn't some world-ending threat. You'll be fine."

MJ sighs. "I have to deal with my parolees, and my wife would kill me."

"Well, I'm going," I say, as if I've thought any of this out. "Even if I have to do all of it myself. I'm not letting you be in danger for the rest of our lives."

"Eventually, they'll all die of old age."

"Freddie, please. I know that you don't want to fight, and I get that, but I'm not asking you to hurt anyone. You've already chosen not to run, haven't you?"

She shrugs. "I don't know. Part of me kind of thought that I'd come here, and you and I would run away together."

"That's really sweet." Would I have done it? Would I give up my whole life to run off with her? Probably not, but I'd consider it.

She sighs. "But I have a friend in town I'm not willing to just abandon. She's going through chemo, and I told her I'd be there for it."

"You have a friend?" I ask, hoping that the jibe will take her mind off things, even if it does make it sound like I didn't listen to her telling me about her friend before.

She rolls her eyes. "You really think we can do this?" She looks into my eyes, but her gaze doesn't linger as she turns to face everyone else.

"Go in, drop the vampire whammy on him, be home in time for dinner," James says. "Seems easy enough. I've heard of more difficult trips to the bathroom."

"How will you even get there?" Larissa asks.

Shit. She has a point. "Well, are you willing to go with me?" I ask Freddie. "We'll figure it all out, but I need to do this for you."

"Scared I'll run if you don't keep an eye on me?" It's said without any scorn toward me. If anything, she sounds upset with herself.

I shake my head. "No, I'm scared you'll get shot a few more times. Don't think I didn't notice the bloodstains."

She winces. "I couldn't afford new pants as well as a new shirt."

How did she manage anything without me? "Larissa, could you see about booking me a private flight? I think there's a pilot who's a fiend somewhere in town."

"I know one," James says. "She fought in Vietnam. Gives amazing head."

"I don't think that skill is relevant."

He shrugs. "Never know. It could come in handy."

I sigh. Why do I let him come to these games again?

Freddie shakes her head, looking between us like we're insane. "I'm sorry, the Community Center, what, has its own airport now?"

"Don't be ridiculous," MJ says. "We just have enough fiends

in town that you can find basically anything you need. So, James, is this the same girl you had fly us to the Bahamas when we were dating?"

"She is. I believe you can attest to her skills."

MJ's sigh sounds increasingly done. How has he put up with James for long enough that they're still friends?

"She'll still have to take us from an airport, though, right?" Freddie asks. "There's no way that would work. You'd be seen."

"Just do the wheelchair thing," Jackie says. "I know you've done it before. I use one when I really need to go someplace."

"I'm too big."

Jackie's gaze flits along my tail. There's no way it'd ever fit under a blanket on a wheelchair. Even if we could convincingly disguise my tail as another person in another wheelchair, there'd still be too much of it left. "You're flying private, right? So you won't see that many people, just have your vampire girlfriend hypnotize anyone you run into."

"That...that could work."

Freddie sighs. "We're really doing this?"

"If you want to not have to look over your shoulder for the rest of your life."

She nods, her shoulders dropping. "I hate this."

"I know." I squeeze her. "James, how much would it be to get your friend to fly us to Berlin?"

"Oh, she owes me a few favors. Just pay for gas and expenses, and I'm sure she'll be amenable."

Do I want to take a favor from James? That sounds risky. "And what will I owe you?"

"Just make sure you come back alive in time for our Shadowrun game."

I will never understand this asshole. "All right. Call her. I'm gonna buy some blood and some pants for my girlfriend." Even now, it feels so good to be able to say.

"And lots of drugs and alcohol."

I'm about to chide her for not focusing on the important part when I remember that we're about to fly across the ocean. She's going to torture herself without even saying a word because I asked her to. "Yeah, I'll get you some drunk blood and all the drugs and booze you want. Larissa?" I ask, with my most pleading smile. "Could we get a ride to the Community Center and then, hopefully, whatever airport James's friend can meet us at?"

"Calling her now," James says. "I'll message you the details. I suspect she'll be able to meet you within the hour."

Larissa stands. "Fine, I guess you get out of the ass kicking I was going to give you. Let's go."

Jackie smirks, having snatched victory from the jaws of defeat.

"That means everyone," I say. "I'm not leaving you all in my apartment while I'm out of the country."

We head outside, and I lock up, and Freddie and I get in the car with Larissa while everyone else takes James's sports car. Just a few errands to run, then I'm going to have to watch my girlfriend suffer.

❖

The car pulls to a stop in front of a private airfield just outside of town. There's a plane idling on the runway. I hadn't expected her to be waiting out in the open for us. I don't even have a name for her or what kind of fiend she is. What should I expect?

"Uh," Larissa says, sounding nervous.

"Don't worry, we'll take care of ourselves."

"No, not that," she says. "Though, good. I am going to worry about my best friend going and fighting the German mafia or something. But I was more thinking about that." She points out the window, and I have to slide my tail out of the way to see. There's another car pulling to a stop a few spots away.

Freddie groans. "I'll talk to them. Go get on the plane."

I can handle fighting for her, but I know she doesn't want to hurt people, and I don't exactly like my odds at this range. All we have to do is reach the plane, and neither of us has to hurt anyone. Yet. I just hope that letting them live won't fuck us.

She grins at Larissa as if our potential death is the farthest thing from her mind. "Thank you so much, Larissa. That threesome offer is still on the table for when we get back. You've quite literally been a lifesaver."

She giggles, and I'm quite certain she's blushing. "It was nothing." Her voice is so much higher than usual. I'm pretty sure that's a yes. At least I have that to look forward to if we survive. I haven't had a threesome in years. In fact, I think she was part of the last one too.

I open the door and start heading toward the plane as fast as I can. I'm faster than a lot of other lamia, as some of them weren't so lucky as to be an anaconda, but having to essentially run with my ribs is not the fastest way to move, and there's nothing to use to speed myself along the way I could in a jungle.

There's a fence in the way, but I can climb that easily enough.

I hear someone shout. I'm not sure if it's about me or Freddie, but I reach the top of the fence and climb back down just as easily, my tail doing nearly all the work, though I have to grab the top.

A gunshot echoes through the night. I want to think it's just a car backfiring or a weird plane noise, but it's too close for me to convince myself it's anything else. They're here. I should go back and help Freddie.

But there's not another shot.

The second I touch the ground, the fence shakes, and footsteps thud next to me. Something grasps my hand, and I cry out, only to hear Freddie's voice. "It's okay. I told them to go home. Had to take out their earplugs first, and they didn't like that. It's just in my arm."

I look over at her and see blood oozing from her bicep. "I have blood in my bag."

"On the plane." She holds my hand, hurrying me along, and we find a figure standing by the plane's door. I'd think it was a trap if the figure wasn't holding her own head in her hand. Now I understand James's joke.

"Maria Douglas, at your service," a cheery voice calls from the head.

"Jesus fuck," Freddie shouts.

The hand turns so the head can glare at her. "There will be none of that kind of talk on my plane. The drugs and alcohol are fine, but I'll have no taking the Lord's name in vain."

"You're a talking head."

She sighs. "I think most people are talking heads by that standard." She sets the head on the open neck and stands up straight. It wobbles but doesn't fall off. "I owe James quite a few favors, but I didn't agree to put up with any bullshit. So if you want to play nice, we can go to Berlin. If not, I can tell him those guys with guns managed to kill you."

"We'll be polite," I say, hoping I speak for the both of us. "I'm Phoebe, and this is Freddie."

Freddie nods and squeezes my hand.

"Welcome aboard. It's a pleasure to meet you. I filed our flight plans—hopefully, that's okay—but I'd rather not be shot out of the air or assumed to be a drug runner. We'll be playing this by the rules, and I'd like you to keep any trouble away from my baby." She lovingly strokes the door frame. "Are you ready?"

"Yeah." I adjust my bag on my shoulder.

We follow her inside. It's nicer than I'd expected. It's plush, white, and stylish. It's a proper jet, rather than the tiny Cessna I'd assumed we'd be in. There are even a few drinks on ice by the leather chairs.

Freddie opens one as she sinks into a seat, and I curl up next to her in my own chair, letting my tail drift into her lap.

"Take-off is right now," Maria announces over a speaker. "It should be smooth sailing."

The plane hums as it comes up to speed, and Freddie grips my tail. When it hurts as much as she told me, I suppose it's hard not to be scared of flying. "It's okay. We've got enough drinks for you." I grab one of the alcoholic blood bags and hold it out to her. She drains it, and the hole in her arm closes instantly, though the blood on her sleeve doesn't go away. I try not to think about how much more there may be by the end of the night and attempt to relax and enjoy the champagne.

She winces as we cross over a river and starts shaking. Even the alcohol must not be enough. I give her the other bag and some opiates. Something has to work. It seems to take the edge off, but once we're crossing the Atlantic, she clings to me. "Fuck…I think it wore off."

I give her another bottle of vodka. "I'm sorry, I thought two would be enough. I still had to pay for the gas for the plane, and I wasn't sure how much I'd need left in my checking. I should've bought four."

"It's okay." She winces. "I thought it'd be enough too. The flight isn't even that long." She tears up, holding tighter to my tail.

I know she normally just drinks her way through it. There's probably enough alcohol. It shouldn't be that bad. But I don't think I can watch her suffer the whole way. "Would my blood work?"

She stares at me.

"I know I'm cold-blooded, but—"

"Yes. I think. You always smell delicious. But we still have some more regular blood."

"Right. I meant for…" I open a whiskey and take some Vicodin with it, downing half the bottle before I gasp for air.

Freddie winces, but she looks as concerned for me as in agony. "You really don't have to. I don't want you hurting yourself."

"Please, I drink this much all the time. You've seen me." Maybe not with all the drugs, though. That'll be different.

She kisses the tip of my tail, and I giggle. God, she really does make me feel like a schoolgirl. And now I have to party like one. I drain the rest of the alcohol and eat some edibles. I close my eyes, feeling it all flow through me. I'm already well past buzzed, and it's barely started digesting. When the edibles kick in, I doubt I'll be able to stay conscious.

Freddie finishes her vodka and looks at me, biting her lip like she's trying to resist.

"Let it take a bit more effect first."

"I know." She takes a deep breath, closing her eyes as she rubs her temple. "It's not that bad. I'll be fine."

"Freddie, just give it a few minutes."

She nods, and another tear runs down her cheek. What does it feel like? I don't see anything happening to her, but she described it as feeling like she's falling apart. "Is it as bad as usual?"

She shakes her head. "No, the blood is still helping." Her voice breaks. "It's not that bad."

My head feels light. That's a good sign. "Okay, just drink. Try to leave me enough to still, you know, live."

Without a word, Freddie lunges for my neck. She must've barely been holding herself back. I stroke her hair as her fangs dig in. God, I've never been that big on biting, but she's making me question that. I expected it to hurt, and it does, but it's oddly magical and incredibly hot. I trail my hand down, gripping her ass, and she moans into the bite, sucking hard.

Fuck. The drugs are really starting to kick in.

She pulls away, licking her lips. "Are you okay? I didn't mean to...please say I didn't take too much."

I blink and find myself grinning. "Dionysus, I'm high."

"That's not an answer."

I lean against her, wrapping my tail around us.

"Phoebe, are you okay?"

I murmur happily, nuzzling her neck.

"Fuck, no, I, oh God." She tears up, her gaze dropping. "Fuck that's a lot of...that's a lot."

"Yeah." I'm low on blood, and full of enough drugs and alcohol to kill a horse. I'm not sure I'm capable of communicating at this point.

"Thank you," she whispers.

I want to tell her that I'd do it anytime, but I can barely form words. And if I do, I have no idea what I'll say. That I'd do anything for her? That I love her? I'm glad I can't talk. I need to stay shut up, or I'll say something stupid. And I'm probably not even in love with her yet. I'm just very intoxicated. And she's very hot. And I'm gonna fight the mob for her. None of that's love. I close my eyes, trying to keep myself from saying any of that out loud. I don't need to embarrass myself. "Anything for you," I mutter. That's not shutting up at all. Just don't say you love her. Just don't say anything even close to that. "You're my little pogchamp." Nailed it. Perfect.

I close my eyes and let oblivion take me before I dare to speak again.

# Chapter Twenty-Five

## *Elfriede*

I pick my unconscious girlfriend up from the back seat of the cab and hoist her onto my back, holding her arms around my throat with one hand as I coil her tail about me. It won't make me look normal, but people probably won't guess that there's a lamia on me.

The driver pulls away as I walk into the condo building and head to the private lift in the back. No one comes down the stairs, so I pull the door closed, put my key in, and press the button for the penthouse. With a shake and a groan, it starts up.

I slide the door open to reveal what was once my home. All of my possessions have been tossed on the floor and torn apart; books are scattered everywhere, some really expensive porn is in pieces on the floor, and a bust of a woman I knew in the 1800s is shattered into dust and barely recognizable. They tore the place apart looking for money I don't even have.

I find the bedroom, where my mattress is sliced open and on the floor. I set it back on the frame and drop Phoebe onto it. She murmurs something that can't quite be described as words.

"It's okay," I say. "I know how long alcohol affects you. Thank you for doing this for me. I had some blood, so I'm fine. I'm gonna try to figure out how we're going to manage this terrible plan while you sleep it off."

Her tail curls around her, and she turns, hugging it like a teddy bear.

I leave her there and head back into the lift, closing the door behind me. But what if someone comes looking for me while I'm gone? If they saw the flight plans, they'll know that I headed home, and this will be the first place they'd check.

I can't leave her alone.

I sigh.

"Fuck." I open the door again and head back inside. This is terrible. What am I supposed to do? We'll be sitting ducks here.

I suppose if anyone comes, I'll take out their earplugs and mind-control them. I'm not looking forward to being shot again, but we still have another couple bags of blood. I head to the fridge and check to see if anything is still good. The milk is questionable, the meat is starting to rot, and all the vegetables are wilted, but there's some tomato juice that looks perfectly fine.

I was hoping to make her breakfast to help wake her up, but even the bread is all moldy. It was only a few days. I didn't think it'd be quite this bad. I suppose I hadn't been sleeping at my place too often.

My cupboard seems mostly okay. The bag of flour is all over the floor, as is some pasta, but the eggs are untouched. They're probably getting close to their expiration, but they should be usable.

And snakes love eggs. I've had a good deal of practice making breakfast, and eggs are always an easy treat. I grab a frying pan and make a nice collection of sunny-side up and poached eggs. I'm not sure which she prefers, but they're both easy and quick enough that I can do both and give her the options.

I carry the plates to the other room and gently nudge her. "Phoebe."

She doesn't say anything, only making a suckling noise and clinging tighter to her tail.

"Come on, Pogchamp."

She bolts upright and grasps her head. "No. I didn't really say that, did I? Fuck, that was so cringe. Oh God, I'm never talking again. Twitch has corrupted my brain, and I am too comfortable with you. And still pretty drunk. Or maybe hungover. How does it feel like both?"

I chuckle and gesture with the eggs. "You need to eat. I could always grab some vodka to help with the katzenjammer. There's a broken bottle in the kitchen that still has some in it, and I have tomato juice."

She shakes her head and takes the plates, setting them on her tail and shoving a forkful into her mouth. "I'm never drinking again. For at least a day. I can't believe I said all that on the plane. Where are we anyway?"

Is she trying to change the topic? "We're at my old apartment. So cringe is bad and...pogchamp is good?" I ask.

She groans. "Kill me now."

"That'd be pretty cringe, wouldn't it?"

She glowers and stabs a sunny-side up egg.

"You're the one who said it."

After another mouthful she says, "Cringe is bad, pogchamp is more affectionate joking, poggers is good. Though usually, you'd say based, not poggers."

"Uh-huh. And where does any of that come from?"

"You know pogs? The, like, poker-chip-looking things from the nineties?"

I tilt my head. "We *had* poker chips in the nineties."

She makes a face that can only be described as contemplating a murder-suicide before going back to eating her eggs.

"Are they...based?"

She takes a deep breath before finally turning to me.

I smile innocently.

"Freddie, I'm not sober enough for this. Please just forget I said anything. You don't need to know how embarrassing Twitch talk is. You don't ever have to watch my stream. Please."

I lean in and kiss her temple. "No promises, but I'll drop it. For now."

She nods, seeming to accept that, and goes back to eating.

"How're you feeling?" I ask when she's all done.

"Like they kinda needed salt."

"You could've said."

She chuckles. "A little better. My head is throbbing, and I'm still kinda woozy. You took a lot of blood."

"I'm sorry!" I could've killed her. I can't believe I went along with her idea. "I wasn't thinking. You just got so into it, and it was really hot and—"

Her tail wraps around my wrist and tugs me onto the bed. "It's okay, Freddie. I'm not upset. I just might need another day to recover."

"All right. I'll give it to you. They probably don't know we're back in town yet." But they could. They could be here any minute. But I'd hear my elevator going down. There's a fire exit, but the regular stairs don't go up here. This may be pretty defensible if we're only going to stay here for a day. "Okay, I think we can do that. I'm just gonna need to be listening for them at all times."

"Thank you." She pulls my hand to her mouth and trails kisses along my wrist. "I know how much it means that you came back here for me. That you put yourself through that flight."

"No, you were right. It's time to stop running."

She sighs. "We just have to hide for a day first."

"You put yourself through a lot to make the trip easier for me. I appreciate that."

"Well yeah, I…"

"Are my little pogchamp?"

"You said you'd drop that. And, no, you're mine."

I grin and climb onto her tail, kissing her gently. "Are you hurting too much for anything fun or just for taking on a criminal kingpin?"

She bites her lip and sets the plates on my nightstand. "I think I could find it in me for something more."

"Good." I lay a soft kiss on the bite mark on her neck. "Thank you so much for coming with me."

She blushes. "I want to be able to have a relationship with you. For that, I need people to not be shooting at us."

I nod and kiss along her collarbone, feeling her tail slide under me until I can straddle her hips. "I want that too."

She pulls me to her and kisses me hungrily, her strength seeming to return. I try to keep an ear out for anybody coming to kill us as I slide her shirt over her head and return to kissing her. She's very distracting.

This sex better not get us killed.

❖

Phoebe's tail unwinds from me as I stand. "Gods, Freddie, I think you fucked away my hangover."

"I am pretty magic in bed."

She gazes up into my eyes, a soft smile on her face, and all I want to do is kiss her again. "You are."

She is increasingly getting close to the best sex I've ever had. She keeps learning every touch that drives me wild. "I wish we could stay in bed doing this all week."

"But we have a crazed murderer to take care of?"

"I wish they were crazed. It would make this easier." I put my sports bra and boxers on and look around for my pants. She threw them across the room. I wipe off the dust and hop into them. "So do we just go into town and ask around?" I ask as I button up my shirt.

Once she's dressed, she says, "Do you not know where they are?"

"Not where the head guy is. I guess I know where a couple loan sharks are that I haven't talked to as much. If they're still alive, maybe they can tell us something."

She gestures at her tail, not needing to say anything beyond that.

"All right, how about you stay in the cab while I talk to them?"

"Perfect." She grins. "But if anybody shoots me, it's your fault."

It really will be. She came here because of me. People are after me, and she'd only be in their way. If she dies, that is entirely my fault. Would there be anything I could do? I already told Vivi that I'd make her a vampotaur or whatever. Can I make a vamia? Lampire? "I'll try not to let you die."

She grins. "I would prefer that."

I call a cab on the new phone with a German SIM card Phoebe bought me from the Community Center, and once the driver lets us know that they're here, we head outside, and I mind-control them. "You don't speak any German, do you?" I ask as she climbs into the back, and I get in the passenger seat.

"I do," the driver says.

He can't read context clues anymore. That's a worrying sign for brain damage. "I know a little. It's been a while, but I think I might be able to get by," she says in perfect German, albeit from the fourteenth century.

"Yeah, don't talk to anybody."

"Is it that bad?"

"No, it's amazing, you just sound like a LARPer."

She chuckles. "I am a LARPer."

Of course she is. Is there anything this geek doesn't do? It's adorable. "I assumed you learned medieval German when it was contemporary. Did you learn it for some game?"

"No. I had a lindwurm friend who taught me."

I didn't know they were real. "Like a dragon or a giant snake or…"

"More snakey."

"Huh." I should stop assuming anything isn't real.

The car pulls to a stop in front of a nightclub. "All right, you two stay here." I blow a kiss to Phoebe like some sort of demented romantic and walk inside. There's a drug dealer here who I've bought from before and haven't always paid, and I know he has some connections to the loan sharks in town. It's probably the same operation. But he could've been killed for me not paying for drugs.

It hasn't even been a week, so I'm doubting he'll have found a new haunt. And I'm proven right. A familiar human with mussed brown hair and a side shave is standing on the second floor, flirting with a few women. They probably just want his coke. "Lars," I say. "It's been too long."

He turns, flashing a friendly smile, only for it to vanish when he sees me, his eyes going wide. "You're…"

That answers that question. "Ladies, I need a minute with our friend, but he'll help you out when I'm done. On me." Normally, I'd suggest they meet me back at my place, but there are more pressing matters to attend to. They grin at me and walk out of earshot.

He shudders, taking a step back. He knows what I can do, then.

No use in beating around the bush. Phoebe is a sitting duck until we find this bastard. "Tell me where your boss is, and then give those women whatever they want."

# CHAPTER TWENTY-SIX

## *Phoebe*

"Of course this is the place," I grumble as the car stops in front of the gates to a mansion. I don't know what I was expecting, but it was probably this. This is about as drug lord/loan shark/kingpin estate as you can get. It's large and grandiloquent, with statues and topiary, but it's out of the way enough that it isn't likely to attract anyone's attention, and the hedges and fence are certain to keep away any curious eyes. "I assume people will start shooting at us the second we climb over?"

Freddie nods in the front seat. "Yeah, seems likely. All right, buddy, wait for us for half an hour. If we don't come out by then, go back to your normal life."

The driver nods, and we get out of the car. I look up at the fence. It's a good ten feet tall. Easy enough for me to climb and her to jump. "Are we sure about this?" I ask.

"It was your idea."

It was, wasn't it? "Okay. Just, please don't let anybody shoot me."

"I won't, Pheeb."

"Really, trying out nicknames now?"

"Pogchamp?"

I groan. "Pheeb is fine." I'm never going to live that down. The only solution is to burn Twitch and take all of them with me.

The fence is as easy a climb as I expect, and at the top, no light comes on, and no guns start shooting. They're not expecting us. That's a surprise. Or they are, and the trap is later on. I really hope it's not that option.

Freddie lands on the ground in front of me. "How did you talk me into this again? This seems like a fighting thing. I should've called and arranged a meeting."

"Where they'd have someone waiting to chop your head off like those cops said they were supposed to do?"

She huffs and crosses her arms. "Isn't there someone better for this? There have to be some fiend soldiers or something. Fine, I get it, as much as I hate it, these guys know too much, and they're a threat to all of us, and they should probably die. Can't we just tell someone at the Community Center that and have it taken care of?"

"There's no one like that that I'm aware of. I think it's up to us." I squeeze her shoulder and gesture toward the compound.

Freddie grumbles but walks with me. Still, no one shoots. This is starting to seem suspicious. It must be a trap.

We reach the front door unimpeded, and I'm so nervous, I can feel my blood pumping in my brain. "Do we just go inside?" I ask.

She shrugs.

Right, I've probably done this stuff more times than she has. Just a few days ago, I was storming my ex's place and threatening her. This is the same thing but on a much grander scale. Except Paula didn't have guns. Or police officers in Toronto on her payroll. I can't imagine what this guy must have in Germany. Even if we kill him, what would he be able to have done to us in revenge?

Her hand rests on the doorknob, and we exchange glances. She jerks her head to the side. It takes me a second to realize what she means. She's worried they'll start shooting the second she opens the door. Is that what happened with the cops?

I slide to the side, and as soon as my tail is out of the way, she opens the door.

I close my eyes, waiting to hear the sound.

Nothing comes. I hear her step inside and wait a few seconds before I follow. "Where is everyone?"

She sniffs. "There are definitely people here. A lot of them. I don't know why we haven't found any yet."

"A trap?"

She shrugs. "I can't say. I don't know anything about how this sort of stuff works. It could be a party. Or maybe they're all waiting just around the corner to shoot us. The place stinks of humans, and I know they're near, but it's hard to place them exactly."

Great. So we know nothing. "Okay, let's keep going."

"Pheeb, I really don't want you to get hurt."

"And you expect me to believe that you're willing to fight them all on your own? Or at all?"

Her mouth opens to reply, but she closes it and stares at the floor. "I don't want to hurt people. Especially when they're only after me because I was an idiot who didn't think through my actions."

"I know you don't. But they're trying to kill you."

"Really ineptly."

"Yeah, until one of them gets lucky. Or a stray bullet hits me."

She nods, a pained expression flashing on her face. "Okay. Fine. Let's…let's find out if this is a trap."

We proceed farther into the compound. At every door, I expect shots to ring out and to find myself dying on the ground, but it doesn't happen. We keep moving for what feels like hours but is probably only a few minutes, until she comes up short in front of a double door. "They're here."

"Everyone?" I ask.

"I'm sure there're some people who aren't. The place is so full of human scents that I can't say much for certain, except that there are a lot behind this door. And listen, don't you hear that?"

I don't have vampiric hearing, so it takes me a second, but I realize there's music.

She opens the door without waiting for me to get out of the

way, but it only leads into another hall where the music is even louder. It's nothing classy enough to match the opulence of the place, but there's a pleasant beat to it.

No trap springs as we walk through the hall and reach another set of double doors. She takes a deep breath and pulls them open, revealing a cavalcade of humans, all drinking, snorting, smoking, and imbibing intoxicants in every way you can imagine, and the music is all the louder.

Somebody screams, but it's not in fear. It sounds joyful, or at least jovial.

And that's going to stop if I go in there. "I can't," I say.

Freddie looks back at me. "You're the one who wanted us to come here."

"But…" I gesture at my tail.

"That's all the more reason. Show them all, and we can scare them into leaving me alone."

"Or they'll kill us. Or sell us to a zoo."

"Right." She sighs and looks through the open door. No one seems to have noticed her yet. Or me. I should leave while I have the chance.

And do what? Would we try to come back another day? Hope that he'll be available to talk at our convenience tomorrow?

"We could wait in another room?" Freddie suggests. "Find someplace to hide out until the party dies down and then look for whoever the guy in charge is?"

It makes sense. We could try that. "But what if the guards sweep the place for any stragglers?"

"Then we get shot. Or I manage to tell them to stop first."

"And what if we go into the party?"

She grits her teeth and looks back at the party. "I don't know. I don't see or smell any fiends. You'd stand out, but I won't let anyone hurt you."

She keeps saying that. I wonder if she's thinking of me or Hertha. Probably both. I don't mind. As much as I think her actions were more than acceptable back then, they still bother her, and she seems to think she can make up for it now. So I'll let her.

"Let's go in," I say. "What else can we do?"

She sighs, nodding. "Well, if we're doing this, let's make an entrance." She takes my hand and guides me toward the door. Every instinct in me tells me to run. I'm moving toward humans. It tends to mean being hunted or seen as an oddity to be fetishized and used.

There's no good outcome to this. But I'm with Freddie, and I trust her.

I follow her out into the dark room, where dozens of people are partying. Maybe hundreds. And I feel nearly every set of eyes in the place fall upon me. Someone screams, and this time, I *am* the cause of it.

"It's okay, bunny." She's still trying pet names, and it's cute, but calling a snake a bunny feels weird. Then again, I am an anaconda, and a bunny would barely even be a snack for even a mundane one, so I suppose it's not like she's comparing me to my prey. That'd be calling me a human. "I'll take care of things." She raises her voice to speak over the clamor and switches to German. "I believe your host requested some entertainment. Or perhaps I have the wrong house."

"It's her," someone whispers. Okay, apparently, German has changed a lot because I wouldn't have phrased anything the way they are.

Someone approaches in my peripheral vision. And against the wall, I see someone else looking around and reaching into his jacket.

"Did you have a plan?" I ask.

"I was hoping I'd manage to get us an audience and maybe some drugs while we were at it."

I sigh and jerk my head toward the one who seems to be trying to get an angle for a better shot.

She grins and nods. It's a party full of the guy's guests. He's not going to shoot into them without being very careful. She runs toward him and whispers in his ear. Did she actually have a plan? Had she figured any of this out?

Does that mean she's had Nazis not shoot her because she was surrounded by people before? That's horrifying to think about, but it makes sense. They wouldn't want to risk killing the nice straight people she'd have been drinking and gambling with.

A gun goes off, and I hear her scream. I look over, but she doesn't seem to be shot. She holds the guy out as a human shield. A man to my side is walking in an arc, his hand on a gun. He must be the one who shot. I snatch him with my tail, and more people scream. Someone finally runs for the door, and it instantly evolves into a stampede. I snarl. "Don't you hurt her."

The guy shudders, and I can feel it run down his body.

"He's here," Freddie says. "This one already told me." She points toward the back of the room where a few people are still clustered, though even more seem to be scrambling now that I'm looking toward them.

When did I become the muscle? I'm not used to being used to scare people. I don't like it, but I suppose if she isn't willing to hurt anyone, it was always going to come down to this. I don't know what else I thought would happen. I'm here to make my girlfriend safe enough that she can be my girlfriend. And unlike her, while I may not love it, I've never been afraid to kill. It's just still a big change from going after my ex with some vampiric muscle at my back to being the scary monster who has to take down the German mob all on her own.

"Let me go," the guard says in German.

I reply the best I can in my archaic German. "Are you going to behave?"

His eyes widen. I wonder if I messed it up? He nods, and as I let him go, the gun drops to the floor. I pull it to me and pick it up. I don't know how to use a gun very well, but they don't have to know that.

"Is your boss back there?" I ask, trying to confirm what Freddie learned. I know she can mind-control, but I'm still worried. What if her guy was wrong? He could've been fed bad information to make sure she walked into a trap. They know what she can do.

But they also didn't know we'd be here so quickly. Or did they?

The guy quivers. Was the other one bait?

I point the gun at him. "Where is he?"

"Enough," a voice shouts, and the music stops.

A wheel squeaks, and I turn to see an old man rolling a wheelchair toward us. "In three minutes, the entire police force will storm this room. Once I knew that she was looking for me, I expected that a party would be the perfect way to attract her attention. It would draw her out, rather than giving her time to figure out a better approach."

He does know my girl well. But why's he telling us this? Right, he's buying time until the police kick down the door and shoot us full of lead.

"So you're the boss?" Freddie asks, dropping the guard in her hand. "I have to say, you sell some great MDMA. I was hoping to do some after we struck a deal."

"I'm afraid it's quite dark in here, and you're far away. If you want me to be able to read your lips, you'll have to come closer." The wheelchair stops, and there's a smirk on the old man's face. His hair is gray, and he's wearing a suit that even Freddie would kill for. "Once I learned what you could do, I'd wondered if it would work on me. Would you care to give it a try?"

She steps closer, her eyes wide. "You're deaf?"

"Ah, much better. Yes."

A man behind him draws his gun.

The old man waves his hand. "It's already done. They'll be dead soon." He chuckles, perfectly white teeth showing in a victorious grin. "Not that they can hear me, of course. I gouged out the ears of a few guards after I told them what to say should you come here."

He did what? I stare at the fucking psychopath.

"You're a monster," Freddie says.

He points at me. "You call me a monster when you walk in here with...what is this creature?"

I cross my arms and glare at him.

"Can we make a deal?" Freddie asks. "I don't want to kill you."

"I know you don't. You're not a killer. It's part of what makes you so weak. So you'll be the one to die. I've told the police you have a sonic weapon. They'll be wearing ear coverings."

Freddie glances toward the door. Did she hear something? "Please."

"Yes, beg. You stole from me, Elfriede Bauer. I don't take kindly to people who steal from me."

"Then let me make it up to you. I'll pay it all back."

"Do you have it on you?"

Her eye twitches. "I lost it. Gambling."

"And paying for your condo, I've no doubt. It's a lovely place. Nice view of the Spree."

"What can I do?"

He smirks. "As I said, you can die. I expect they'll make you suffer. Perhaps that will teach this town a lesson."

She closes her eyes and takes a deep breath, and when she speaks, it's with the tone she always uses to control people. "You will call off the police, forgive my debt, and let us leave."

His smile only grows. "Funny. I'd expected something more impressive."

"Enough of this." I wrap my tail around the pathetic old man and lift him from his wheelchair. He's too cocky. Just because the cops are on the way doesn't mean that he'll survive. "Call them off, or you die." My tail starts to tighten, but before I get that satisfying crunch, I see movement in the corner of my eye and jerk my head toward the guard already raising his gun.

*This is going to hurt.* It's the only thought I can manage before a bang echoes through the room, and people start screaming.

I don't feel any pain.

I let out a shuddering breath and stare at the guy with the gun only to find blood pouring out of him, the still-smoking gun, along with his arm, several feet away on the floor, with powdered debris wafting from a bullet hole. And Freddie shaking, staring at the gushing stump. "No," she whispers. "No. No. I…I didn't."

Whatever adrenaline that kept the guard from reacting must have worn off because he screams and cries, making my ears ring as he runs for the door. Footsteps thud outside, coming closer. Freddie *had* heard something. The cops are already here. And she quite possibly just killed someone.

The old man coughs, shaking against my tail. I'd almost forgotten I was holding him. I must've tightened my grip. I turn him to make sure he can read my lips. "Call them off," I say again. I know he can't hear the desperation in my words, but he can certainly feel how close I am to killing him. If it wasn't for him, Freddie wouldn't be in danger, and she wouldn't have hurt anyone.

"I didn't mean..." she says again, her voice breaking.

"You're too late," he says. "They're just outside, and you'll die. Even if you take me with you."

"And you don't think your life is worth it?" I ask, the words coming out so rushed that I'm scared he won't be able to tell what I'm saying. "Come on. Call them off. You can keep running your evil empire, and we can go home. No one has to die."

He shakes his head, that wretched smile returning. "She stole from me."

"Then leave her out of it," Freddie shouts, rushing over until she can face him. Her face is covered in tears, but there's a resolve in it that I've never seen before. "You can have me. They can kill me. I don't fucking care. But she's not involved. She didn't steal from you. I'll turn myself in. Just let her leave."

The smile only grows. "It's too late for that." The bootsteps in the hall confirm just how correct he is. "Besides, look at what she's done to me." He'd probably be gesturing if I didn't have his arms pinned. "She deserves it just as much as you do. Another monster attempting to make a fool of me."

I tighten my grip and hear bone crunch. His eyes widen. He didn't think I'd really do it, did he? "Last chance to reconsider," I say.

He narrows his eyes again and spits something in German that I can't quite understand.

"Just let her go!" Freddie says again. "It's not worth your life. Both of you can walk out of this."

"We're all walking out, or he dies," I say simply. She can save the selflessness for the bedroom. I'm not letting her throw her life away for me.

"I don't think two of us can walk," he mutters. There's blood trickling past his lips. I've done a lot of damage already. He must be in agony. The fucking bastard is willing to die just to spite us.

I look around for any means of escape. I can hear the boots thudding closer. Someone shouts something through a megaphone, but it's so distorted and my German is so rusty that I can't tell what they're saying.

He chuckles, more blood spilling out. "I'll see you in Hell." His bloody teeth show in a victorious smile.

I tighten my grip until the smile goes away, and I feel his bones turn to dust in my grasp. His body drops to the floor in a puddle. He refused to call them off. And I have no idea how we would. Maybe he's right. Maybe it is too late.

I look to Freddie, hoping against hope that she has any ideas beyond just getting high and waiting to die.

She returns my gaze, pain clear in her eyes, avoiding glancing anywhere near the old man's body. "I don't want to hurt anyone."

"I know."

There's a loud ringing and more distorted words. I think it's something to the effect of "This is your last warning, come out with your hands up," but it's so difficult to tell.

"He's dead," she says, her voice sounding hollow. "Do you think that means his people won't come for me anymore?"

I wish I knew the answer to that, but they may be out for revenge now. "I don't know. But we have to get out of here."

She nods and glances around, covering her mouth when her gaze finally settles on the body. A sob rattles her body, and she looks a bit green. I hear gagging, but she takes a deep breath and doesn't add to the puddle on the floor.

More footsteps thud, and before I can say anything, I feel her hands on me, and I have to cling on for dear life, my tail flying behind me as I feel her run for it. I knew she was fast, but I've never felt anything like this. We fly through a wall and out a window in the next room, concrete and glass bouncing off my tail and scratching my face as I close my eyes and feel the wind rushing past. By the time I open my eyes again, we're standing outside of her apartment, and she looks ready to collapse.

I take her hand and lead her inside. "I think we still have some blood in the fridge."

# CHAPTER TWENTY-SEVEN

## *Elfriede*

How the hell did she talk me into this? I said we should leave town while they were scrambling to figure out who replaces the crazy old kook she straight-up murdered, but, no, she insisted that that would only delay our being killed, and as we're going to be around for millennia, a delay is barely even a drop in the bucket for us. I just want to go home.

I blink, staring at the wooden table. Did I just call Toronto home? *This* is home. I look toward Phoebe with her tail snaking around her chair. How am I already this far gone for her? It hasn't been a week since I left, and Berlin isn't even home anymore. It's been my home for half of the last eight hundred years, and all of a sudden, that's changed. Because of her.

I guess that's how she talked me into this. I sigh, leaning back in the chair. We broke back into the same manor we just killed someone in yesterday. This is a terrible idea.

"It'll be okay," she says, but her smile doesn't quite make it to her eyes.

"The last time we were here, I ripped someone's arm off, and you killed a guy."

A pang of guilt flashes on her face. "I know. I didn't want it to go that way."

"We could've run," I say, like we haven't already had this conversation a million times and agreed that this is the only option.

She reaches out and takes my hand. I sigh. I hate this. I lace my fingers between hers, squeezing her hand, needing to feel her presence.

Footsteps sound in the hall. This time it isn't the regimented, combat-booted steps of the police coming to kill us but loafers and heels. The door opens, and a young man with slicked-back hair steps in; his eyes widen and keep widening as he takes in Phoebe. Her tail isn't quite hidden beneath the table. "You must be the dragon," he says. "I've been expecting you."

"I'm sorry?" she asks, in her ever-stiff, archaic German. I should've said I'd do the talking. It hurts.

He stiffens and straightens his tie, but rather than saying anything to us, he leans out the door and whispers to someone. If it wasn't for the fact that I have super hearing, I'd worry it was a trap, but all he says is, "Could you fetch us some coffee? And make sure you knock first."

He closes the door behind him and sits across from us at the table. "I thought perhaps you'd use the front door, but I suppose that would hardly be easy with your friend. Several party guests said that a dragon had broken in and killed my grandfather. I assume that was your work?"

"That's me. Big scary dragon." She'd probably be baring her fangs if she had any, but all she does is smile. Her teeth are slightly sharper than a human's, so maybe it's a little intimidating, but I think it just makes her look cute.

He nods, tapping his fingers on the table. "Well, then, it would seem I owe you a good deal. As do most of my employees."

"And how's that?" Phoebe asks, her tone conversational.

There must have been some memo about hiding our shock that I didn't get, as I'm staring at him in confusion. "What? You're not out for blood?"

He snorts, and a knock sounds at the door. Phoebe shifts next to me, but there's a lot of tail and only so much table. "Come in."

A woman opens the door and wheels in a tray with coffee and cups on it. Her eyes widen when she sees us. "You're the one who killed the bastard who deafened my husband."

Oh. Understanding finally dawns on me. Phoebe probably

already figured it out, but I can be a bit slow sometimes. I hurt one person, and I'm not sure I'll be able to live with that, but he hurt so many of them in his quest to get revenge on me. "It's my fault," I say. "He only hurt them because he was after me."

She shakes her head as she sets our drinks before us. "He's done worse for far less. It's about time Lukas was able to take over."

The man, who I have to assume is Lukas, smirks. "Thank you. That'll be all."

She smiles at us and ducks out of the room. I take a sip of the coffee. It could really use some whiskey. "Well, I'm glad we could help you get your dream job."

He chuckles. "Elfriede Bauer, isn't it?"

That's never a good sign. "My reputation precedes me."

"You're the one he was obsessed with. He thought you were a witch. And you even summoned a lindwurm to kill him."

"I'm a very scary witch."

I can feel Phoebe rolling her eyes even without looking over.

"You still owe us a good deal of money," he says. "And you killed my predecessor. I'm going to look weak if I don't do anything about that."

"But we got you this job, so I think we can call it even." I hope I'm playing this right. Phoebe was handling this so much better, even with her terrible German, but she's not the witch.

He sips his coffee, considering it. "They're going to say it was a coup, that I let you off the hook to kill him."

This better not be poisoned. It wouldn't do anything to me, but it might to Phoebe. At least she doesn't seem to have touched hers yet. "It sounds like people would like for that to be the case. Why not let it be the story?" Should I compel him? No, he's not wearing earplugs or anything, so I should at least hear him out first. I can force him if it comes to it, but clearly, he wants something. He doesn't seem dumb enough to talk to me without protection if he was going to act against me. After all, I *am* a terrifying witch.

"The two of you made the front page. This isn't something I can cover up. So I'm going to roll with it. I'll let people think I have a witch on my payroll. If they cross me, then they're going to pay, and they'll know it."

I narrow my eyes. Maybe I should mind-control him. "I'm not going to hurt anyone for you."

"All I need is for people to think that you will. My assistant is likely telling everyone she knows that she just met an actual dragon. And I'm sure they'll blab as well. Before long, everyone in Berlin will know that I had a meeting with you."

Why is he acting like this was his idea? We broke in here. Was he seriously expecting us? A chill runs up my spine. Maybe he did plan it. But from how far back? Since we were in Berlin? Did he make sure we knew about the party? Or was he the one who sent the cops after me in the first place? He used us as his personal assassins.

"As far as the rest of the world is concerned, your debt has been forgiven in exchange for you acting as our enforcer. I'd offer you the job for real, but I assume you're not interested."

"I'm not hurting anyone," I snap.

He chuckles, holding out his hands. "Easy, easy. You don't have to do a thing. Your debts are wiped away, and you're free to leave or do as you will. Though if you could make appearances once in a while at our clubs, to keep the myth going, I'd appreciate that."

"I don't intend to stick around."

He swirls his coffee, studying me. He likely knows that if he pushes for anything, this will stop being a negotiation, and I'll get whatever I want. "Whatever suits you. I'll inform all the drug dealers in Berlin that you're on our payroll. I'm sure that'll be enough to make sure you pop in from time to time."

Phoebe snickers, and I shoot her a glare. She smiles innocently.

"Was there anything else you wanted?" he asks. "I have an empire to run, and I do need this office for an actual scheduled meeting."

"No," Phoebe says, rising. "We'll get out of your hair."

"There's a car waiting for you out front. It'll take you back to your loft."

Always the power plays with this guy. I mutter, "Thanks," as he leads us out into the hallway. No one escorts us out. It's weird. And it makes it look like we can freely come and go. Because we work for them. Great, his plan is already working.

We climb into the car, only proving his point, and the driver takes off without a word. "Wow," Phoebe says, chuckling as we pull onto the road. "I can't believe that worked."

I sigh and lean against her shoulder. "I feel used."

"But it worked out, didn't it?"

I shrug against her. "I guess. I just don't like being used to hurt people."

"It wasn't you. I'm the one who killed him."

"Well, you shouldn't have had to, either."

She wraps an arm around me. "You're worth it."

No one else ever seemed to agree. "I *am* your little pogchamp." I smirk. I need the satisfaction of annoying her. It'll make me feel better after all that.

She groans. I know I shouldn't have said it, but her reaction is always so priceless. "I love you."

I blink and try to pull up to look at her, but her arm doesn't move. I could sit up easily, but she may not want to face me quite yet. "I love you too," I admit, settling against her chest. "I know it's early, and I didn't even know I still could, but…"

"But after risking our lives for each other and going through all this, it's hard not to."

I nod, and she squeezes me to her. "I guess we should head home," I say. "Er, to Toronto."

She finally releases me, and I find her smirking. I keep calling it home. "I promised I'd be back by Thursday, so we still have a few days. If you wanted, I thought maybe you could show me what you like about this town."

As much as I'm already starting to think that Toronto may be home, it's hard not to appreciate that idea. I do love Berlin. "Are you sure?"

"I can take a few more days off from streaming, and besides, we get free drugs." She takes my hand, trailing kisses along it. "Show me where Berlin's fiends party."

# CHAPTER TWENTY-EIGHT

## *Phoebe*

The place is dingy and wet. It makes dive bars look like five-star restaurants. And Freddie is grinning ear to ear as she leads me inside. She's wearing a perfectly tailored suit that emphasizes all her best features, and she looks amazing in it. Her new sunglasses aren't rose-tinted, but the mirrored shades are just as excessive. And she looks like the weight of the world has been lifted from her shoulders.

She gestures around the bar, still beaming, and I take it in.

This is probably the closest thing she had to the Community Center. A pale figure that must be a fair one snorts cocaine off a dryad at a grimy, torn-up booth, while something furry with massive claws sips a can of beer at the bar, across from what I'm pretty sure is a tengu wearing an apron and buffing a stain that looks to be a few decades old.

There are a couple other fiends at the far end of the bar, a booth full of young women with various horns and fangs celebrating what sounds like a bachelorette party, if my German is right, and a few people with various limbs and appendages dance to some poor-quality techno that's blaring throughout the place loud enough that I can taste it. "This is the place," she says. "There are a couple others, but this is the big one."

It wouldn't even pass for a particularly slow afternoon in Toronto. I'm spoiled. "Let's get a drink."

She leads me to the bar where the tengu seems to be satisfied that the stain is thoroughly polished and looks up, his red face contorting in a smile.

"Friede," he says, his voice deep, thick, and German. "I haven't seen you in days." He slides drinks over without us even having to order. Is it Freddie's usual, or is there not actually a selection? Does she have a tab?

She snickers. "Oh, some people were trying to kill me, then I fell in love." She takes my hand and smiles at me. "It's been a busy week."

The furry creature a few seats away chortles. I expected it to sound bestial, like when I heard my upstairs neighbor yelling at someone, but this creature is oddly soft-spoken. I almost have to strain my ears to hear him over the music. I suppose it shouldn't surprise me at this point, when I've known so many fiends whose appearances belie their true selves, but it's hard not to expect someone who looks like a werewolf to be a little feral. "No. I refuse to believe it. There is no way you're in love." He sounds amused rather than angry, so that's a good sign. "You've been coming here for the past century, with all kinds of women on your arm, and suddenly, it's more than a casual fling?" He turns, his fangs showing in a jovial grin. "So who's the woman who finally tamed our favorite vampire?"

"Hi," I try. "I'm Phoebe." In times like this, I wish I had a last name. My ID says it's Walker, but that's just for taxes and my own sense of humor.

"I'm Elias. Friede, I had no idea you had a thing for snakes." He chuckles.

Rude. Maybe?

Freddie shrugs. "I'm not sure I have much of a type beyond women. But I can certainly say that I have found the right one."

She really is smitten with me. And I'm as absurdly into her. I can still scarcely believe it's all real. But she also seems to be struggling with trying to show this new side to her old friends. I wish I knew how to help with that more. Maybe a lot of drugs. "I swear, save a girl from the mob, and suddenly, they're in love with you."

She grins at me and pulls me into a kiss. "I don't think it took you that much."

I giggle and find myself wishing we were back at her loft. Then again, if this is her sort of place, we may be able to fuck right here. But I'm bashful, and I'd rather not show all that off to a bunch of strangers, so I pull away, just a little. I don't want to be too far from her.

The bartending tengu grins at us. They really are all perverts. "I'm Max. It's a pleasure to meet the one who finally tamed our girl."

"I wanted to show her what life is like back home. Elias, you holding?"

Elias chuckles. "Am I ever not?"

When in the former Holy Roman Empire...

I have absolutely no idea when she ends up topless, but someone cheers as I snort a line off her tits. I don't know how she lives like this. Granted, I've had a few game nights end up not too dissimilarly—and with even fewer clothes—but usually, it's at least not someplace so gross.

I rub my nose and look around. The girls from the bachelorette party came over to join us at some point. If I'm not careful, Freddie's probably going to end up inviting them to an orgy, and we haven't even had the chance to clean up her loft.

Then again, is there any reason to? She's coming home with me to Toronto, isn't she? We haven't actually talked that much about our plans.

She leans back against the bar and wraps her arm around me, and I can't help but hug back, my tail twining around her legs. "See, Berlin might not have the Community Center, but fiends still manage to have some fun here."

I roll my eyes. I want to protest, but it's hard to pretend the Community Center is any different from this dive bar. "I think the drugs are usually better quality there."

Elias clutches his chest, his eyes going wide. "That really hurts. I share with you, and you insult my supply."

I shrug. "Sorry."

"Don't mind him, he's a drama queen," Freddie says.

"After all the time I spent cutting it myself."

She rolls her eyes. So he is joking, then. It can be so hard to tell in a language I'm not as fluent in.

One of the women clears her throat, and I turn to her. She's small, maybe four feet tall, with a beautiful dress that seems to be woven from the forest itself. It's strange, like it's simultaneously linen, tree bark, and leaves. "This might be a weird question but...are you on Twitch?"

I gulp. God, no. Please, not another stalker.

"I just recognized your voice. You did a playthrough of Inscryption that I loved. The beginning was too creepy for me to bring myself to play it on my own."

So just a normal fan? I can take that. Maybe. And she's a fiend, so it's not like she'd out me to the rest of the world. "Yeah, that was me. It's an interesting game."

She giggles, grinning and shaking her head. "I just love your content. I had no idea you were actually a...well, a real live lamia. I thought it was just an avatar."

I chuckle, still a little nervous, but find myself relaxing. She's harmless. "Yeah, that's kinda the point. It lets me be me so out in the open that there's no way anyone would ever suspect a thing."

She giggles. "Well, I think it's brilliant. I'd been considering streaming myself, though I don't think I'm anywhere near as good as you. Maybe I'd make mine a little pixie or something, to seem appropriate."

"That'd be cute. Message me if you start one. I'll give you a raid."

"Poggers!" She grins and looks like I absolutely made her day. I've only met one fan in real life before. Maybe this is what it's supposed to be like. It's relieving, almost cathartic. People who love my content don't have to be terrifying.

I should have let my fans know I was going to take all this time off. "I kind of miss streaming," I whisper to Freddie. "I forgot how much it means to people."

She rubs my back, looking genuinely concerned. "Can you do it back at my flat?"

"I need my computer and everything."

She sighs, but there's a faint smile there. "Well, we do have to get home before too much longer."

I take the opening. "You keep calling it home."

She blushes. She's so adorable when there's fresh blood in her. "I'm not saying I have to move in with you or anything. We already said I was staying in Toronto."

"Oh, we're definitely U-Hauling if you're moving there, but are you sure? Even now that it's safe to be back in Berlin?"

Her fingers slide between mine. "I love you, Phoebe. I love Berlin, and maybe I'll come back here someday, but I want to be with you. And Toronto is your home. And it's Vivi's home, and I told her I'd be there for her for chemo. She has another appointment Wednesday, and I was hoping to make it back in time."

It's already Monday. She was planning on going home that soon. It's even earlier than I'd expected. "Well, then, we shouldn't keep Maria waiting."

"You just want to hurry up and stream."

I huff. "I miss my job. And it's not the only thing I'm excited for. I'm starting a life with you."

She kisses me, her hand roaming over my tail. I love how much attention she pays to it. How complete her love is. "Let's go home."

I'll never get tired of hearing her say that. "You sure you're all done here?"

She grins. "Well, I did kind of want to invite that bachelorette party over."

I roll my eyes. She's so predictable. I kiss her neck and whisper, "I guess we can leave in the morning."

Her smile only grows, her grip tightening on me. I don't know what I did to get lucky enough to find someone so perfect for me. She kisses me again, pulling me flush against her, her tongue meeting mine, and we have one last perfect night in Berlin before finally returning home and starting a life together.

# About the Author

Genevieve McCluer was born in California and grew up in numerous cities across the country. She studied criminal justice in college but, after a few years in the field, moved her focus to writing. Her whole life, she's been obsessed with mythology, and she bases her stories on myths from around the world, with a sprinkle of real life experiences.

She now lives in Arizona with her partners and cats, always chasing after the next novel. In her free time she enjoys going on walks, playing video games, and refining her culinary prowess.

# Books Available From Bold Strokes Books

**A Heart Divided** by Angie Williams. Emmaline is the most beautiful woman Jack has ever seen, but being a veteran of the Confederate army that killed her husband isn't the only thing keeping them apart. (978-1-63679-537-9)

**Adrift** by Sam Ledel. Two women whose lives are anchored by guilt and obligation find romance amidst the tumultuous Prohibition movement in 1920s California. (978-1-63679-577-5)

**Cabin Fever** by Tagan Shepard. The longer Morgan and Shelby are stranded together, the more their feelings grow, but is it real, or just cabin fever? (978-1-63679-632-1)

**Clean Kill** by Anne Laughlin. When someone starts killing people she knows in the recovery world, former detective Nicky Sullivan must race to stop the killer and keep herself from being arrested for the crimes. (978-1-63679-634-5)

**Only a Bridesmaid** by Haley Donnell. A fake bridesmaid, a socially anxious bride, and an unexpected love—what could go wrong? (978-1-63679-642-0)

**Primal Hunt** by L.L. Raand. Anya, a young wolf warrior, finds herself paired with Rafe, one of the most powerful Vampires in the Americas, in an erotic union of blood and sex.(978-1-63679-561-4)

**Snake Charming** by Genevieve McCluer. Playgirl vampire Freddie is on the run and a chance encounter with lamia Phoebe makes them both realize that they may have found the love they'd given up on. (978-1-63679-628-4)

**Spirits and Sirens** by Kelly and Tana Fireside. When rumored ghost whisperer Elena Murphy and very skeptical assistant fire chief Allison Jones have to work together to solve a 70-year old mystery, sparks fly—will it be enough to melt the ice between them and let love ignite? (978-1-63679-607-9)

**Aubrey McFadden Is Never Getting Married** by Georgia Beers. Aubrey McFadden is never getting married, but she does have five weddings to attend, and she'll be avoiding Monica Wallace, the woman who ruined her happily ever after, at every single one. (978-1-63679-613-0)

**A Case for Discretion** by Ashley Moore. Will Gwen, a prominent Atlanta attorney, choose Etta, the law student she's clandestinely dating, or is her political future too important to sacrifice? (978-1-63679-617-8)

**The Broken Lines of Us** by Shia Woods. Charlie Dawson returns to the city she left behind and meets an unexpected stranger on her first night back, discovering that coming home might not be as hard as she thought. (978-1-63679-585-0)

**Flowers for Dead Girls** by Abigail Collins. Isla might be just the right kind of girl to bring Astra out of her shell—and maybe more. The only problem? She's dead. (978-1-63679-584-3)

**Good Bones** by Aurora Rey. Designer and contractor Logan Barrow can give Kathleen Kenney the house of her dreams, but can she convince the cynical romance writer to take a chance on love? (978-1-63679-589-8)

**Leather, Lace, and Locs** by Anne Shade. Three friends, each on their own path in life, with one obstacle…finding room in their busy lives for a love that will give them their happily ever afters. (978-1-63679-529-4)

**Rainbow Overalls** by Maggie Fortuna. Arriving in Vermont for her first year of college, an introverted bookworm forms a friendship with an outgoing artist and finds what comes after the classic coming out story: a being out story. (978-1-63679-606-2)

**Revisiting Summer Nights** by Ashley Bartlett. PJ Addison and Wylie Parsons have been called back to film the most recent *Dangerous Summer Nights* installment. Only this time they're not in love, and it's going to stay that way. (978-1-63679-551-5)